HATE LIKE HONEY

CORSICAN CRIME LORD, BOOK TWO

CHARMAINE PAULS

Published by Charmaine Pauls

Montpellier, 34090, France

www.charmainepauls.com

Published in France

Cover design by Rachel Christley of The Author Buddy

ISBN: 9782491833251 (Paperback)

 Created with Vellum

CHAPTER
ONE

Sabella

The library is quiet. Most students are gone for the holiday. I revel in having the space to myself. The gray winter light that sifts through the windows catches the dust particles in wedges. The smell of leather, paper, and ink reminds me of my dad's study, a place where I felt secure and loved.

Yet something is off. The long lines of shelves crammed with books form an ominous labyrinth. The aisles between them are hiding places where danger can lurk. I don't like that I can't see between them. The lamp throws a ring of light around my books and laptop that doesn't reach farther than the edge of the desk. The corners of the hall are cloaked in darkness.

A creak sounds overhead. I jerk my head toward the upstairs landing. There's no one. It's probably just the wooden floorboards expanding or shrinking due to the changes in temperature. A shiver slides down my spine. I pull my cardigan tighter around myself as I prick up my ears, focusing on every sigh and groan of the old building.

The medical section with its priceless oil paintings and precious antique books displayed in glass cabinets is my favorite room. For some reason, the faces of Hippocrates and Pasteur stare menacingly at me from the wall today. I should go back downstairs to where the librarian has her desk. I can do with the comforting presence of another human being.

My mind made up, I gather my books and notes. Just as I slide my laptop into my bag, the door squeaks open, cutting a triangle of chalky light into the space. I jump. Footsteps fall hard on the floor. Like in a bad dream, I'm frozen in place, watching with growing dread as the form of a man takes shape in the darkness.

The hair in my nape stands on end, and my palms turn clammy. My mind screams at me to flee, but my body is paralyzed with fear. I inhale deeply, fighting for reason. I'm being silly. Students come here all the time. It's not unusual for a man to walk into the room.

Like a ghost manifesting from thick, black fog, he advances toward me. Life finally returns to my limbs. I push back my chair, ready to bolt, but then he passes in front of the window, and the grainy daylight illuminates his shaved head and meaty hands.

Roch.

I'm simultaneously relieved and scared. He walks to me with determined steps, each falling like a warning on the floor, and stops next to me with his hands balled into fists. From close up, I can make out the angry light in his pale eyes and the furious strain in the hard angles of his face.

It's unreal to see him standing there. The man my

tormentor pays to keep an eye on me hasn't showed himself in months.

I look up at him, swallowing away the tightness of my throat. "What's wrong?"

His nostrils flare. He inhales. Exhales. "They're dead."

My voice comes out breathless. "What?" I scoot my chair to the side, putting space between us. My first, incoherent thought is, *Not Angelo. Please, no.* "Who's dead?"

He flexes and clenches his fingers. "Teresa and Adeline."

I blink. "Who?"

"Angelo's mother and sister," he says through clenched teeth.

Shock slams like a fist into my stomach. The punch steals my air. "W-What?"

Pain glitters cold and hard in his gaze. Anger makes it sharp. "Car accident."

"Oh my God." The metal of the armrests is cold under my palms. "When?"

"An hour ago."

An hour ago.

The statement is like a blade slicing through my heart. It's too fresh, too terrifying. Too raw. I can't imagine how Angelo must feel. Enemy or not, this isn't what I want for him. Or for anyone.

"I didn't know he had a sister," I say, thinking out loud.

"His twin," Roch says, the words strangled.

His *twin*? I can't imagine losing Mattie or Ryan. Coldness settles in my body. I feel sick. How did I not know he had a twin?

Oh, Angelo.

How does anyone cope with such a tragedy?

"I thought you should know," Roch says, trying to force

an impersonal tone, but his brutal emotions come through in his voice.

Turning on his heel, he stalks away.

Long after his footsteps have faded, I'm still sitting there. I haven't lost anyone close to me. I hope I never do, because I feel awful. Haunted and tormented. For a man I don't even like.

My hand shakes as I reach for the phone in my bag—the one Angelo gave me—and wake up the screen. There are no messages. There haven't been any since June last year.

Why didn't he let me know?

Then again, why would he?

Pain is private.

Why would he share something so intimately hurtful with a person who hates him? Not that he doesn't hate me too. The only thing he loves where I'm concerned is tormenting me. Letting me know about his grief doesn't serve that purpose.

I remain there until the day has gone dark, searching for the right words, but I can't come up with anything appropriate. No language can communicate what I want to say, how sorry I am that this happened to his family. To him.

Finally, I settle for simply, *I'm sorry for your loss*.

CHAPTER
TWO

Angelo

The house is brimming with people wearing black. Everyone is here—my uncles and cousins, people who served with my mother on charity boards, friends of my sister from university, our business associates, and a shitload of others I don't know.

They sip the drinks my mother imported for the wedding and nibble on the refreshments Heidi prepared while talking in hushed tones. Every now and again, a name drops. My mother's. My sister's.

I should say my late mother and sister. It takes getting used to.

The dining room is shrouded in darkness. The shutters are closed, dispelling the harsh summer sun. The AC does the job of keeping the room cool, but the gloom seems fitting.

Breaths and perfume mingle around me where I stand

next to my father's chair at the head of the table. He sits quietly, staring straight ahead. We each have a glass in our hands. His is empty. Mine still contains the four fingers of Scotch he poured.

The end of his cigarillo burns red as he drags on the tobacco, puffing the smoke into the already stuffy room. The air is thick with the heady scent of the white lily wreaths on the mantlepiece, sideboard, and table. Thick with mourning. Every mouthful of oxygen I drag into my lungs chokes me with grief.

In between loading their plates with Corsican pates and tapenades, people file past to pat my father's shoulder.

Their voices are demure. "We're sorry for your loss."

They nod at me, avoiding looking into my eyes, perhaps because of what they see there.

Someone opens the window and grabs the latch of the shutter.

"Leave it," I say.

A woman. "It's so dark in here. Letting in some light will help—"

"Leave it," I say again, harsher this time.

The woman jumps. She closes the window and scurries away.

My cousin, Toma, enters. He catches my gaze from across the room and gives a slight nod.

My father stands.

People step aside. They clear a path as we make our way to the study and continue their conversations when the shuffle is over.

Toma enters first. My uncles are already inside.

I close the door.

My father goes to his desk, his face a mask of loathing and wrath.

Every muscle in my body draws tight as I stop in front of my family.

"Is it done?" my father asks.

I clench my hands in anticipation of the answer.

"Yes," Uncle Nico says, his manner resigned. "He talked."

My father narrows his eyes to slits. "Is he alive?"

"Yes," Uncle Enzo says. "Like you instructed."

I look down. My hands are empty. I should've brought that drink. But I don't want to blur my reason. I want to be lucid. I want to—*need* to—remember every detail of this day.

My father curls his fingers into a fist on the desk. My uncles wait. When my father dips his head to indicate that he's ready, Uncle Enzo speaks.

"Cusso cut the brake cables." Uncle Enzo hesitates as if he's too afraid to continue.

Uncle Nico speaks. "As for you, Angelo, he was supposed to paint thallium on your steering wheel. When absorbed through the skin, death is slow and painful. The only reason he hadn't done it that morning was because the delivery of the parcel was delayed.

"The guy who brought it in via boat from Marseille had engine trouble on the way. We intercepted him at Cusso's house. He didn't know what was in the parcel or who paid him. He said the arrangements were made over the phone and no names were mentioned. Fifty percent of the payment was deposited in his bank account upfront. The parcel arrived by mail. All he knew was that he had to drive the boat to Bastia, rent a car, and make a drop-off at Cusso's house. Nevertheless, we didn't want to take any risks. Both him and his boat are now on the bottom of the sea."

"We checked the rest of the cars thoroughly," Toma

says. "The mechanics work fine. Nothing else has been tampered with."

"Who paid Cusso?" my father asks, his even tone not masking the hatred riding on those words.

Uncle Nico holds my father's gaze. "Benjamin Edwards."

It's who we suspected, but all the fury of hell is nothing compared to the rage that erupts inside me. Edwards meant to kill my father and me. That's the answer he sent in response to my instructions. That's how he wanted to repay my wedding invitation. Instead, he killed my mother and my sister.

That motherfucking coward. He couldn't even look us in the eyes while pulling the trigger. Like he always used us to do his dirty work, he paid someone else to do his killing.

I shake with the emotions I try to contain. For this reason, I didn't interrogate Cusso myself. I would've killed him too easily, long before he talked. The task of torturing him was safer in my uncles' hands.

My voice is miraculously calm. Steady. "Is he conscious?"

"Yes," Toma says, sneering. "The bastard is praying. Gianni is keeping an eye on him."

"Good."

Leaving them in the study, I go to the basement to finish the job.

CHAPTER
THREE

Sabella

Angelo still dominates my mind a week later when I visit Mattie in Stellenbosch. Mom is there for the weekend. Dad couldn't make it because he's drowning in work.

When I called my dad after the incident in the library, he didn't mention anything about the accident. I couldn't ask him without confessing how I learned about the news. As I can't explain Roch's presence, I had to contend myself with what I could find on media sites.

Apparently, the late Mrs. Russo lost control of the car she drove and plunged down a cliff. Both mother and daughter were killed on impact.

I dared to bring it up in a conversation with Ryan, saying that I saw the news, but he told me in his typical stoic manner not to make it my business, and then he changed the subject.

Angelo never replied to my message, not that I expected him to. That wasn't the objective. The double funeral was only two days ago. I took the bracelet they'd given me for my sixteenth birthday from my jewelry box. I haven't worn it since my seventeenth birthday, since the day Angelo betrayed me. No. Since the day I *discovered* he betrayed me. He'd been betraying me long before then. He manipulated me right from the start. He used me to steal incriminating evidence from our house to blackmail Dad into signing over a part of his business to the Russo family. I don't know why I haven't returned the bracelet to Angelo. After everything that happened, I should've, but now is hardly the time.

"You look far away," Mattie says, sinking into one of her art deco chairs in a sunny spot in the lounge and resting a hand over her stomach.

Attempting a smile, I say, "I was just thinking. How are you feeling?"

"Ugh." Her grin is rueful. "Do you really want to know?"

Mom enters with a tray of rooibos tea and rusks that she puts on the coffee table. "The nausea will disappear at the end of the first trimester."

"If I'm lucky," Mattie says. "Celeste was queasy for the whole nine months."

"Celeste just wanted sympathy from Ryan."

"Mom," I say. "That's not nice, and you know it's not true."

Mattie laughs. "Well, if that was the case, it worked. She only had to say the word craving, and Ryan jumped."

"Do you blame him?" I ask. "He's crazy about Celeste. Jared must be the same with you, Mattie."

She sighs. "He tries."

"Yup. I didn't exactly peg him as the romantic type."

"He'll go to the store if I tell him to," Mattie says. "He just won't take the initiative himself."

My mom hands Mattie a cup of tea. "When I was pregnant, your father never pampered me. He was proud, of course, but in those days, men weren't as involved as they are today. Women just had to get on with it while men built their empires and played golf."

"Dad isn't that bad," Mattie says. "He's always been very present in our lives."

"With you kids, yes." Mom sniffs. "I only regret one thing, and that's not making a life for myself. When your father and I got married, I sacrificed having a career so that he could start his business. Now that all of you left the house, I'm sorry I never did anything for myself."

Mattie sips her tea. "What job would you have chosen?"

Mom sighs and turns a wistful gaze to the window. "I always wanted to be a pediatrician, but it's too late for that."

"How about taking up natural medicine?" I ask. "You can get a diploma in four years. One of Colin's friends is doing a correspondence course, and he's loving it."

"I'm fifty years old." Mom picks up her cup, lifting a pinky in the air. "That ship, I'm afraid, has sailed."

"There's always voluntary work in the medical field," Mattie says. "There's no shortage of possibilities in the area."

Mom shakes her head. "It's not the same."

"What about you, Mattie?" I ask to change the subject. Continuing with the discussion will only end up with Mom becoming depressed. She'll make a decision that works for her when the time is right. She always does. Regurgitating things she can't change doesn't help.

"What about me?" Mattie asks.

"You're so young. Doesn't a baby at twenty scare you?"

Her smile is serene. "Jared and I want to be young with our children. I'm happy being a housewife, and I'll be ecstatic being a mommy."

"I didn't mean it in a negative way." My mind jumps to that night with Angelo and the wrongness of what we shared. "I just can't imagine being tied down when there's a whole world to explore."

"Everyone's ambition is different." My sister shrugs. "It doesn't mean one is better than the other."

"Of course not," I say quickly.

Mattie and my mom launch into a discussion about the baby shower arrangements. I should be more interested, but I can't help how my mind wanders. I worry about my dad. He's been so closed-off and distant after Ryan's birthday. Like Mom, he's more absent from home. I imagine him sitting alone in his study, going over his accounts or balancing his checkbook. Will he eat a proper lunch if Doris or my mom isn't there to cook? He'll probably just munch on a few pretzels.

A wave of tenderness washes over me. I have a sudden desire to be with him, to sit on the sofa with a blanket over my knees and a book on my lap while a fire crackles in the fireplace and his presence warms the room.

Mattie and my mom don't seem to notice when I stand and take my phone from my bag. I walk onto the terrace, soaking up the welcome winter sun as I dial my dad.

"Hey," he says. "Is everything all right?"

"Of course. Why wouldn't it be?"

"I thought you're spending time with Mattie and your mother."

"I am." I lean against a pillar. "They're discussing baby shower stuff."

"Ah. Try to give some input. It's important to your sister."

"Sure," I say half-heartedly.

"Is there something you wanted to talk about?"

"I just wanted to check up on you."

He chuckles. "You don't have to worry about me. I'm old enough to take care of myself."

"I know you don't eat when you're alone."

"I'm at the office. I'll pick up a frozen meal on my way home. Happy?"

I laugh. "You're working too hard."

"It comes with the territory."

"Are you there by yourself?"

"What do you mean?" he asks, his voice scraping in his throat.

"Is someone helping you at least?"

"I don't make the staff work on weekends. You know that."

Biting my lip, I consider what to say without making it sound as if I'm babying him.

"I've got to go, Bella. I still have a ton of reports I'd like to finish before tonight."

"Okay," I say, for some reason reluctant to let him go.

"Love you, darling," he says.

"I love you too, Dad."

The line goes dead.

I catch a glimpse of Mattie and my mom through the window. They're conversing with their heads close together, no doubt talking about a color scheme and baby shower themes. They don't need me. They're happy doing this together.

Making a quick decision, I go back inside. "I'm going to see Dad."

Mom lifts her head. "What about your tea?"

"Sorry." I kiss her cheek. "I'm just a little homesick."

"Now?" Mattie asks.

"It's early. I'll get there before dark. I can sleep over and drive back tomorrow."

"It's far to drive alone," Mom says.

"You drive the same road all the time, Mom. I'll send you a message when I arrive to let you know I'm safe."

"All right," Mom says slowly. "But if I don't hear from you by four o'clock at the *latest*, I'm sending a search party."

"Do you mind if I leave Pirate here?" I ask Mattie. "I'll pick him up on the way back. He doesn't like traveling in the car that much."

"Sure," she says. "Leave his food out in the kitchen."

"Thanks." I kiss her cheek. "I appreciate it." Remembering Roch's visit at the library, I hesitate. I hate that he's still following me. "Do you mind if I take your car? You're not planning on going anywhere, are you?" I grab the first excuse that pops into my head. "I forgot to charge mine. It won't make it to George."

"You shouldn't forget to charge your car," Mom chides. "What if you have an emergency and you're stuck?"

"No problem," Mattie says, coming to my rescue. "The key is in my bag."

I shoot her a grateful smile before escaping. Mattie's car is parked in the garage. The windows are tinted. To be on the safe side, I bundle my hair under a cap and nick Mattie's sunglasses from her bag. This way, Roch won't recognize me, and I can get away without worrying about having him on my tail.

After throwing a change of clothes into a bag and giving Pirate a cuddle, I hit the road.

In George, I stop for fish and chips at my dad's favorite fast-food restaurant. It's only late afternoon, but we can pretend it's dinner time. I'll surprise him at the office. He'll be happy that he doesn't have to nuke a ready-made meal from the supermarket when he gets home.

It's freezing when I get out in front of his office building. The wind that blows from the mountain cuts through my jeans and lightweight parka jacket. My nose and fingers feel frozen. I should've taken a scarf and gloves. In my rush to get here, I didn't even pack a beanie.

Grabbing the paper bag with the food, I walk with a brisk pace to the door. The guard that usually mans the entrance is absent. I don't visit Dad at the office often—very seldom, actually—but he's a stickler for security. He has guards on duty twenty-four-seven. Maybe he decided it's safe enough in George or that the alarm is adequate protection.

I climb the three steps to the double French doors. Edwards Imports and Exports is situated in a historical building with a stone façade, arched windows with red metal frames, and a black iron rooster on the chimney. The building was used as the province trade headquarters until a century ago. After falling into ruin, my dad bought and restored it. The building stands almost right on the street, flanked by two giant oak trees. A large green lawn and a parking lot with an ornate iron fence stretch out at the back. The gate is locked on weekends, which is why I parked in the street.

The light on the intercom panel next to the doors is dead. I push the call button to test it, but the bell doesn't ring. The power isn't down, because a light burns in the reception area. Weird. I feel the door handle. The door swings inward soundlessly.

It's not like Dad not to lock the doors. Then again, he's been more forgetful of late. Mom says he sometimes forgets to set the house alarm before going to bed. He's not getting younger, but he's not old enough to be that negligent yet.

"Dad?" I call, taking the stairs to the upper level two by two.

His office spreads over half of the first floor. The spacious room boasts blackwood floors, a corner chimney, a crystal chandelier, and a genuine nineteenth century pressed ceiling. The wide windows frame the Outeniqua Mountains. Together with a skylight, they let in plenty of light. The decoration is a mashup of steampunk and factory-loft styles. The whole building is a work of art.

"Dad?" I say again, quickening my steps down the hallway.

Overhead lights with industrial trumpet shades throw circles on the teak floor. The bulbs reflect in the stained-glass wall that gives a view of the inner courtyard below.

"Surprise," I say, sticking my head around the doorframe. "I brought—"

The scene that greets me cuts the rest of my sentence short. The food drops from my hand. The bottom of the bag breaks. Fries and packets of condiments scatter around my feet. Those objects I can process. Not the blood and gray matter on the floor. Not my dad lying in that puddle. Not Santino Russo towering over him. And not Angelo crouched next to my dad, wearing black leather gloves and holding a gun in his hand.

CHAPTER
FOUR

Angelo

Sabella stands in the door with a scream trapped in her throat. She doesn't give sound to it, but it's there. It's in her eyes. It's in the way horror transforms her features. But she's frozen. She wants to run. Cry for help. Deny what's in front of her. She can't. Her body and brain are locked by a terrifying spell of shock.

I know.

I've been there.

She's a fragile picture of a delicate object that's been violently broken. A beautiful vase. Shattered. Shards of paper-thin glass. And even when she picks up the pieces, she'll never be the same.

I know.

Food lies around her feet, wasted. That's why she's here when she wasn't supposed to be. She wanted to surprise her father. She brought him lunch. Or dinner. It's too late for lunch and too early for supper. Too late to unsee what she's witnessed.

There's no choice. I have to finish the job. Even if she screams, no one will hear her. The office buildings around us are closed for the weekend.

Tearing my attention away from her, I place the gun in Edwards's hand and fold his lifeless fingers around the shaft.

My father looks down at the body with contempt as I straighten. He adjusts his jacket, steps over the blood, and walks to the door.

"Finish her," he says, holding her gaze as he shoves past her.

Finish her.

Because she's a witness.

Because we don't need her any longer.

But *I* need her. God knows, I hate her for it, but I do. I don't even know when it became so imperative that her father kept his promise. Maybe when I first saw her. Maybe before, when she was nothing but a distant knowledge and a vague concept of my future. Maybe when I kissed her. Definitely when I fucked her. Undeniably when I branded her with my seed in her pussy and my mark on her skin.

Finally, she finds her voice. What escapes from her lips is more of a raw sound than a scream. Instead of running away, she rushes to her father and falls on her knees beside him. She reaches out, groping.

Before she can touch him, I grab her arm and drag her up. It's cruel. It's inhumane to withhold this from her.

I know that too.

I have to, lest she disturbs the scene or steps in the blood and leaves prints.

"Don't look, *cara*." I drag her toward the door. "Goddamn. You shouldn't see this."

"No." She fights like a wild animal. "I need to help him."

I shake her. Hard. "You can't help him."

She claws, her nails leaving burning paths on my neck and cheek.

"Let me help him!"

Grabbing her wrists in one hand, I pin them behind her back while holding her in place with my free hand wrapped around her nape. We're standing face to face, pressed up against each other, our expressions naked and exposed. Hers is panicked, terrified, bewildered, crazed… I can heap on a mountain of descriptions. Between good and bad or love and hate, they'll all be on the darkest end of the spectrum.

Me? All I have left is cold anger. My senses are still sharp from the kill. If I could feel, I'd experience everything with more intensity. Now, I only see what lies behind and in front of me clearer.

"No. Please." Her eyes are dry. Demented and feverish. She's looking but not seeing. "You have to let me—"

Her mind is blocking out the reality, protecting her psyche from a truth that will wreck her. There was no choice. My family had to destroy hers like hers destroyed mine.

An eye for an eye.

Sabella and her father for my mother and sister. I hate how her father made that decision for us.

Her gaze darts to the floor, to the blood seeping into the rug. "I have to call an ambulance."

I turn our bodies, blocking the view with mine. "Stop it, Sabella." My words are violent, but my hold is gentle. Willing the meaning to sink in, I say, "He's dead."

It does. The truth registers.

Her expression twists into a mask of agony. "Not true."

"Yes." I don't shrink from holding her gaze, from letting her see who I am. "It had to be done."

"You did this to him," she says between a sob and a gasp. "You shot him."

"No." My voice is flat. "I wish I had. That justice was reserved for my father."

"You did this." She twists in my hold, turning feral again. "You did this to him!"

"It was justice for my mother and sister," I bite out.

She's not listening, not even when I tighten my grip so much it must hurt. She's shaking from head to toe, screaming herself hoarse.

Letting go of her nape, I slam a hand over her mouth. There's still no risk of anyone hearing her. I just can't stand the sound of her grief.

Her eyes grow round. She sags a little, either from the crush after the adrenaline high or because she believes her turn is next.

I want to take her with me. I should.

I don't.

I had a funeral. It didn't change shit, but it did bring a warped sense of finality. Closure, I suppose. She deserves the same. She deserves to be there for her family like I'd been there for mine.

It's only fair.

What do I do with her in the meantime? Where do I take her? I can't get into her house. I could take her to our hotel, but my father won't understand. He'll need time. The idea has to grow on him. It's not ideal, not at all, but I have to leave her here.

The fight has left her. All that remains are sobs and fear. The sobs are racking her shoulders. The fear makes her tremble. She heard what my father said.

"Shh, *cara*. I'm not going to kill you." I lower my lips to her ear. "I should, but I won't."

She shakes harder but cries more quietly.

I continue in a hushed tone. "Just remember, I spared your life." Pressing a kiss on her temple, I tell her how it works. "Now, I own it."

Straining in my hold, she tries to lean away. I lift my hand from her mouth. She gasps, sucking in air. When I caress her nape with my gloved fingers, she shakes her head.

"No, no, no, please," she begs through her tears, already knowing what I'm going to do.

This time, I don't apologize. I find the right spots on her neck and squeeze. Her eyes dim. The light in them doesn't fade. The brown pools don't turn glassy when her eyelids flutter closed. Not like my mother's. Not like Adeline, who we buried without eyes or a face. I don't tell her I'm sorry because I'm not. The only thing I regret is that she witnessed something she was never supposed to see.

She goes limp in my hold, her body succumbing to the mercy of unconsciousness.

Scooping her up in my arms, I carry her downstairs—as far away from the upstairs office as possible—and lie her down on the sofa in the staff room. I push a cushion under her head and cover her with a throw, making sure the ends are tucked beneath her body.

When I'm sure she's comfortable, I step outside and call Roch.

"Why the fuck didn't you tell me Sabella came to George?" I ask when he answers.

He sounds baffled. "In George? She's at her sister's place in Stellenbosch. She hasn't left the house since she arrived. Her car is still in the driveway. I'm looking at it as we speak."

I scan the street. Matilde's car is parked on the curb. "She took her sister's car."

"Fuck. I couldn't know that. She tricked me."

"Get your ass down here now. Edwards is dead. Sabella walked in on the scene."

"Fuck," he says again. "I'm on my way."

"She's in the office building. Make sure she stays safe, but keep your distance."

"If she saw what you did, why don't you take her with you?"

"Because she deserves a funeral," I say in a clipped voice before hanging up.

I glance at the Mercedes that's parked on the opposite side of the street. My father's profile is visible through the passenger window. He's waiting, expecting me to carry out his order.

I've never disappointed him. I've always done as I was told. This is the first time I disobey him.

Making my way to the car with brisk steps, I send a text message to Ryan, informing him where to find Edwards and Sabella.

CHAPTER
FIVE

Sabella

I wake up warm and comfortable, not cold and shivering like…

Like when?

Caught between a deep, dreamless sleep and wakefulness, I stretch under the blanket that covers me. No, not a blanket. A throw. Not a bed. A sofa. In my father's study. Wait. This is his office. I'm lying on the sofa in his staff room.

And then it all rushes back—the nightmare. I'm relieved it was just a dream. At the same time, the most horrible fear that it's real cripples me.

When I sit up and plant my feet on the floor, it feels real, but that's how dreams are. You believe they're true until you wake up. You're trapped in the dream, dreaming you're awake.

I'm no longer warm and cozy. I'm frozen to my core.

Pulling the throw around my shoulders, I stand. I'm wearing my socks. My sneakers stand next to my bag on the floor.

I pad through the room and enter the reception area. The light is on. It's dark outside. I can't tell the time because it gets dark early in winter, already around five-thirty.

My legs carry me up the stairs and down the hallway under the canopies of industrial lampshades. Every step takes me deeper into the dream. My heartbeats fall out of rhythm, each thud hurting my chest.

I clutch the ends of the throw not because of the cold but because I need to hold on to something. My mind screams at me to stop. I don't want to go farther, but I have to know.

A shadow falls over the threshold of my dad's office and bleeds into the hallway. Petrified, I freeze. I'm terrified the owner of that shadow is Angelo. I'm praying he won't appear like a scary vision from my dream. I'm praying the man attached to that shadow is my dad, that he'll give me a delighted smile and a hug before asking what I'm doing here.

Please, wake up.

Ryan exits the office, wearing his habitual weekend attire of jeans and a sweater, but the way the clothes sit on his frame is wrong. Askew. His face is pale and his hair disheveled. The unsettled look in his eyes is out of place. It doesn't fit his stoic disposition.

He steps over the spilled food littering the floor and stops short when he notices me. "Jesus, Bella." The words gush from his mouth. "You're alive." Quickening his steps, he closes the distance and fastens his hands on my arms. "Sweet Jesus." He hugs me tightly. "You're all right."

That's when it hits me. The truth crashes into me when

I realize I'm alive but not all right. When I admit that it's not a dream, reality settles like the aftermath of a violent storm, cold and cruel.

I try to move forward, but my brother holds me back.

His voice is firm. "No, Bella."

"Ryan."

"Shh." He rubs my back. "You're alive. That's what matters."

It's not what matters. I pull away and lock my hands in his sweater. "I saw him. Them. Angelo and his father. They… It was them. I saw it." From a distant corner of my mind, I register that I sound hysterical. "We have to call the police."

"No." He curls his fingers around my biceps and catches my gaze. "You have to forget what you saw." His manner is steady, forcing calm. "It's a suicide."

"It's not. Ryan, we have to call the police. He couldn't have gone far. The airport. They have to hold the flights."

"Listen to me, Bella." Ryan tightens his hold on my arms. "We can't call the police."

"What are you talking about?"

"Dad was involved in a murder. A double murder."

Dad was involved in a murder.

I hear the words, but I don't understand. "What? You're not making sense."

His expression is sympathetic. No, it's pitying. "Dad ordered the hit that killed Angelo's sister and his mother."

It can't be. Not my dad. That's not who he is. *Was.* I slip out of my brother's touch and back up. "You're lying."

"Bella, listen to me." He spears his fingers through his hair. Frustration and urgency lace his tone. "Dad paid someone in Santino's employ to cut the brake cables on Santino's car. Santino was the target, not Teresa and Adeline. The fact that Teresa drove her husband's car that day was a sad and unforeseen twist of circumstances."

I take another step away. "I don't believe it." My voice is shaky. "Dad would never do something like that."

Angelo's words whisper through my mind.

It was justice for my mother and sister.

"No." I shake my head, retreating farther. "It's not true."

Ryan looks me straight in the eyes, showing me the truth with his steadfast stare as he declares solemnly, "I was there when he commissioned the job, Bella. I made the transfer for the payment."

The payment. Ryan and Dad. They paid someone to kill Santino. I can't wrap my mind around that. But then an image of Ryan and Dad at Ryan's birthday party springs into my head. I remember the message Dad read on his phone and how he looked at Ryan, how that scared me.

There are a million things I could ask, but the question that slips from my lips is, "Who? Who did you pay?"

"You don't need to burden yourself with the details. There's no risk of him talking." He dips his head, measuring my reaction. "The Russo family executed him."

The storm his words unleash is trapped in my chest. It tears me apart, uprooting who I am and every foundation I built my life on. Not finding a way out, it wreaks havoc with every part of my being.

"How?" I've gone from hysterical to eerily calm, the storm now living inside me. "How do you know this?"

"Angelo informed me when he sent me a text to tell me they'd taken their vengeance." He swallows. "Of where to find you and…"

Dad.

"I wish I didn't have to tell you," Ryan continues. "Now you understand why we can't go to the police."

"No." The world tilts beneath me. I grab the rail to support my weight. "We can't let them get away with this."

Ryan raises his hands. "If this comes out, everything comes out. Think about Mom, about how the scandal will ruin her life. Think about Mattie and the baby. Celeste and me. Brad."

The rational part of me understands his logic. The rest of me battles to process what's happening. What *happened*.

"Why?" I whisper-cry. "This isn't—" I swallow a sob. "This wasn't Dad."

He drops his arms at his sides. "There are parts of the business you don't understand. Illegal parts. If any of this comes to light, we're all fucked, Bella. Do you understand?"

Slowly, like muck drifting to the bottom of a muddy river, the truth sinks deeper. The bribes weren't the only unscrupulous dealings in the business. That nasty, unsavory bit of reality was only the tip of the iceberg. I shudder thinking what lies beneath.

Ryan advances cautiously. "I'm going to call an ambulance. You have to be strong now. Understand?" His gaze drills into mine. "You came here to surprise Dad. Instead, you discovered the body." His speech is steady and grounding. Like me, he's carrying his storm inside. "You fainted. Blacked out or something. The shock can do that to a person, especially someone as young and sensitive as you. It's believable. When you didn't call Mom as agreed to let her know you arrived safely, she got worried. She called you and Dad, but neither of you answered your phones."

This part must be true. The missed calls will be registered on our phones.

He stops short of me, cupping my shoulders in his palms. "Mom called me. I came looking for you. I found you here, disorientated and in shock. Then I called an ambulance."

He waits, searching my eyes for agreement or understanding.

I'm not sure I can do this.

He gives me a shake. "Think about the family, Bella. This is bigger than us. You have no idea just how big. It goes all the way to the government and higher. The media will have a field day with the truth. It'll ruin every one of us and any future our children can ever hope to have. Dad made a call that destroyed Angelo's family. Angelo did the same to us. It can end here. Be over. Or we can go down a path that will be a thousand times worse than what happened today. You may as well put a gun against our heads and pull the trigger. Can you live with that? Can you live with doing that to Mom and Brad and Mattie's baby?"

I'm trembling by the time he's done. "What's wrong with us, Ryan?" I point toward the office. "We're talking as if Dad isn't lying dead in there."

"Nothing is wrong with you, Bella." He wraps his arms around me and pulls me close. "Dad tried to protect you from this. It's us. Me. The guilt is mine."

No. If I lie, the guilt is just as much mine.

"You've got this." He holds me at arm's length. "You're strong enough."

I'm not.

"Dad made sacrifices for us you can't begin to comprehend." He squeezes my shoulders. "Don't let it be for nothing." Letting me go slowly, he takes his phone from his pocket. "I'm calling, all right?"

I open my mouth, but there's only silence. The havoc is stuck inside.

"I have to call now, Bella. We've taken too long already. You can do this."

It's a lie. Everything is a lie. There's only one truth here.

Dad is dead.

Oh my God.

Dad is dead.

The circles of light sway in my path. Their brightness isn't enough to expel the darkness that steals over me. The floor gives way, and then I fall into a blissful night where monsters don't exist.

CHAPTER
SIX

Angelo

The news about Edwards's suicide will soon be all over the news. I remain in South Africa to do damage control if necessary while my father flies back to Corsica. Damage control includes killing anyone who dares to reveal the truth, and the only people who know the truth are us and the Edwards family. Taking into consideration what's at stake, I'm not worried about anyone running to the authorities. Still, I take nothing for granted.

I'll hang around until after the funeral. That should give Ryan Edwards enough time to prepare for his sister's departure. As her father didn't apply for her passport like I instructed, I arranged for delivery through a third-party company. I paid them enough to get it in less than a week.

The wedding will no longer take place as planned. There won't be a white dress and a cake or a big celebration with flowers in the garden. That turned into a funeral. We'll get married at the marriage office with my father and close relatives as witnesses. There won't be a honeymoon like my mother wanted, but I intend on taking everything from Sabella Edwards that's been denied me save for that one night when she turned eighteen.

My phone rings when I arrive at the hotel in George after dropping my father off at the airport. It's Roch. My gut tightens as I take the call.

"It's Sabella," he says.

I grip the phone hard. "What happened?"

"She collapsed. An ambulance took her to the hospital. Her brother is admitting her as we speak."

Little makes my heart speed up these days, but this news has that organ pumping. "Where?"

"Here in George."

"Send me the details."

I disconnect the call and head straight back to town.

The parking lot is almost full when I arrive at the general hospital. It's the evening visiting hour. I park in the first empty spot and run inside the building.

"Sabella Edwards," I say as I rush up to the receptionist. "I'm her fiancé."

She gives me a sympathetic smile before checking her computer screen. "Room one hundred eleven. First floor."

In too much of a hurry to thank her, I push a few people loitering in the corridor out of my way and take the stairs. When I exit on the first floor, I spot Ryan in the hallway, talking to a doctor. I stroll toward a vending machine, keeping an eye on them as I pop in a few coins and get a coffee.

Ryan nods at something the doctor says. The doctor leaves, and Ryan enters the room. Sipping my coffee, I make my way to the nurses' station on the floor.

The nurse on duty looks up when I stop in front of the desk. "Can I help you?"

I smile. "Just waiting for family."

"There's a visitor's lounge down the hallway."

"Thanks," I say, raising my cup.

She ducks her head and resumes her work. I saunter toward the lounge, taking stock of the rooms as I go. The door of one of the rooms stands open. A young woman in a hospital uniform is pulling the sheets off the bed and dumping them in a laundry trolley. When she leaves with the trolley, I slip inside.

The night is moonless. I look at the dark, star-studded sky through the window. My breath makes vapor against the cold panes of the glass. Taking my phone from my pocket, I send a message to my father. He'll only get it when he lands in Marseille, and he won't be pleased that I'm extending my stay. I don't explain about Sabella. It's best that we have that conversation in person. It's not going to be easy. My father will never be able to look at her and not want to kill her. As I said, he'll need time.

I wait until the bustle in the hallways grows quiet before I crumple the empty cup in my fist and chuck it in the trashcan. Pushing the door open, I look around the doorframe. The visitors are gone. People are no longer walking up and down the corridors with flowers and fruit baskets.

I'm not particularly cautious as I leave my hiding place, but the nurses' station is empty. I open the door of Sabella's room and step inside before closing it behind me. She lies small and pale in the bed, machines beeping around her. I've never seen her looking so vulnerable. So small. Frail.

Taking the chart from the file pocket at the foot-end of

her bed, I read the doctor's observations. I recognize Ryan's signature at the bottom, authorizing the treatment.

Motherfucker.

I clench my teeth and return the chart. Then I round the bed and take her hand. Her skin is cold. I bend down and brush my lips over her forehead.

My promise is sweet. Ominous. "I'm here."

I kick off my shoes and lift the covers. I'm careful not to disturb the IV tube, the nasal prongs, or the heart rate monitor when I get in next to her and pull her into my arms.

"I'm going to take good care of you, *cara*."

CHAPTER
SEVEN

Sabella

The darkness of water is bliss. It's weightless. Freedom.

This darkness is different. It's heavy. A prison. It pins me down and glues my eyelids shut while dunking my head under the surface. All I want is to come up for a breath. I'm fighting, but it's stronger than me.

It takes every ounce of energy I possess to swim up from that bottomless pit of inky black liquid. Every movement is a battle against the density of the mass that keeps sucking me down. How can anything be so tiring?

Celeste's voice reaches me from the top of the well. "I don't think keeping her drugged is a good idea."

My brother replies. "It's a radical treatment but no different than one used for depression."

Mattie surfaces somewhere. "…think she has depression?"

Ryan again. "She's suffered severe trauma, that's for sure."

A woman cries softly. My mom. "It doesn't help that we can't give the doctor the full details. How is he supposed to treat her properly? And bribing him to do this to her?"

Something stirs in my memory, something that compels me to fight harder.

"Shh." Ryan's voice is hushed. "Not here."

"But two days?" Celeste's voice drifts back to me. "Two days in an induced coma sounds severe."

"It's for the best. At least it delays the police interrogation."

"…shock treatment. It gives the body and brain time to recover from an overload of…"

"Wait." My mom. Alarmed. "She stirred. I think she's waking up."

"…too soon. Get the nurse to…"

I'm reaching for the voices, trying to grip the edge of the well, but I'm sinking deeper again.

No.

Don't leave me here. .

I swim harder, using all my might, but invisible fingers wrap around my ankle and pull me back into a dark hell from which I can't escape.

———

THE FOG LIFTS A LITTLE. I'm dreaming. I'm on the bottom of the ocean. It's dark around me, but I'm not alone. I sense his presence. He comes closer. I sense this too, even before the smell of cedar and citrus pierces the water. This isn't the cruel Angelo. This version of him is the one from before, the kind one who pretended to like me. The man who gave me a phone for no other reason than to get to know me is pulling me onto his lap and wrapping his arms around me.

He rocks me gently as I cry for that man, the one I lost. No, the one I never had, because he's not real.

"Shh, *cara*."

His lips are warm on my temple. It's comfortable in the heat of his embrace. I burrow deeper, losing myself in the safety of his arms. It's good not to swim so hard against the stream. I just want to rest here for a little while.

I DRIFT CLOSER to the surface. It's unbearably hot. How can I be burning up in the water? No. The fire comes from inside me.

The water smells like cedar and citrus. It doesn't douse the flames, but it soothes me. I inhale deeply, wanting to drag that fragrance into my lungs, and choke on a mouthful of seawater.

I'm drowning.

Panic grips me until a soft, warm mouth presses on my parted lips and feeds me air. Soothing hands hold me as I grab that air greedily, violently fighting to breathe.

"Easy. I've got you."

Something cool and wet presses on my forehead. Calloused fingers caress my neck. Refreshing drops dribble down my chest and roll over my stomach. I'm a starfish on the surface of the sea. I'm five years old, laughing while Dad teaches me to float on my back in the pool. The sounds of sobs reach my ears. Why am I crying?

I sink again. The hands that catch me are different. They're not Dad's. Angelo's face flickers through my memory. I recognize those hands, the only hands that touched me with pleasure. I give in to those hands, letting them carry me.

SHARP LIGHT INFILTRATES my closed eyelids. Someone lifts my eyelids.

The light hurts. I open my eyes and blink a few times. The faces of the people around the bed come into focus. Ryan, Mattie, and Jared.

A woman I don't know switches off the penlight in her hand and removes nasal prongs from my nose. "There you go, sweetheart. Take it easy. I'm Dr. Stein, your anesthesiologist." She looks at Ryan. "Everything looks fine. Take a moment to get her settled." She pats my hand. "Your doctor will be here shortly."

Nothing makes sense.

Ryan takes my hand when she leaves. "Hey." He smiles. "How are you feeling?"

"Thirsty."

Mattie catches a tear under her eye with a finger and hands me a cup with a straw. The water tastes like honey. I've never sipped anything sweeter.

I look around, taking in the white walls and strange bed and starched linen. I have an IV tube in the back of my hand and a heart rate monitor clipped onto my finger.

My voice is croaky. It's difficult to speak. "Where am I?"

"In hospital," Mattie says, brushing the hair from my forehead.

I frown. "What happened to me?"

She looks at Ryan, bites her trembling bottom lip, and turns away.

Jared puts his arm around her shoulders.

Ryan is the steadfast one, the person who answers. "Your memory will come back slowly. The doctor says that's perfectly normal."

The note of caution in his voice scares me. What I should remember frightens me the most. I'm in the dark, even now in consciousness, and it's a scary place to be. I don't want to be there any longer.

A memory flashes through my mind, a picture of my dad lying in a pool of blood on the floor in his office.

It's horrible. Terrifying.

I blink it away.

The picture that replaces that dreadful image is one of Angelo sitting on the bed and holding me in his arms. Another flash of him giving me a sponge bath rushes to me from nowhere.

I squeeze my eyes shut.

The same image reappears, but this time, Angelo is kissing my forehead. I hear his voice.

Easy. I've got you.

And then he kneels over the body of my dad with a gun in his gloved hand, his black gaze blazing with a cold fire as he looks at me.

My eyes fly open. Bile pushes up in my throat. I gag. Ryan grabs something from the nightstand and pushes it in my hands. A metal bowl. Convulsions fold me double. My stomach is empty except for the few sips of water. Like the storm trapped inside me, nothing comes out.

Dragging in ragged breaths, I try to calm the heaving.

Ryan rubs my back. "Feeling sick is a normal side-effect of the drugs they gave you. It'll pass in a bit."

My eyes burn from dryness and memories. "I remember."

His face takes on a regretful expression.

"Where's Mom?" I ask. "How is she?"

"She's been here for most of the day," Ryan says. "I sent her home to get some rest."

I don't miss that he's not answering my question.

How is she?

Does she know? Does she know who killed her husband? Does she know that Dad didn't commit suicide?

Scrubbing my hands over my face, I push the questions and recollections aside. "I want to go home."

"Where is that doctor?" Mattie's eyes are red and swollen. "What's taking him so long?"

I look between my sister and my brother. "How long have I been here?"

Mattie shoots Ryan an accusing glance. "Two days, honey."

"Two days?" I exclaim. "Why?"

"You suffered severe trauma," Ryan says. "The doctor thought it wise to induce sleep to allow your body and mind to recover from the shock."

"I'll get the doctor," Mattie says, taking Jared's hand and pulling him to the door.

Jared gives me a strained smile. Straightening his glasses, he says, "I'm glad you're better."

Better.

It sounds so simple, so easy.

When they're gone, I look at Ryan, really look at him. The strain around his eyes isn't new. It's always been there. I just haven't noticed it before. Whatever my dad was involved in, my brother knew about it. Was he the only one who shared Dad's secrets? Or am I the only person in the family who's been left in the dark?

"Mattie shouldn't be here in her condition," I say.

"She's fine. The baby is okay. Jared is taking good care of her."

"We need to talk."

The set of his mouth is resigned. "At home."

The doctor enters, followed by my sister and brother-in-law.

"You're awake," the doctor says in an upbeat tone. Taking a penlight from his pocket, he flashes it in my eyes. "Your red blood cell count was on the low side when you were admitted. I'm going to run a few tests to make sure your mineral levels are normal. I'll prescribe an iron supplement, but you should also consult a dietician to work out a balanced meal plan.

"I'll have lunch delivered to your room. You've been on an intravenous drip for two days. Start with lots of liquids and go slowly with the solids until your digestive system has adapted. It's best to stick to bland food for the first week. Don't forget to make sure you're well hydrated.

"We'll keep you under observation for another couple of hours after you've eaten. If you keep the food down and your tests come back normal, you can go home. But I want you back here for a checkup in another couple of days."

My family gives us privacy while he takes a blood sample, checks my vitals, and tells me that my blood pressure is fine. They return when a nurse wheels a trolley with soup, a glass of juice, and a bowl of jelly and custard into the room. The doctor scribbles the name and number of a psychiatrist on a prescription sheet and gives it to Ryan.

"I recommend that you schedule a visit as soon as possible," he says with a pat on Ryan's back and a smile directed at me before he leaves.

Despite myself, I'm starving. I don't remember ever being this hungry. The food is tasteless, but I finish every morsel under Mattie and Ryan's scrutiny.

After eating, I'm suddenly exhausted again. Ryan

switches on the television, and Jared offers to get everyone coffee from the vending machine.

I'm drifting in and out of awareness, doing my best to just survive and not to think for now.

It feels like hours later when the doctor returns to inform me that my test results are normal and that he authorized my discharge. A nurse removes the IV tube and tells me that I can get dressed.

"We'll wait outside," Mattie says.

Ryan's manner is quiet and calm. As always, it grounds me. "Your clothes are in the closet."

Mattie pushes Jared through the door. "Call if you need us, honey."

When we're alone, I turn to Ryan. "I think he was here."

He stills. "Who?"

"Angelo." The name gets stuck in my throat. I swallow around it. "I think he was here in the hospital."

Compassion softens my brother's face. "You were dreaming. Hallucinations are a known side-effect of the drugs."

"No." I shake my head. "This was different from dreaming."

"He wouldn't dare come here." A shutter drops in front of his eyes. "Not after what happened." Putting on a bright smile, he says, "Get dressed so that we can take you home."

Walking through the door, he closes it softly behind him.

I rub my hand where the IV was inserted. The needle left a small puncture mark. The skin around it is bruised, the blue already turning a greenish yellow.

I don't want anyone to help me dress—I hate feeling like a helpless child—but I'm dizzy when I sit up and swing my legs over the bed. The world spins a little as I make my way to the closet where I find a clean pair of jeans, a T-shirt, a sweater, underwear, and my toilet bag. Mattie or my mom must've been thoughtful enough to bring my toiletries and clothes.

I go to the en-suite bathroom to use the facilities, freshen up, and change. I'm dying to have a shower and wash my hair, but I'm eager to go home. For now, brushing my hair and my teeth will have to do.

My reflection stares back at me in the mirror. I don't recognize the woman with the pale skin and dark circles under her eyes. I don't want to look at her too closely because I'm afraid I'll hate what I see.

Not making eye contact with that woman, I brush my teeth and pull my hair into a ponytail. Then I untie the hospital gown at the back, free my arms, and let it drop to the floor. At the sight of my naked body, I freeze. I go cold. Colder still. So cold that it feels as if my veins are filled with ice.

The curls between my legs are gone. I'm bare, shaved clean. At the apex of my sex, the embossed white circle of Angelo's mark screams the truth.

CHAPTER
EIGHT

Sabella

R och stands outside the door of the hospital room. My muscles tense. He returns my glare with a cool look.

"It's all right," Ryan says, touching my elbow to catch my attention.

"You know him?" I ask under my breath.

"Since the last two days."

"What's he doing here?" I ask, not bothering to keep my voice down.

Ryan takes my arm when I don't show any signs of moving. "He and I want the same thing, which is to keep you safe. That's the only reason I'm allowing him near you."

"Or to keep me from talking," I bite out, glancing at Roch from over my shoulder as Ryan pulls me to the exit.

"Bella." Ryan's voice holds a warning. "Not here."

I shut my mouth, but my anger escalates when Roch shoves his hands in his pockets and saunters after us. His casual gait is borderline taunting.

Once we're in the car, I turn in my seat to face my brother. "He's one of Angelo's men."

Ryan pushes the ignition button. "I know."

Does he know Roch has been shadowing me for the past two and a half years? Will it make a difference if he does? As there are too many things I can't explain about the last thirty months of my life, I keep quiet. It's unfair, especially as I'm going to demand answers from Ryan, but we're going through enough as it is. I'm not going to load the secrets I locked away deep inside me on my brother's shoulders as well.

We don't speak for the rest of the drive. When we get home, I'm scared. I'm frightened to go inside, terrified that I won't be able to handle the memories. The house doesn't seem like home without my dad.

Doris, our housekeeper, waits on the front steps. Thankfully, she doesn't greet me with meaningless words. She only pulls me in for a quick, bruising hug before ushering me inside.

Mom, Mattie, and Jared wait in the lounge. Jared stands in front of the window, staring out at the sea. Mom sits on the edge of the sofa while Mattie is reclining deeper on the seat next to her. I'm glad they're not in the study where we usually have our family meetings. I wouldn't be able to handle that. I can't go there yet.

"Bella," Mom says, standing when we enter. She crosses the floor and kisses my cheek. "I'm so happy you're home."

Like Mattie, she wears signs of crying. Her eyes are puffy, and the whites are bloodshot.

Ryan drops my bag on a chair and closes the door. "I think we can all do with a drink."

"I'll pour," Jared says, already making his way to the wet bar. "Spritzers?"

"We need something stronger," Mom says.

My gaze falls on the bottle of Scotch. That was Dad's favorite brand. I have to look away lest I break down and burst into tears.

Instead, I focus my attention on Ryan. "Do they know?"

The question is loaded. I don't have to explain. He understands I'm referring to Dad's murder.

He nods.

Mom sits again, her expression forlorn and her gaze absent.

Walking to the sofa, I face my mom and my sister. "Did you know about Dad's real business, whatever that was?"

Ryan answers. "They didn't. Mattie only knew about the bribes. You know how Dad kept his professional and home lives separate."

"To hide what he was involved in from us," I say, unable to help the bitterness that slips into my tone.

Ryan's voice is quiet. "To protect you."

My words hold an accusation. "Yet *you* knew."

"I've always been involved in the business." His smile is patient. "Dad had to prepare me for taking over someday."

Jared puts drinks in Mattie and my mom's hands.

I cross my arms. "I'd like to know what exactly that business entails."

"Bella." Ryan observes me from under his lashes. "It's better that you don't know."

"No." I shake my head, declining the drink Jared offers me. "If I'm lying about Dad's murder, I want to know why I'm doing it."

Mom makes a choking sound.

I shoot her an apologetic look, but I stand my ground. No more ignorance. No more staying in the dark.

"She has a right to know, Ryan," Mattie says. "She's not a child any longer."

I look between them—Mom, Mattie, and Jared. "You all know?"

Mom's face is pale. "Ryan told us."

I turn an expectant gaze on my brother.

He takes a gulp of his drink, rolling it in his mouth like Dad used to do, and casts a glance at the closed door before speaking. "Arms smuggling."

I must've heard wrong. A single word slips off my tongue and bursts like a bubble in the air. "What?"

"Part of the business is bringing illegal arms into the country."

My legs wobble under my weight. I plonk down in the nearest chair.

"The import and export business became a good front," Ryan continues. "We make most of our money by facilitating shipments of arms. That's where the bribes come in. We pay high-ranking officials and government employees to turn a blind eye."

My mouth is so dry it's difficult to speak. "How high-ranking are we talking?"

His tone is even. "All the way at the top."

I can't breathe. "As in…"

"Presidents and ministers," he finishes for me.

"Weapons destined for where?" I ask.

"Zimbabwe. Angola. Central and North Africa."

God.

Pressing the heels of my hands on my eyes, I rub away the dryness. The sting. No wonder Ryan said the truth couldn't come out. The reality is much worse than I expected.

"Angelo?" I ask, dropping my hands on my thighs.

"Do not say that name in this house," Mom says in a shrill voice.

"Sorry, Mom." I look at Ryan again. "I have to know."

"That's part of their business, yes," he says. "However, they're more involved in clearing the way for us, so to speak."

Clearing the way. I can only imagine what that means. Getting rid of people in the most literal sense, no doubt.

A shiver crawls over my skin. Now it makes sense why Dad was involved with them. That's why he warned me, why he told me they're bad people. He tried to make me understand, but he couldn't tell me everything.

Shit. That makes us bad people too.

I'm going to be sick again.

"This house," I say. "Everything."

"Don't think like that." Ryan's demeanor is gentle. "There's also the legal side of the business."

Is that supposed to make us feel better? A laugh catches in my throat. The only thing preventing me from letting it out is consideration for my mom. My dad lied to us. He did something terrible, something unimaginable, by putting weapons in people's hands for sinister purposes I don't even want to think about. If I want to puke, how must Mom feel?

"Do you understand why this can never come out?" Ryan asks. "If it does, we'll be hunted by governments and powerful arms dealers."

My family's expressions are mostly resigned. Mom's mouth is turned down, her bottom lip quivering. They've all had time to come to a decision on how to handle the awful situation. They're only waiting for my compliance.

"Why don't we stop?" I ask, looking around the room. "You can cut out the illegal part and carry on with the legitimate business."

Ryan's smile holds sympathy, the kind that an adult reserves for a child who doesn't have a concept of the harshness of reality. "Do you think for one minute the arms dealers will simply accept that? Do you believe they'll shake my hand and say, *Thank you very much for doing business with us for the past ten years. We're going to miss you. But don't worry, we'll easily find someone else to smuggle our weapons into your country.*"

I go cold. Of course not.

"No," Ryan continues. "They'll make us do it. Do you know how? Jesus, I don't even want to go there. Perhaps they'll torture me. Or maybe they'll kidnap my son. Hey, why not kill one of us?" Swirling the liquor in his glass, he walks to the window and says more to himself than to us, "At least they're paying us now. If they force our hand, they may realize payment isn't even necessary."

All those scenarios he mentioned make me break out in a sweat.

"Do you have to be so graphic?" Mom asks in a tremulous voice.

"What?" Ryan shoots her a look from over his shoulder. "Do you prefer that I hide the ugly facts from you like Dad used to do?"

A sob tears from her lips.

"Ryan," Mattie exclaims, scowling at him as she wraps an arm around Mom.

"Fuck." Ryan pinches the bridge of his nose. "I'm sorry. The last few days were tough. I'm letting the situation get the better of me."

"This is too much, Ryan." I say. "Even for you. You don't deserve this."

None of us deserves the heritage Dad left. And for what? For a pretentious house on a hill by the sea? For fancy cars and glitzy parties?

"We've all been questioned, Bella," Mattie says. "The doctor was kind enough not to let the police interrogate you at the hospital. He said it was better done at home in an environment where you feel safe. You'll have to give a statement too. We just have to make sure we all tell the same story."

"Like the one I briefed you," Ryan says. "Stick to the truth as much as possible. That's the golden rule of lying."

"We have an appointment at your father's lawyer's office the day after tomorrow for the reading of the will," Mom says. "It'll have to be tomorrow."

Ryan turns his back to the window. "It'll be this afternoon. The authorities weren't happy about waiting until after Bella's discharge. I doubt they'll wait longer."

"They don't suspect murder, do they?" Jared asks.

"No." Ryan frowns. "But Bella discovered the body. Questioning her is protocol. I arrived on the scene more than four hours later. They'll want to know why Bella didn't call an emergency service immediately."

Mattie's tone is gentle. "What happened, Bella? Can you tell us?"

I wring my hands in my lap. "When I..." I swallow. "When I walked in on..." I can't say it. "Angelo manipulated my neck." I point at my nape. "He pressed on points that made me black out."

"Son of a bitch," Ryan says with gritted teeth.

"He no doubt did it to prevent you from calling for help," Mattie says. "He couldn't risk getting caught near the scene."

"Or it was an act of mercy," Jared says. "Maybe he

wanted to give Ryan enough time to get there, preventing Bella from having to deal with everything."

We all stare at him. Under Mattie's cutting look, his expression drops.

Mom's tone is cold. "There was nothing merciful about that man's actions."

Jared mumbles, "Sorry," and carries his empty glass to the wet bar.

Ryan walks over and places a hand on my shoulder. "You'll just tell the truth of that part then. You blacked out, and when you woke up, I was there."

Swallowing again, I nod.

"The biggest question the police are asking now is why the alarm at the office didn't work," Ryan says. "Mom told them how Dad was getting forgetful of late, sometimes not setting the alarm at home before going to bed. If they pose the question, don't act like finding the alarm inactive surprised you."

I stare at my brother. "What about the guard? Why wasn't there anyone on duty?"

"The guard testified that Dad dismissed him."

"Do you believe that?" Mattie asks.

Ryan hesitates.

"We need to know, Ryan." Mattie shifts to the edge of the sofa. "We better know if we're to keep our stories straight."

Ryan's reply is reluctant. "Angelo paid him to keep his mouth shut."

Mom makes a sound of distress before pursing her lips as if to prevent more sounds from escaping. My heart breaks for her.

"What if he decides to talk?" Mattie exclaims.

Ryan meets her gaze with a calm that belies the situation. "Angelo also paid him to switch off the alarm.

That makes him an accomplice. He's not going to talk, but I'm keeping an eye on him."

"Did he tell you this?" Mom asks with flaring nostrils. "That devil of a man himself?"

"Yes," Ryan says levelly.

"You're covering up for Angelo?" The realization leaves me breathless. "Are we going to turn into killers now too?"

Ryan's tone is soothing. "No, but you know what's at stake."

Wait. What am I saying? We're already killers. We pay criminals like Angelo to *clear the way*, and we put illegal arms in people's hands.

"Dear God," Mom says, looking away.

Mattie rubs her back. "We'll get through this. Dad did what he did, however wrong that was, but our name isn't Edwards for nothing."

"There's a lot to manage in the next few days." Ryan sounds tired. "I'll cover the finances and make sure the bills are paid. Can you handle the funeral arrangements?"

"Yes," Mattie and my mom say in unison.

It's all so business-like, as if we're discussing a takeover in the boardroom instead of my dad's murder.

"What about his life insurance?" Mom asks.

"If the cause of death is certified as suicide, they won't pay out," Jared says.

"Don't worry about money." Ryan leaves his empty glass on the side table. "You'll be set up for life."

Mom dabs at her eyes with a tissue. "Money is the least of my worries."

"It's tough to think about the bills in the midst of grief," Jared says, "but you should. You don't want to find yourself in a dire financial situation when the funeral is over."

Mattie glares at him. "Thank you for that piece of solid advice. Maybe you should just keep the comments to yourself."

Jared's shoulders sag. "I was only trying to help."

"No one has to worry about our financial situation." Ryan shoves a hand in his pocket. "I'll take care of the money."

I get to my feet. "I'm going to look for Pirate." I need a cuddle like never before. "You did bring him, didn't you Mattie?"

Mattie shoots Jared a panicked look. Ryan's expression is strangely sympathetic.

"What?" My stomach contracts into a ball. "Why are you looking at me like that?"

"Bella, honey." Mattie cups her stomach. "I'm afraid something happened."

"What?" I say again, my heart tripping over its own beat.

"He got away," my sister says. "Jared tried to stop him, but he ran over the road and…" She bites her lip. "I'm sorry."

I don't believe it. This can't be happening. Is the universe punishing me for something? What did I do? Is it because Angelo manipulated my mom into letting me keep the cat?

Tears build behind my eyes. Pirate was my first and only pet. Sometimes, it felt as if he was the only one who accepted me unconditionally.

I swallow down the tears, not showing my pain. I know my mom never forgave me for arm-wrestling her into keeping him here.

"Where is he?" I ask, my voice steady because I learned how to keep those storms under the surface. "I want to bury him."

"Oh, honey." Mattie flinches. "Jared had him cremated."

"There wasn't much to bury," Jared says.

"Jared," Mattie exclaims. "For God's sake."

"Sorry," he mumbles.

A knock falls on the door. It opens to reveal Doris in the frame. "Excuse the interruption, but the police are here to see Bella."

CHAPTER
NINE

Sabella

My life is falling apart.

Dad is gone. So is Pirate.

Guilt consumes me. I should've left Stellenbosch earlier. If I arrived in George ten minutes before I did, I could've stopped Santino from pulling the trigger. Dad could've been alive. I should've taken Pirate with me. He wouldn't have liked the long car ride, but if I hadn't left him at Mattie's, he would've still been here.

Sometimes, I think I'm still trapped in that bad dream, the one in which my tormentor showed up to soothe me. How can everything so hurtful and utterly devastating happen at the same time? Karma is obviously trying to tell me something. I only hate one person more than Angelo Russo, and that's myself.

Not wanting to add to my family's heavy burden, I mourn my losses in private. If only I could cry, but the stormy emotions remain trapped in my chest. At night, alone in my childhood bed, I'm sucked back into that deep, dark pit until I surface from my sleep gasping and with my body covered in sweat.

Our lawyer was present when the police interrogated me to make sure my legal rights were protected. He was happy with how the questioning went. The hospital psychiatrist told the detective in charge of the investigation that the shock most probably caused a short circuit in my brain, which made me black out.

The fact that I fainted again when Ryan arrived counts in my favor. It proves that my mind opted out because it couldn't cope with the harsh reality. The detective seemed satisfied for now, but he said he'd file a report once the forensics team submitted their results.

In the meantime, we carry on as best as we can. Ryan sent Celeste and Brad home before I was discharged from the hospital. He didn't want to expose them to the ugliness surrounding Dad's death. Now he leaves for Cape Town to bring them back to Great Brak River for the funeral.

The arrangements keep Mom and Mattie busy. Doris feeds us at every chance she gets. Cooking makes her feel useful. Neighbors and colleagues of Dad pop in with flowers, frozen meals, and condolences. A few reporters camp out on the pavement, waiting for us to leave the house.

When Ryan returns with Celeste and Brad, he's swamped with work. His many clandestine alliances all want a chunk of his time, demanding assurance that no foul play or information leaks are involved and that business will continue as usual.

Colin returns early from his holiday when he learns about the news. I haven't shared the tragic event with anyone. I can't bring myself to talk about it. It's bad enough that I receive curious messages from the students in my class. During this time, Colin and I grow close again, even closer than when we were kids playing cops and robbers on the beach.

On the day Dad's will is to be read, Mom dresses in a simple but elegant black dress with a matching faux-fur hat. I couldn't care less about what I wear, but Mattie ordered a long-sleeved shift dress for me. The journalists and photographers are still hanging around outside. In our world, appearances are everything, even in the midst of grief.

I pair the dress with long black boots and a fitted coat. My make-up is light but effective, hiding my grief from the media vultures and the spectators. After twisting my hair in a bun, I have enough time left to help Mattie straighten her hair and to play with Brad while Celeste gets ready. Doris offers to take care of Brad at home, saying a lawyer's office is no place for a child.

We set off for the solicitor's office in two cars. Ryan and Jared are driving. Paparazzi follow us into George, trying to get a few shots of the family through the vehicle windows.

The solicitor hired guards to keep the building entrance clear. It's a decoy designed to mislead the reporters who crowd on the pavement while we park in the underground lot and take the elevator to the top floor.

A secretary in a crisp, blue dress meets us when we exit. She shows us into a boardroom and offers us refreshments, which we decline. The silence in the room is subdued as we take our places around the table. Ryan and Mattie flank Mom while Celeste and Jared sit next to their spouses. I'm at the end of the table.

The solicitor enters when we're seated. He's a stately gentleman with white hair and a ruddy complexion, wearing a three-piece suit. He shakes our hands, making eye contact with each of us before taking the chair at the head of the table. A leather folder, fountain pen, notebook, and glass of water are set out in front of him, every object perfectly aligned.

After expressing his condolences, he's all business. He opens the leather folder and takes out a stack of papers bound with a spiral spine. Then he starts reading in a monotone voice.

"Mrs. Margaret Rose Edwards, spouse of the late Mr. Benjamin Joseph Edwards, is the sole heir of the property situated at number seven Orion Street, Great Brak River, and of the property situated at number fifty-five Jacqueline Drive, Bloubergstrand, Cape Town."

Celeste lifts her head quickly, looking at my mom.

"Mr. Ryan Edwards, son of the late Mr. Benjamin Joseph Edwards, will retain habitation rights of the property situated at number fifty-five Jacqueline Drive, Bloubergstrand, Cape Town, until such time as he voluntarily evacuates the property, purchases the property at the market value defined at the time of the purchase from Mrs. Margaret Rose Edwards, or is declared deceased by an official state death certificate."

He drones on, reading my dad's last wishes in formal terms and with an emotionless intonation. Besides the houses in Great Brak River and Cape Town, Mom also gets a retirement fund that will pay a monthly allowance from the date she turns sixty. Ryan inherits the business.

Poor Ryan.

I catch his gaze across the table. Does he even want the burden? Did he ever? Or did Dad make those decisions for him—for all of us—when he decided to do things under the table?

Dad set up investment funds for Mattie and me that

will pay out when we respectively turn twenty-five. I don't care what I get. I don't need anything. All I care about is the fact that Dad is gone and that I can't think about the man who did it for fear of breaking down so effectively I'll never come back from it. All I can think about is the farce and the lies and the terrible sword hanging over our heads. I can only think about the untruths and the fear we'll have to live with for the rest of our lives.

"…the vintage collection of cars be sold and the profit donated to a charity of Mrs. Margaret Rose Edwards's choice."

I tune out as the solicitor goes into the finer details of how my dad's belongings should be divided. The sailing boat he kept in Cape Town, the one he hardly ever used, goes to Ryan. Dad's collection of old coins goes to Brad, as well as some cash. Brad and Mattie's unborn child each receives a college fund. It goes on and on.

It's only when he mentions a property in Hout Bay that I pay attention again, not only because we don't have a house in Hout Bay, but also because of the short hesitation in the solicitor's otherwise flowing presentation and especially because of the way he clears his throat and takes a sip of water.

He sticks a finger in his collar and loosens the knot of his tie. "Ownership of the property at hundred eleven Fish Eagle Avenue, Hout Bay, is transferred to Mrs. Laura Remington."

Mom frowns, pale and startled. Ryan sits quietly, expressionless. Mattie takes Jared's hand where it rests on the tabletop as if she needs the support.

"Excuse me," Celeste says. "Who?"

The solicitor clears his throat again. "An investment fund to the value of ten million rand goes to Miss Daisy Remington."

"Ten million?" Mattie exclaims. "That's double the amount of Bella's and mine put together. Who is this person?" She twists in her chair, leaning forward to look at Ryan. "Is that someone at work?"

"No," Ryan replies, his tone flat.

"Can you please explain?" Celeste asks.

The solicitor briefly glances at my mom before fixing his gaze on the document in his hands. "Miss Daisy Remington is the daughter of Mrs. Laura Remington and the late Mr. Benjamin Edwards."

CHAPTER
TEN

Sabella

T he two vacant chairs next to the solicitor suddenly make sense. They're reserved for these women, Laura and Daisy Remington.

The information refuses to sink in.

She's the daughter of Mrs. Laura Remington and the late Mr. Benjamin Edwards.

Dad had an affair. Or a one-night stand. He has a daughter with someone else.

So many questions flood my mind that I feel dizzy. When? Why? How old is she? Why didn't Dad tell us?

Mom is frozen in shock. Mattie clamps a hand over her stomach as if wanting to protect their baby from the violent way of discovering the news. Jared rubs her back. Celeste gapes. Ryan scrubs a hand over his face.

The solicitor gets to his feet. "I understand that this

isn't the best time or way to meet Mrs. Remington and her daughter, but they requested to be present." The slightest hint of an apology slips into his professional tone. "Alas, it's their legal right."

He goes to the door and opens it. "You can come in now."

Dread fills me as he steps aside.

An attractive woman with shoulder-length blond hair and clear blue eyes enters. The soft lines around her eyes and mouth tell me she's in her late fifties. A powder-pink Chanel dress hugs her slim figure. Heels in a matching shade of pink adds an inch to her average height and shows off her well-toned calves. A handbag in the same patent leather as the shoes hangs over her forearm. She wears a compassionate smile and a warm expression. There's no malice or anger in her features, only concern and affection as she waits for the second person to enter.

The young woman who follows is more or less my age. It comes as a shock. I don't know why I expected a child. Maybe because I don't want to admit how long my dad concealed this secret. With wheat-blond hair and gray-blue eyes, Daisy takes after her mother. She's beautiful and regal, looking like a queen in simple black slacks and a silk blouse. She offers her mother a smile, one that says, *I'm okay*, before meeting our gazes with a confident air.

Behind them, the solicitor coughs. "I'll give you a couple of minutes before we continue," he says before leaving discreetly.

Laura Remington leads her daughter to the table. Her voice is pleasant and serene. "I wish we could've met under different circumstances."

We stare at them, none of us seemingly sure how to handle the situation.

"You must have questions," Laura says, taking her seat next to the solicitor's chair. "Why don't we get those out of the way before we let Mr. Dickson continue?"

Daisy sits and folds her hands in her lap. They observe us with a strange mixture of sympathy and curiosity on their faces.

As always, Mom gets to her senses first. She's not as composed or compassionate as Laura. Her face isn't a mask of serenity and warmth. She's battling to hide her shock, anger, and confusion. She's not hiding the loathing in her voice. "Did you have an affair with my husband?"

Laura utters a sigh. "I wish you didn't have to find out like this, Margaret. Really, I don't. It was Ben's wish to keep us a secret." She glances at Daisy, another soft smile transforming her features. "We loved him enough to respect his wishes."

"It's Mrs. Edwards to you," Mom says, sitting ramrod straight in her chair. "And you can spare us your apologies. The only things I'm interested in are the facts."

"Oh, I'm not apologizing for what we shared with Ben," Laura says. "Our feelings were genuine and pure, just like yours, I'm sure. Ben and I weren't a fleeting, dirty affair. Daisy and I were his second family."

"Second family?" Mattie exclaims. "What does that even mean?"

Laura turns her attention to Mattie. "You must be Matilde. I hope everything that's happened isn't putting too much stress on the pregnancy. It's not ideal, but your father always said you're as strong as your mother. You're even prettier in real life than in the photos I saw."

Mattie flinches. "He discussed us with you?" Her voice rises in volume. "He showed you photos?"

"Of course he did." Laura gives her a sad look. "He loved you. Very much."

"Like he loved you?" Mattie asks with a wry chuckle.

Laura's answer is patient. "Yes. He loved us too. I guess that was the problem, why he couldn't choose."

"How long?" Mom asks, pressing her lips into a thin line. "How long have you been sneaking around behind my back?"

Mattie cups Mom's hand, a gesture no doubt meant to urge my mom not to lose her composure and dignity.

"Daisy and Sabella are the same age," Laura says with meaning.

The cruelty of it is too much. I can't stand to look at them, but I can't look away either.

Mom isn't to be deterred. "How long were you together before she was conceived?"

Laura sighs again. "Eight years."

Oh my God. That was before Ryan was born. My brother's face turns chalky as he processes the news.

"I know what you're going to ask next," Laura continues, "so I'll just tell you everything. We met at a fundraising event. I was a journalist for a pony newspaper in George back then. We didn't expect to fall in love or for the bond between us to grow so strong. I knew from the start that Ben was my soulmate, but I tried to keep my distance.

"I guess some things are simply too strong to be kept apart. When the relationship got serious, Ben asked me to leave George. He was protecting you, you see. He didn't want any rumors to start that could hurt you. He bought the house in Hout Bay, and I moved there."

"All this time," Mom says. "You knew. You knew he had a real family, yet you continued to play house with him."

"We didn't play. Far from it. We were his real family too. The only difference is that you got his surname."

Laura chuckles. "I've always been a little jealous of you for that."

"You're right," Mom says, pushing to her feet and pulling herself to her full height. "That's everything I wanted to know. Now that I do, I don't ever want to see you again."

"Margaret—" Laura catches herself and corrects her mistake with a small smile. "Mrs. Edwards, this is not how I wanted the reading of Ben's last wishes to go."

Ryan gets up too, standing in solidary support next to Mom. "Why *did* you come here, Laura? What's your real agenda, except for ruining my family's lives and stealing whatever peace we could've found in our grief?"

"Don't forget, Ryan," Laura says, "Daisy and I are also grieving. We're mourning a father and a life partner who we loved dearly. As for your fears, you needn't worry. Ben left us with enough to live comfortably and to take care of ourselves. We're not here to make claims on your money."

"No." Ryan narrows his eyes. "Why would you? Daisy is ten million richer, isn't she?"

A half-smile curves Daisy's mouth. She holds Ryan's heated gaze, hers cool in turn.

"Daisy didn't ask for anything," Laura says. "Neither did I. It was Ben's decision to take care of us."

"As was his duty," Mom says, lifting her chin. "I, on the other hand, owe you nothing." She picks up her bag and walks to the door.

Ryan glares at Laura and Daisy as he takes Celeste's elbow and helps her to her feet. Mattie, Jared, and I follow. We're far from being a perfect family, but we do stand together when it matters.

Mom opens the door. The solicitor stands on the other side of it, talking quietly to his secretary.

He gives a start. "We're not done."

"Well," Mom says, stepping around him. "It would seem that I am very much done here."

CHAPTER
ELEVEN

Sabella

I didn't know an emotion can fill your chest with so much ache that the bruise feels physical. That every breath you take hurts.

How do I deal with the betrayal? I've barely had time to process Dad's cold-blooded murder. I'm still digesting the fact that the man who raised me, the dad I loved and admired, was a criminal. That the man I had sex with killed him. Now I discover that I never truly knew my dad. It makes me question everything we shared. Which parts were real? Which parts were deception and lies, covering up an illegal business and a second family?

A second family.

Mom locked herself in her bedroom when we got home. Jared is making tea. Mattie does what she always does in a crisis. She remains cool and collected, throwing herself into the funeral arrangements. Ryan is tightlipped, and Celeste is asking too many questions, questions to which none of us want to know the answers.

Because it hurts too damn much.

Because it's too painful to admit that our whole life up to now was a farce.

My dad, the man I placed on a pedestal, the man who taught me with so much patience to ride a bike and to drive a car, lied to my face for as long as I've been alive.

Mom is hiding. Mattie is organizing. Ryan is closed-off. Celeste is playing with Brad. Those are their go-to coping mechanisms. Mine is swimming.

It's cold outside, but I don't care. I'm always swim fit, even in winter. I pull on my swimsuit and climb down the dune to the beach.

The coldness of the water comes as a shock. I welcome the iciness that steals my breath. It numbs my body and my senses. It dulls the feelings I can't express, and it freezes the havoc in my chest. When my muscles contract with cold, I don't feel the hollowness in the pit of my stomach. I don't feel the sickness that pushes up in my throat.

I swim and swim, putting distance between me and my life. But no matter how hard I kick and how fast I swing my arms through the water, I can't outrun what's trapped inside me. I carry it with me into the deepness of the water until the heaviness of the burden pulls me down.

At first, I fight. Hard. I fight the cramps and the fatigue and the onslaught of emotions. I fight long past knowing it's too late, knowing I exceeded my limits.

For a terrifying moment, there's only darkness and finality, but the dark and the cold have always been my safe place. The water is where I'm free.

Sinking.

It's not like when I was drugged in the hospital and I wanted to surface. It just feels so good to stop fighting.

To be free.

Alive.

I gulp. My lungs fill with water.

I'm drowning.

The realization pumps a rush of adrenaline through my veins. Everything vanishes—the storm, the numbness, the tiredness. Only one thing remains. A will to live.

I kick with all my might, using my arms to drag myself through the water, but my muscles are uncooperative. Useless. My ears pop painfully. An engine sounds somewhere, a thread that connects me to life. It's like a lifeline to reality. I can almost taste the diesel fumes of a boat. An urge to vomit the water in my lungs contracts my shoulders. Spots explode in my vision.

A fist punches through the surface. And another. A man dives into the water with his arms stretched out in front of him. No shoes or jacket. Just a shirt and trousers. Those arms grab me. They pull me toward the surface, back toward breath.

CHAPTER
TWELVE

Angelo

The motor boat approaches the shore by the time I make it to the beach. Roch's bald head shines in the sun. Sabella sits on the side, clinging to the ropes while the wind whips her hair around her face. She's wearing nothing but a one-piece swimsuit. It's fourteen degrees Celsius outside and the water is twelve degrees max. She must be freezing.

Not taking the time to remove my shoes, I half-run and half-slide down the dune. It's faster than taking the bridges via the island and swimming through the river. I thank any gods willing to listen not only for Roch's foresight to keep an inflatable boat in the cave but also for his navigational skills.

He reaches the break as I arrive at the bottom of the dune. My gut tightens. The surf is big today. It's high tide, plus a strong wind blows in from the sea. Roch keeps the boat parallel to the waves. When the swell lifts, he makes a ninety degree turn and rides it out. The wall of water curls, bends, and crashes around them, white foam bashing the boat.

Fuck.

Miraculously, the boat stays afloat.

Sprinting across the sand, I forget to breathe. All I see is a car racing toward a hairpin bend on a mountain road. All I feel is the impending doom of a crash. I'm knee-deep in the water before I register the icy pricks that assault my skin.

Roch repeats the maneuver, steering the boat between the waves before turning the nose head-on into the break. After what seems like forever, he makes it to the shallow water, diverts left to avoid some rocks, and launches the boat smoothly onto the sand.

I run like never before, scraping my shins against the sharp edges of abalone shells that cling to the rocks, but I hardly feel it. Roch cuts the engine. His soaked clothes are plastered to his body. He reaches for Sabella, trying to pull her to her feet.

Her hysterical words reach me over the deafening crash of the breakers. "Don't fucking touch me!"

Roch freezes with flaring nostrils and a clenched jaw. His baritone voice carries louder than hers. "The least you can do is thank me for saving your life."

"I told you to stay the hell away from me," she yells.

"Roch," I call in warning, a few steps away from the boat.

If he hears me, he doesn't react. "Fine," he shouts, shoving her with both palms on her shoulders as he continues at the top of his lungs, "Then get the hell out of my boat."

Sabella falls backward over the side and lands with her ass in the shallow water.

"I should've left you in the fucking water." Roch points a finger at her. "If that's where you want to be, be my guest and stay there."

Spluttering and gasping, she braces herself on her arms.

I hook my hands under her armpits when I reach her and hoist her to her feet. "Fuck, Sabella." Her skin is icy. She trembles like a flimsy sheet of paper in a violent storm. "Are you all right, *cara?*"

The question is automatic. Of course she's not all right.

Wrapping one arm around her shoulders and the other under her knees, I lift her into my arms.

She tries to wrestle herself out of my hold. When I only tighten my grip, she fights like a wildcat. "Get off me."

Her teeth chatter so hard I barely make out what she says.

Roch jumps out of the boat and grabs the rope, his movements jerky and careless.

I carry Sabella out of the water and lower her to the ground. The moment her feet touch the sand, her legs fold under her. Fatigue and shock take over, stealing her fight. I strip off my jacket and hang it around her shoulders. She huddles under the fabric on the wet sand, looking wretched and exhausted and half-dead.

In two long strides, I'm next to Roch. My fist connects with his jaw before he sees it coming. The blow makes him stumble back a step. I land another punch in his stomach that makes him fold double.

Adrenaline born from rage and fear pumps through my veins. "Apologize," I snap.

Roch grimaces as he straightens. It takes him a

moment to find his breath. "I'm sorry. I'm not myself." He works his jaw. "It's the scare. I didn't think she was going to make it. I thought I was too late."

His words put me on edge. I've lost too much. I'm not prepared to lose her as well. If I do, the deaths of everyone this war already claimed will be futile. I won't allow that. I won't allow my mother and Adeline's deaths to have been for nothing.

For good measure, I punch Roch again. He had a fright. So did I. It's no excuse for how he behaved.

Cold fury laces my tone. "Apologize to Sabella, not to me."

Roch turns to her, rubbing a hand over his jaw. "I'm sorry. I shouldn't have pushed you and said things I didn't mean." He lifts his gaze to me. "I've been on babysitting duty for two and a half years."

"You're relieved of it," I say, grinding my teeth.

"Angelo." He raises his hands. "Mr. Russo. Two and a half years without a break."

"Do not try to justify your actions." Each word is measured. "Get the fuck out of my sight before I kill you."

He ducks his head, pushes the boat back into the water, and jumps inside.

Sweeping Sabella into my arms, I hurry with her to the shelter of the cave. The engine of the boat sounds when I reach the rock enclosure, but I don't bother to look back. I sit, pulling her onto my lap.

"Get away from me," she says, trying to break out of the cage of my arms.

I rub her biceps through my jacket. "You need to get warm."

"What I need is for you to stop touching me," she screams, finally managing to scurry off my lap.

She lands on all fours, my jacket slipping off her

shoulders. I reach for her ankle, but she claws her way like a crab through the sand to the other side of the cave and pushes her back against the wall. There, she sits shivering, watching me with a terrified expression.

"I'm not going to hurt you." I raise my hands in a placating gesture. "I already told you that."

She spits the word at me. "But?"

I make to move. "But you need to get warm."

She flattens herself against the rock. "Stay away from me."

"Sabella." Frustration rides on my words. "I want to help."

"Help?" She utters an ugly laugh. "Like you helped my dad?"

A sob racks her shoulders.

Using my most reasonable voice, I say, "You know why it had to be done." I don't want to mention my mother or my sister. I don't want those memories to cloud my judgment with anger. Not now. Not now that she needs me.

Her accusation bounces off the roof of the cave. "I can't even go to the police. You must be fucking ecstatic about that."

"I'm not ecstatic about anything."

I try to advance again, but she shakes her head so vehemently that wet tendrils of her hair stick to her cheeks.

My patience is running out. I make myself stern. "Be reasonable, Sabella."

"Reasonable?" She laughs again. "Why? Because you're so reasonable, you heartless, deceitful, murdering son of a bitch?"

I grit my teeth at the insults, but I let them slide. After all, I earned every name she called me. "You'll catch pneumonia."

Her upper lip curls. "Like you care."

"You know I do."

Her tone is biting. "Is that why you came to the hospital?" Then sarcastic as her volume rises again. "Because you cared? No, wait. It was only to shave me. You're a sick pervert."

"I wanted to see my mark." As if the thought alone is a magnet, my gaze is drawn to her lower body. "It healed nicely. Very pretty." And like the pervert she accused me of being, that thought makes me hard.

She picks up a handful of sand and throws it at my face. "Go fuck yourself."

My reflexes are good. I duck in time. "We've been through that, haven't we?"

"Are you getting off on this?" she asks, sparks shooting from her eyes. "Is that why you're tormenting me?"

"Tormenting you has never entered the equation." I add with warning, "Not yet, but if you keep this up, it may."

"Just—" She spears her fingers through her hair and cups her head. "Just stay away."

"I can never stay away from you."

She drops her hands and curls her fingers like claws into the sand. "What the hell else do you want from me? You've taken all my firsts. Everything. What else can you possibly want?"

The answer is simple. "You."

"Why?" she cries out. "What have I ever done to you?"

"Wanting you isn't a punishment, Sabella. We were always meant to be together."

Hatred darkens her eyes. "Here's a newsflash. We're enemies. I may not be able to give the police the names of my father's murderers because I just found out that he was a murderer too, but we will never be together." She emphasizes the last part, using the rock for support to straighten as she throws those words at my feet.

Now isn't the time to convince her of anything. It's an even worse time to inform her of her fate. What worries me the most, is, "Did you go that deep into the sea on purpose?" The question constricts my throat and twists my mind. "Did you plan on coming back?"

Her eyes flare. Her chuckle is mocking. "Do you think I'll drown myself over the likes of you?"

I watch her narrowly, noticing how cold she is, inside and out, how full of bitterness and hatred. "What would've happened if Roch weren't there?"

She shrugs, mocking me. "Who knows?"

I don't like it. I don't like her gambling attitude toward life. "Why did you do it? Why did you go so far?" I add in a quieter tone, "It wasn't the first time."

She clenches her hands at her sides. "I'm not a fucking quitter."

"No?" I tilt my head. "Then explain it to me."

"I don't owe you any explanations," she bites out.

That's it. I've had it. I lunge, grabbing her arm before she can escape. "Don't forget, *cara*, your life belongs to me. I have every right to demand an explanation."

Angry tears simmer in her eyes. "I regret the day I laid eyes on you."

"You don't have to," I say, rubbing my thumb in a soothing gesture over the soft skin of her wrist. "There was a time you liked me. With a little effort, we can go back to that."

"I never liked you," she utters with a sneer. "How could I? I didn't even know you. The person you pretended to be wasn't real."

"One day, you'll understand." Now isn't the moment to come clean about her father's broken promise.

"Oh, I understand." She yanks on my hold. "Perfectly."

"I can be that man for you again." I drag her closer, making our bodies collide. "All you have to do is ask me."

Her brown eyes narrow, and her lips thin. Contempt shows in every line of her features. "Hell will freeze over before I ask you for anything." She lifts her chin, holding my gaze with false bravado as she commands in a calm, controlled voice, "Now let me go."

I don't miss the effort it takes her to force that control or to pretend not to be scared. Her whole body is shaking with the effort. Uncertainty flickers behind the anger shimmering in her eyes. I take notice of other things too, of how her body fits against mine and how hard her nipples are from the cold.

Pushing her backward, I follow her down and catch her body to break her fall before she hits the sand. I'm on top of her in a wink, spreading out over the length of her, and nothing has ever felt so right. Finally, I can warm her. What I really want to do is possess her.

She fights me, slamming her fists into my ribs and clamping her teeth onto my shoulder. I don't stop her. I let her use me as the punching bag she needs to get this poison out of her system. I'm not restraining her. If she wants to, she can flip us over and punch me in the face, but she doesn't. Not that she's holding back. No, she tries to inflict damage to the best of her ability.

I let her carry on until she tires. When she sags onto the sand with a defeated sob, I catch her wrists and pin them above her head. The look in her eyes changes. It turns from uncontrolled fury to uncontrolled carnality. I can't tear my gaze away from the way she watches me like a female praying mantis about to mate a male before making a meal out of him.

What passes between us is simple physics. Energy can't be destroyed. It can only be transformed. All that anger fueling her now doesn't vanish. It simply changes into a different sentiment. I can take away her fury as little as I can change the law of energy. I can, however, offer her an escape, if only for a short while. She was my first, and she'll be my last. What we are isn't pretty, but we're meant to be together.

Dipping my head, I hold her gaze as I press my mouth on hers. She tastes cold and salty and wild. She bites. I let her. When I part her lips with mine, she doesn't resist. She meets the strokes of my tongue, getting tangled in my body and in our kiss. She's using me like I'm using her, groping blindly for a remedy to ease the pain. In our case, the medicine is lust.

I let go of her wrists, wanting her to make this choice. She does. She fists her hands in my hair and holds on. For better or worse. For whatever we can get. Even if the relief lasts for a fleeting moment. I'd rather she finds it here in a cave with me than on the bottom of the ocean.

My movements are jerky when I pull the straps of her swimsuit over her shoulders to expose her small, firm breasts. She pants with feverish breaths as I close my lips around a nipple and suck the icy, hard tip into the warmth of my mouth. She tastes good on my tongue. I take her deeper, unable to get enough. Then the other breast. The iciness of her skin melts underneath me. Heat burns between us, but I know from experience that nowhere does it burn hotter than between her thighs.

Making quick work of stripping off her swimsuit, I spread her legs. I'm eager. Hasty. I want to do this before the fog of grief and fury lifts enough for her to change her mind. I'm already unzipping as I kiss the soft spot between her legs. My mark looks perfect just above it. I'm aching to trace the outline of that picture with my tongue, but I don't want to call her attention to it. Not now. For now, I only want her to think about pleasure.

I dip my tongue inside, lapping her up. I'm on fire, but so is she. She arches her back when I suck. I tease enough to make her toss and moan without taking her over the edge. If she comes down from the high of a climax, she may push me away before I have a chance to get inside her. I lick and nip, making sure she's lubricated, but she doesn't need my help. She's soaking wet for me.

Freeing my cock, I guide it to her opening and part her with the crest. She cries out, wrapping her legs around me. I don't waste time. I surge forward, sliding deep. Five months. Five months since I had her, since I had relief. It's the sweetest torture, but I rock inside her instead of thrusting, making this last.

My girl isn't shy about showing me what she needs. She lifts her hips and takes me deeper. How hard her tight, hot pussy grips me almost makes me go out of my mind. I forget why we're here. Or that I should use a condom. Almost. I try to pull out, but she locks her ankles behind my ass and wraps her arms around my neck. When her inner muscles squeeze my cock, I lose my shit.

I pump into her like a madman. Making a soft sound of frustration, she pushes on my shoulders. I pin her to the sand with both my movements and the advantage of my weight, taking care not to crush her, because there's no way I'm letting her go. Until I understand what she wants.

When I let up, she pushes me over and straddles me. The sight of her sitting naked on my cock is so hot I forget to move. Her tanned body is toned. Sand sticks to her skin and her hair. Her breasts bounce gently as she takes over the rhythm, her pussy stretching to swallow my cock. I'm fixated by the sight. Mesmerized. When she wraps her fingers around the root of my cock, I nearly come then and there. It's hot and dirty. Sacred. Us. Our moment.

She leans back, keeping her weight on one arm, and moans. Finally snapping out of it, I let loose. Her cries of pleasure echo in the cave. We're crazed and desperate, but our movements are coordinated. We're doing this dance so well. Our bodies are locked together, hers naked and mine clothed.

I follow her lead, quickening my pace. It's impossible to hold back any longer. Not with five months in between. Taking advantage of her exposed position, I rub her clit. She goes over first, her hot, velvet pussy milking my cock as spasms contract her muscles. Her climax triggers mine. I palm her breasts, digging my fingers into the soft curves and holding on for life as I empty myself inside her. I'm delirious with pleasure, even when I'm done, dry-fucking her with a semi-hard cock.

Not willing it to end, I roll us over without pulling out and push her down on the sand with my body. Locking my hands around her wrists, I plant them next to her face and kiss her. This time, I'm not rushed. I want to explore the contours of her mouth. If I carry on kissing her, I'll grow hard again. I can stay inside her, and we can keep on fucking in this cave where the outside world doesn't have to exist. Just a little longer.

But reality is already seeping through the cracks. Turning her face to the side, she breaks the kiss. Even as I let her escape, I miss her taste. I pull back a little, giving her the distance she wants.

She looks at me with wide eyes and parted lips. "What have I done?"

I squeeze her wrists with a gentle warning. What we did is too sacred for regret. "The most natural thing in the world."

Just like that, the heat evaporates from her gaze. We never stopped being angry. We only used our anger differently. I see the exact moment the shame sets in.

"Let me up," she says, her voice shaky.

It goes against every grain of my being to let her go. Only the superhuman willpower I cultivated through the years allows me to unlock my fingers from her wrists. I sit up. We both look at where we're joined. Her cheeks flush when I pull out and stand on my knees. My seed leaks down her thighs. So dirty. So pretty. The sight sends a surge of possessive satisfaction through me.

Tucking my cock back into my pants, I say, "We didn't use protection." I don't tell her I have a condom in my wallet. I don't say that I should've stopped to fit it, because, even though I understand her objections, I don't want anything between us when I'm inside her. Not even a thin layer of rubber.

"It doesn't matter." Her voice is oddly flat. "My period is due any day. Actually, it's overdue. Nothing is going to happen."

I get off her, zip up, and offer her a hand.

She accepts my help, avoiding my gaze.

I pick up her swimsuit. "You can't put this back on. It's still wet. You'll freeze outside in the wind." I grab my jacket from the sand, dust it off, and hold it open. "Here."

Not arguing, she slides her arms into the sleeves and allows me to button it up.

"I can bring the car to the island," I say. "I'll grab some clothes for you on the way."

Hugging herself, she shakes her head. "I'll go back via the dune. It'll be quicker."

I motion at her attire. "You can't walk around your neighborhood like that."

"No." She pulls the jacket over her head without unbuttoning it. "You're right."

Snatching her swimsuit from my hand, she turns her back on me and pulls on the wet garment.

"Sabella."

"I don't know what came over me," she says, refusing to look at me. "Fucking the murderer of my—"

"Stop it."

My harsh tone shuts her up. I make an effort to soften my voice. "Choose me. That's all that stands between you and happiness. You can have everything you ever wanted, everything you dreamed of. All you have to do is say yes."

She spins around. "Choose you?" She laughs, the sound cold and mocking. "How can I choose a man I hate?"

"To hate or not to hate, *cara*, can also be a choice."

Observing me with a too perceptive gaze, she says, "Tell me you don't hate me, not even a little, for what my family did to yours."

I clench my jaw. I can lie, but I don't want to. Not to her. Not about us.

Her smile is victorious. "That's what I thought."

When she makes to turn, I catch her wrist. "Choose me now, *cara*, while you can." My words hold a warning. "Because there will come a day that you won't have a choice any longer."

"Never," she says, jerking free from my hold and walking like a queen with her head held high from the cave as if we didn't just fuck like animals.

CHAPTER
THIRTEEN

Sabella

The mug of tea I'm cradling between my palms where I'm sitting on the veranda doesn't warm me. Neither does the blanket covering my legs. I showered and changed into a cashmere sweater and sweatpants, but the heat burning on my skin doesn't come from my clothes. It comes from shame. Inside, I'm frozen.

Mattie exits from the lounge, wearing a black wool dress that shows off her round belly. How does she manage to look so classy and unruffled in the midst of everything that's happening?

She walks over and sits down next to me. "Hey."

I scoot to the side to make space for her and offer her half of the blanket.

"Thanks." She draws the blanket over her knees and heaves a sigh as she looks toward the sunset. "It's pretty, isn't it?"

Even though I haven't noticed the view, I nod. I'm not out here to admire the rose-gold reflection of the sun on the water as it sinks like an orange ball below the horizon. I'm hiding from what I did and from the despicable person those actions make me.

"The police closed the investigation," she says. "The pathologist released his body. At least now we can set a date for the funeral."

I look at her quickly. "They did?"

"They concluded that the strain of Dad's affair and keeping his *other* family hidden from us and the world was a very likely motive for suicide. I suppose it helps that the police are understaffed and that the high crime rate keeps them busy." Her expression is grim. "The media is already running headlines that living a double life finally took its toll."

Feeling sick, I stare at her in horror. "How did the affair leak out? From Dickson's office?"

She sighs again. "Laura Remington came clean. She told her story in an exclusive media interview."

"What? When did this happen?"

"She went straight to a local newspaper after the reading of the will. It's breaking news. I wanted to tell you before you saw it on social media or on television."

"Oh my God." I set my mug on the table. "Why would she do such a thing? I don't expect her to give a damn about us, but why ruin whatever dignity Dad had left when she claimed to have loved him so much? And why would she expose herself and her daughter to public scrutiny?"

"She told the journalist the same thing she told us, that she has nothing to be ashamed of. She said she respected Dad's wishes while he was alive, but now that he's dead, she wants recognition for Daisy who grew up under exceptionally difficult circumstances."

"Whose fault was that?" I cry out. "Didn't Laura consider the hardships of being a part-time single mother before she decided to have a child with a married man?"

Mattie wipes a hand over her brow. "Laura is evoking sympathy by telling the country how Daisy was teased in school for not having a father. She's using the bullying card. She wants the world to recognize Daisy as Ben Edwards's daughter and not just another bastard child."

My chest squeezes. No child is a bastard. No child should have to grow up with a *part-time* father.

Mattie sounds tired. "According to Ryan's PR agency, fifty percent of the viewers and readers are sympathizing with Laura and Daisy."

Hollowness settles in my stomach. "They're choosing sides?"

"How can they not? People are judgmental by nature. Very few are going to sit on the fence about the scoop."

"Shit. This is terrible. How's Mom?"

"Strong. Brave. Holding her head high and keeping up appearances. What choice does she have?"

Pulling the blanket up to our waists, I say, "I wish there was a way of making this easier for her."

"That's what I came to talk to you about. We're going to be bombarded by the media for the next few weeks, at least until the sensation wears off. Our family should have an aligned strategy on how to deal with the scandal. We decided that our response will be no response. It's the quickest way to put out the fire."

"No comment," I muse.

"Exactly. The funeral can be as early as Friday. The sooner we put this behind us, the sooner Mom can move on."

I steal a glance at my sister. Like Mom, her make-up

and hair are perfect, but the strain shows in the tight set of her mouth and the dark circles under her eyes.

Putting an arm around her, I hug her against me. "You shouldn't have to deal with this in your condition. Let me take over. I'm on break until July anyway. What else am I going to do while hiding from the media?"

"Not hiding." She pulls her back straight. "An Edwards never hides. We just don't engage. We won't throw them a bone to fight over."

"Right."

She leans her head against mine. "Thank you for the offer anyway. I'm good at organizing, and Mom needs this. If she doesn't keep busy, she'll probably have a meltdown."

"What if she melts down after all the arrangements are done? Aren't we just prolonging the inevitable?"

"Then we'll be there for her. At least prolonging a breakdown will help her to maintain her dignity while the media dissects her every move."

A beat of silence passes before I ask carefully, "What do you think about them?"

The set of her features hardens. "Laura and Daisy? No matter how Laura justifies her affair with Dad, what Laura and Dad did was wrong. Dad married Mom, didn't he? He chose Mom before he met Laura. If he fell out of love with Mom and divorced her before getting together with Laura, I would've understood. But keeping a second family in secret? What they did to us is inexcusable. The worst is leaving us to deal with this alone."

My chest tightens painfully. "Dad didn't die on purpose."

"No, but everyone dies. He knew his relationship with Laura would inevitably be exposed. He even constructed his will in that manner. Letting us find out like that…" She swallows. "Letting us handle the aftermath of his infidelity? I'll never forgive him for that cruelty."

"What Dad did is wrong, but Daisy *is* our half-sister."

Her words are harsh. "I have no interest in getting to know her. Even if I did, I'd never do that to Mom. Can you imagine how that would make her feel?"

Rubbing her arm, I say, "I'm sorry. I'm so sorry this is happening when you're only supposed to feel the joy of being pregnant with your first baby."

"Oh, Bella." She lifts her head and gives me a soft smile. "I know this is harder on you. Of all of us, you and Dad were the closest. You were always his favorite."

"That was wrong too. Parents shouldn't have favorites."

"Sometimes, they do. The two of you were accomplices, so similar in your likes and behavior." She pats my hand where it lies on top of the blanket. "Besides, I've always been Mom's favorite."

Biting my lip, I stare at the distance. The sun has sunk below the ocean, leaving streaks of pink across the sky. "I don't know which parts of what I had with Dad weren't fake. Sometimes, I wonder if anything was real. I didn't even truly know him. That's the hardest part." I swallow back tears. "That I don't know. That now, I never will."

"Don't think like that." She nudges me. "His love for you was always real. That's what you have to remember."

Taking a shaky breath, I consider that. The problem is that his lies make me doubt his affection. Is that how someone who loves you behave? Then again, who am I to judge? After what I did to my family by falling for Angelo, I don't have the right to criticize anyone's behavior.

Someone raps on the glass of the sliding door. Mattie and I turn our faces in that direction. Mrs. Taylor and Colin stand on the threshold.

Mrs. Taylor wears a sympathetic expression. "Doris said we'd find you here." She holds out a basket with wine, fruit, and biltong. "I brought some nibbles to see you through between meals. I also wanted to ask if you need help with anything, maybe with the catering for the funeral?"

Mattie moves the blanket aside and stands. "That's very kind of you, Mrs. Taylor." She takes the basket. "Mom will be happy to see you." Leading Mrs. Taylor into the house, she asks, "Would you like a cup of tea?"

Colin walks over, his hands shoved in his pockets. "I'm sorry. We should be offering to make you a cup of tea."

I try to smile, motioning at my untouched tea on the table. "I already have one."

"Care for some company?" he asks with a compassionate smile.

"Sure."

He sits down next to me. "I saw the news."

"Yeah. Quite the scandal."

"I hate that you're going through this."

"Thanks." What else can I say?

"I just want you to know that I'm here for you, Bella, and that I'll never judge you, no matter what happens."

"I know." Shifting closer, I borrow some of his warmth. "What would I do without you?"

He shivers. "It's cold out here."

I shrug. "I needed some space."

"From people? I can go if—"

"From me."

He catches my chin and turns my face to him. "You're not blaming yourself for any of what happened?"

Pulling free, I jump up and escape to the garden.

Colin's steps crunch on the gravel path behind me. "Bella?"

The breeze blows my hair into my face. "Maybe I am." I drag my hands over my hair and grab the strands in a ponytail at the base of my neck. "I should've realized what Dad was up to. There were signs. Many signs. Like at Brad's name giving party. Dad was talking to someone on the phone, and he cut the call short when I approached. Come to think of it, he did that often. He was in such a rush to get back to George from Cape Town, he couldn't even enjoy the family gathering. He couldn't make the time to take me to the aquarium. When he got here, he left straight away. He dropped us off, and after seeing us home safely, he left to spend time with them, his other family. I should've realized then, but I didn't. I should've realized at Ryan's birthday and at all the other gatherings where my dad was distant and more on his phone than with us."

Colin grips my shoulder and turns me around. "It wasn't your duty to question your father or to mistrust his motives. It wasn't your duty to uncover the truth. The obligation to be honest was your father's alone."

If only he knew. "I'm not a good person, Colin."

He pulls me into a hug. "Nobody is perfect. Don't be so hard on yourself. The best thing for you right now is a good dose of self-love."

I wish I could tell him what happened in the cave. I wish I could confide in someone. I want to open my mouth and let this storm out of my chest, but not even the psychiatrist can know what truly happened.

Mattie was right when she said I'm just like Dad. Am I not keeping secrets from the world too, secrets that will destroy my family if they find out? How will Mom and Mattie and Ryan react if they know I slept with Angelo in a drunken state on my eighteenth birthday and worse, after his father killed mine? They'll see me for the pathetic traitor I am.

"Come on." Colin releases me. "Let's go inside where it's warmer."

He makes his way back to the house. I hover on the edge of the lawn, reluctant to abandon the freedom of the open space for the prison of the house. At least I can breathe here.

My gaze is drawn to the cave on the beach. The man who stands at the edge of the water makes a gasp catch in my throat. He's too tall, too large, too present. Too deeply under my skin.

He stands with a proud stance, his hands shoved in his pockets. He's nothing but a black outline in the dusk. However, when I rest my gaze on the shadow of his face, I can swear he's staring straight back at me. When he turns and strides toward the lagoon, I sense his smile. The worst? After everything he's done, as he walks away, he takes a piece of me with him.

Angelo

Roch waits in the parking lot of the hotel when I get back.

He straightens from leaning on the hood of his inconspicuous city car as I park and get out.

"I left the boat on the island." He grunts. "It may come in useful."

"Pack your stuff," I say in passing him. "Make sure you're on the next flight home."

"Mr. Russo." He runs to keep up. "I screwed up today. I'd like another chance."

"You heard me. I don't want to see your face again unless it's on Corsican soil."

I leave him standing there, too livid to look into his eyes. If Roch was any other man, I'd chop his hands off and throw him into the sea. The only reason he's alive is that he's a distant cousin of my mother, and she loved him.

I stalk to my room, order room service, and have a shower. The dinner arrives while I'm dressing. I opt for a casual suit and a fitted shirt. Wolfing down the food, I hardly taste the steak and grilled vegetables. After eating, I email a local security company with detailed instructions. I built a good relationship with the owner after researching them well. Even as I instructed Roch to watch out for Sabella, I already had a backup plan. A few, actually. I never do anything without a plan B, C, and D.

Once that's in place, I do a quick check to see what's circulating on the news about Edwards's death. What I find is shocking, even to me. Edwards kept a mistress for years. He had a daughter with her who's Sabella's age. Daisy. He set his mistress and his illegitimate daughter up in a luxury mansion in Hout Bay and divided his time between the women. The mistress, an attractive blonde with style and class, has an arm around the waist of her daughter on the newspaper photograph that's published on every internet news site.

Fuck me.

Edwards hid his infidelity well. My father warned me that Edwards was a snake, but Sabella's father was much slyer than I took him for. I never saw the move he made to kill my father and me coming. If I had, my mother and sister would still be alive. For that, I'll never forgive myself.

Sabella didn't say a word about her father's affair. I can only imagine how the news turned her already messed-up world further upside down. For that mess, we're both responsible, she unknowingly and me very much consciously. For that chaos, I'm prepared. I have my own doctor on standby in Corsica. I have all my weapons lined up—tranquilizers, groveling, money, sex, and discipline. Even a lock and key if that's what it will take.

But *this*? Edwards's double life may be the straw that

breaks the camel's back. No wonder she swam as if she was heading for Robben Island today. What she did concerns me. She almost fucking drowned herself. It worries me that I don't have a plan for *that*.

Making a spur-of-the-moment decision, I head to the hospital. It's way past closing time when I barge into the office of the attending doctor who treated Sabella. His secretary has long since knocked off for the day. He's there though. He always works late. I had time to observe him when I sneaked into Sabella's room at night.

"Mr. Russo." He jumps to his feet. "My office is closed."

"I know." I cross the floor and take a seat at his desk. Pointing at his chair, I say, "Sit."

He does so reluctantly. "If this is about the bill, the administration desk—"

"I already settled the bills."

He pushes his glasses up his nose. "In that case, what's the emergency?"

"I need to talk to you about Sabella."

"Miss Edwards?" He folds his hands on the desk. "Discussing a patient is highly irregular."

"I already told you, I'm her fiancé, and this concerns her welfare."

"It's preferable that she's present."

I smile. "Not going to happen. Do I need to remind you that I also made a significant donation to extend your ICU wing? How many beds will that add to your hospital?"

He clears his throat. "What would you like to discuss?"

"You read the reports from the psychiatrist."

"The initial one after she was admitted and examined, yes. With regard to her treatment, I'm not privy to that information."

I raise a brow. "Her treatment?"

He frowns. "Didn't she tell you? Naturally, after what happened, I recommended psychiatric treatment. Left untreated, the trauma she suffered can only cause damage that may manifest in her behavior later."

The bit about the treatment is news.

Concern creeps into his expression. "I hope she's heeding my advice and seeing someone to help her deal with the trauma."

"You know her diagnosis. Do you think she's capable of suicide?"

He doesn't as much as blink. "I'm not at liberty to discuss—"

"Her wellbeing is at stake."

He searches my face. "Did something happen?"

"She went far into the sea today, so far that she wouldn't have made it back if I didn't have a bodyguard watching out for her."

"I see," he says, his frown deepening. "That's a matter you should discuss with her psychiatrist."

"It's your opinion that interests me."

"I'm not a qualified psychiatrist or—"

"I don't care. You treated her. You must have an opinion. Is she capable of suicide?"

He blows out a sigh. "I can't say yes or no. All I can say is that she suffered such severe emotional trauma her brain short-circuited. It's rare, but it happens in very violent cases."

"And?"

He fixes me with a look. "And there's a history of suicide in the family."

That false belief, I ignore. "Based on only the trauma, it's possible then."

His smile is patronizing. "Anything is possible. Whether it's probable is a different question."

"How high is the probability in your opinion?"

"That, I can't say." He steeples his fingers as he scrutinizes me. "If you think she's a danger to herself, admitting her to a psychiatric hospital is an option."

"I'm not going to lock her up in an asylum." I dig my nails into the padded armrests. "All I'm asking for is a risk assessment."

"Look, as I said, I'm not a psychiatrist, but what I can tell you is that Sabella is vulnerable on all levels right now —emotionally, physically, and mentally."

"What will help? Medication?"

"Perhaps. I saw the news about her late father's so-called second family. She's just been through death and learning some shocking news about someone who was very close and dear to her. She can't demand explanations from the deceased. She'll be left with questions and doubts. What she needs now is a lot of patience and stability."

"What kind of stability?"

"No drastic changes."

"Such as?"

"Anything known to have a major impact on stress levels."

I clench my jaw. "In other words, taking her back to Corsica after the funeral wouldn't be conducive to her state of mind."

"Definitely not. I advise against any major changes in the near future, and moving countries counts high on the list of major changes. First of all, she'll have no friends or family, no social safety net in a new country. That's not ideal for her mental state of mind. What she needs right now is her circle of support. She'd have to learn a new language and adapt to a new lifestyle. All of this takes enormous emotional investment—making new friends, learning to commute, to communicate, to get a new job, to earn a rightful place in society, to find a sense of belonging, to combat the outsider syndrome, to—"

"Fine," I say with something close to a growl. "I get it."

He raises his hands. "You asked. That's my personal opinion as a medical professional and not as a psychologist."

My phone vibrates in my pocket. I take it out. It's Uncle Nico.

"Thank you," I say, getting to my feet.

"I hope that helps with your decision."

Not really. I know what a good man would do. To be separated from her again doesn't sit right with me. If the last two years of waiting were hell, the past five months of sleeping alone after I finally had her in a hotel bed were an inferno. I want her close to me, day and night. I want to get these goddamn obstacles out of the way so that I can put that ring I promised her on her finger and tie her to me with a vow and my name.

Don't you hate me, even a little?

She's mine. Yet a part of me will always hate her for the blood that flows in her veins. Logically, I know she's innocent, a pawn caught in a game. Rationally, I understand it's not her fault that my mother and sister are dead. I hold her accountable for nothing, but I blame her for everything. She didn't give the order. Edwards did. However, he did it for her. Everything that happened is for her. Because of her.

Maybe my motives aren't as clear-cut as I pretend them to be. Maybe the part of me that hates her wants to punish her as much as possess her.

My phone vibrates again.

I greet the doctor and take my leave.

Outside, I return Uncle Nico's call.

"Angelo," he says in a strained voice. "I have bad news. Your father had a heart attack."

Fuck. I make my way to the car with big strides. "How serious is it?"

"It doesn't look good. You know his health issues, how he fell back onto his bad habits after your mother—"

"Tell him to hold on." I get into the car. "I'm on my way."

Dumping the phone on the passenger seat, I start the engine. My heart pounds in my chest as I race to the hotel.

As it turns out, circumstances once again took the question of what to do with Sabella out of my hands.

CHAPTER
FIFTEEN

Sabella

I knock on Mom's door on Friday morning. It's early, but she's awake. I heard her sniffling when I went downstairs to make coffee.

"Come in," she calls.

I enter and close the door behind me. She stands in front of the mirror, studying her reflection.

"I brought coffee." I leave the steaming mug on her dresser. "I thought you might need some."

Her smile is automatic. "Thanks."

The black knee-length dress and A-line jacket look good on her. She dyed her roots and blow-dried her short hair to give it volume. A fashionable hat is pinned on her head and a net attached to the front hides the puffiness of her eyes. The color of her lipstick is a natural pink instead of Mattie's bright red.

"I hate that I have to worry about how what I wear is

going to look in the media photographs," she says. "I feel like I'm putting on a show instead of taking time alone to deal with everything."

"You are putting on a show," I say gently. "All eyes will be on us today. After that, we'll mourn in private."

"I still can't believe he's gone." Her bottom lip quivers. "What he did… It seems unreal. It's not fair that everyone is sticking their noses in our private lives. It's not fair that he left me to do this alone." Bitter, angry tears glitter in her eyes. "How could he subject me to this humiliation? And the way he died… How am I supposed to live with that?"

Not knowing what else to do, I wrap my arms around her. "We'll get through this."

She soaks up the hug for a moment before pushing me away. Pride makes her back stiff. Anger is the mask she adopts to hide her moment of weakness. "My whole life with him was make-believe. Nothing that came out of his mouth was true." Her expression hardens. "Lies are all he gave me, and betrayal is the only thing he left me with."

Borrowing from Mattie's wisdom, I say, "You have to focus on the parts that were good."

"Ha." She yanks a handbag from the dresser. "Which parts would that be?"

"The affection and the love."

She snorts, stuffing tissues and lipstick into her bag.

"Mattie and me." I lower my head to catch her gaze. "We're part of the good that came out of your marriage, aren't we?"

Her face softens only for a moment before she dons her armor again. "Let's just get this ordeal over with."

Marching to the door, she leaves me to follow.

Ryan and Celeste wait downstairs. Jared and Mattie went ahead to make sure the flowers are set up in the church. Colin and his parents meet us outside. Clara,

Colin's sister, is on vacation with her friends. Just as well. The less people who witness our humiliation amidst our grief, the better. I go with Colin while Ryan drives Celeste and my mom.

Even though Mom decided to keep the service a private family affair, the lawn outside the church is packed with spectators and media. Cameras flash when we make our way inside as proudly as we can. A few opportunistic journalists shout questions at us, but Ryan had the foresight to hire a few guards who keep the press and curious people at bay. A television crew runs behind us, filming our entry until a church elder closes the doors.

Outside, Mom was strong and proud. When she finally shifts into the front pew facing the pulpit, she all but collapses. The organist is playing a Psalm on the organ. The deep notes vibrate with somber dignity through the acoustic space. The minister enters from the vestry. He gives my mom a sympathetic nod before mounting the pulpit.

The organ music fades and dies. A moment of silence stretches. Just as the minister opens his mouth to speak, the doors open again.

We turn in our seats. Dressed in black silk and lace, Laura and Daisy enter arm in arm. My mom goes rigid. The lines around her mouth turn hard. She makes to stand, but Ryan, who sits next to her, places a hand on her arm to stop her. The look he gives her says, *Don't make a scene.*

That's what everyone outside is waiting for—a juicy show to exploit in their newspapers and on their online sites.

Mattie glares at the women as they take a seat in the back of the church. Celeste stares until Ryan puts an arm around her and gently nudges her attention to the front.

The minister takes a sip of water from a glass that's conveniently left on the pulpit. Keeping his head down, he launches into a sermon about forgiveness and redemption, but I only listen with half an ear.

While concern, guilt, and grief swamp me, it's Laura and Daisy who steal my focus. I can't help but home in on them, feeling their presence even though I'm not looking in their direction. I can't help but blame them for taking this moment from my mom too. Mom deserves to grieve without the bitter reminder of Laura's presence. This is already hard enough as it is.

The minister keeps the service short. Afterward, he wisely doesn't greet the mourners at the door as per the custom. How can he? He can hardly shake Laura's hand and tell her how sorry he is for her loss while my mom is looking on. He can't ignore her either. She and Daisy lost someone dear to them as well. He can only slip away, leaving us to deal with another painful situation.

The media stay on the outskirts at the graveyard when the coffin is lowered into the earth. That doesn't stop them from snapping photos of Laura and Daisy on one side and us on the other. It's a nightmare. Keeping up a brave show takes its toll. I'm grateful for Colin's arm around my shoulders that keeps me steady. Through it all, I'm scanning the surroundings for a dark, tall man, frightened that I'll recognize his features in the sea of faces.

As the minister says a prayer, the scene of Angelo bending over the body of my dad flashes in front of me. The memory comes uninvited from nowhere, wreaking that silent havoc inside me that will neither let me breathe nor drown. Instead, I'm trapped in a horrible place of suffering.

It's hell.

I imagine snatching the gun from his hand and pushing

it against his head, but even in my fantasies I'm a coward, because when it comes to the part where I pull the trigger, I can't do it.

All I can do is hate myself more.

By the time the ordeal is over, Angelo hasn't showed up except in my head, and I'm a mess, empty and hollow inside.

CHAPTER
SIXTEEN

Angelo

When I arrive on Corsican soil, my father is dead. Disappointment and dread fill me as I walk into the hospital, but my sorrow and dejection weigh heavier.

I'm too late.

My family wait in the hallway outside the room to which a demure nurse directed me. Someone stacked chairs along the wall. It's highly irregular to let that many visitors into the ICU, but my father *was* dying, which meant they would've made an exception, and we're not just any family.

Uncle Nico sits with his head hanging between his shoulders. Uncle Enzo has his fingers steepled together as if in prayer.

Prayers won't help any of us. It won't bring my father back. It won't make the last moments of my mother and sister's lives less terrifying, and it won't bring peace to anyone.

Uncle Enzo straightens when I approach. Toma and Gianni jump to their feet. Uncle Enzo's face is somber as he stands to greet me.

I grip his hand with a firm shake, accepting the support he offers. My vocal cords feel as rusted as if I haven't used them in years. My voice scrapes in my throat when I speak. "When?"

"Just after two," he says, squeezing my fingers while grasping my shoulder in his free hand.

The muscles in my jaw bunch. Violence boils inside me, demanding an outlet. Vengeance demands justice. Killing Edwards wasn't enough. My whole family is gone, just like that. My father was sick, but he was doing much better. The operation added another few years to his life. The cigarillos and the fatty meat didn't kill him. It wasn't the cancer that finally got to him. Grief did. That's why he gave up.

"He went peacefully," Uncle Nico says. "He got what he wanted."

Justice.

He got to push a gun against Edwards's head and look him in the eyes before pulling the trigger.

My vengeance is long from being satisfied. I haven't even scratched the surface. The monster lurking inside me wants more. It's not happy with the simple transaction of an eye for an eye. The only currency it's interested in is measured in pain and suffering. It doesn't care about fairness or justification. That's the nature of monsters. They're selfish.

Uncle Nico lets me go. "We waited for you before moving the body."

His quiet, respectful words pull me back to the present.

I nod, burying the harshness of my feelings under a layer of curtness. "Did he suffer?"

"It went very fast," he says, lowering his head.

I nod again. "I appreciate that you were here for him."

"We'll give you a moment," Uncle Enzo says, patting me on the back.

To pay my last respects.

Toma and Gianni file past, each shaking my hand with a courteous show of compassion.

"I'll start the funeral arrangements," Uncle Nico says, turning down the hallway.

Again, I can only nod. My voice doesn't cooperate. My chest feels too small for the darkness bleeding out into every corner of my being.

Their footsteps echo down the corridor, and then I'm alone. All that's left is the bright, white silence that reeks of disinfectant and the door in front of me. I grip the handle, push it down. The overhead tungsten light crackles. It stutters almost unnoticeably before going back to humming like static noise. My hand on the cold metal doesn't falter. It pushes the door open, letting that generic lifelessness of a too bright, too white hallway into the space.

The private room is as white as the rest of the ward. The only splashes of color come from the flowers in the vase on the trolley at the foot-end of the bed. My father lies pale under the covers, his hands folded on his chest and his eyes closed.

I'm grateful for that, grateful that I don't have to look into the lightless eyes of my mother again. Going to the bed, I sit down in the visitor's chair that's pushed up to the side. The doctors here know us well. *Knew* him well. They'll give me a moment, as long as I need.

I rest my elbows on the bed and take my father's cold

hand. No moment can be long enough. This is how Sabella feels. But I harden my heart, because in this very significant moment, I hate her more than I've hated anyone, and it's the hatred that ties us together. In a strange way, it's the hatred that makes me feel closer to her. Bonded. It's the hatred that makes me want her more. For what reasons, I'm not in a state of mind to examine.

Pressing my mouth to the back of my father's hand, I kiss his ring, the one that's identical to mine. Knowing there's a woman out there who wears that mark both settles me and makes me restless. It soothes the man I once was while stirring the beast.

I have an inkling these feelings will forever be at war in my chest where my promised bride is concerned. I desire and despise her in equal measures, a situation of my own making. However, the monster doesn't care. The selfish part of me that survived the massacre of my sentiments can only register that the man who raised me is gone. The man I admired and loved blew out his last breath while I was consulting a doctor about the welfare of a woman whose family destroyed mine.

Here, at my father's deathbed, a realization shoots like a well-aimed arrow straight into my brain. Sabella and I were always destined to destroy each other. There's no other way. There's no turning back. We both paid too dearly. The cost of being together is too high to give that goal up now. Neither of us have a choice in the matter any longer. We're already barreling down this path of destruction, and there's only one end to this game.

We're going to finish it.

No matter how long or what it takes.

CHAPTER
SEVENTEEN

Sabella

I shoot Ryan an uncertain glance when he parks in front of a villa in Cape Town that overlooks the beach at Camps Bay. Celeste raises her eyebrows when we get out of the car. The villa is architectural in design. It's modern and spacious, exactly what I like. Perched on the cliff, the double-story house has a prime view of the sea.

Unlocking the door, Ryan says with enthusiasm injected into his tone, "Shall we take a tour?"

He's been like that with me ever since I came home from the hospital, trying too hard to please me.

"Sure," I say, matching his eagerness.

It's all just a show, and the acting is tiring. I only want to kick off my shoes and curl up on a bed. I don't care which bed. Any reasonably comfortable corner in some place with a roof will do.

A small entrance gives way to a huge living space with

a kitchen and bar on the right and a lounge on the left. Sliding doors open onto a covered veranda with a narrow, rectangular pool balancing on the edge of the cliff. The blue color of the water looks like an extension of the shiny surface of the ocean. A Jacuzzi and deck chairs take up one corner of the veranda while an outdoor lounge with classy white sofas occupy the floor space on the other side.

It's breathtakingly beautiful. Under different circumstances, I would've appreciated the sight. Fallen in love with it even.

"Wow," Celeste says, flicking on a light switch even though sunlight streams in through the floor-to-ceiling glass walls.

Dim lights cast the room in a soft, golden glow.

"Is this secure?" She crosses the lounge and taps on the glass. "Isn't it easy to break?"

"It's bulletproof glass." Ryan directs his smile at me. "It's not that easy to break. Plus, the security system is top notch." He points at a computer panel in the kitchen. "All the walls are equipped with reinforced steel shutters that you can lower in a second with the press of a button."

The plush rugs covering the polished hardwood floors absorb the clack of my shoes as I go over to inspect the panel.

"Have a look around." Ryan motions at a staircase next to the breakfast nook. "The bedrooms and bathroom are downstairs."

"How many bedrooms does this place have?" Celeste asks, gawking at the contemporary art on the walls as she heads for the stairs.

"Only two," Ryan says. "A master and a guest bedroom."

"Only?" She huffs a laugh before saying on her way

down the spiral staircase, "That's more than enough for most people, let alone for a student."

"She's right." I face my brother. "This place is way too expensive."

"Hey." He grips my shoulder. "You're an Edwards, right? We have standards to uphold."

I wince at the attempted humor. Sometimes, I wish I could forget that I'm an Edwards.

He sobers. "Letting you live alone isn't ideal." Dropping his hand to his side, he says with meaning, "Not now."

I brush the statement away. "I'm almost nineteen years old. It's about time I stand on my own two feet."

His eyes crinkle in the corners. "That's not what I meant. I wish there was another way, but I have to take over the business in George."

Concern tightens my stomach. "How does Celeste feel about moving into the big house with Mom? You know they don't get on."

"Celeste is looking forward to having Doris and Mom there to help take care of Brad. That way, she can go back to doing more voluntary work." He drags a hand over his head. "To be honest, I'm not sure about leaving Mom on her own after everything that's happened. With Mattie in Stellenbosch, she can do with family close by."

"You're right." I smile. "Moving back is very noble. I just don't want the relationship between you and Celeste to suffer. We both love Mom, but you know how she can be." I lower my voice. "Especially with Celeste."

"Don't worry," he says with a wink. "Celeste can take care of herself. She knows how to handle Mom."

Ryan looks so much like Dad when he winks that I have to swallow and look away.

I hide the sudden onslaught of emotions by pretending to study the interior. The furniture is sparse but comfortable. A couple of cream leather sofas frame a glass coffee table. The focal point of the room is a freestanding fire pit with a black metal extractor chimney leading to the ceiling. A desk and a built-in bookshelf in the corner make a cozy spot for studying. The kitchen and bar sport stainless steel countertops and cable lights hanging from the ceiling. The decoration favors natural colors with light wood fittings. It's stylish and tranquil.

The noise of the waves rushes in, expelling the quiet. I turn toward the view. Ryan opened the sliding doors. The glass must be double-pane for the silence inside to be so complete.

"It's going to be a bitch to keep these glass walls clean," Celeste says as she comes back upstairs.

Ryan shoves a hand in his pocket. "The rent includes a cleaning service."

"Of course it does." Her heels clack over the kitchen floor. "Does it include a chef too?"

"Maybe it should, smart mouth," he says, his lips quirking.

"Hey." I look between them. "I know how to cook."

My feeble protest is lost on them. They're sharing one of their private moments when Ryan ushers his wife outside with his hand on the small of her back.

I follow them onto the veranda.

Staring at the flat surface of the sea, he says, "It's something, isn't it?"

I glance at him sideways. "Like I said, it's too much."

His signature smile is intact when he tears his gaze from the view and fixes it on me. "Don't you like it?"

"Of course I do, but I don't need so much space." Not to mention that Camps Bay is one of the most expensive neighborhoods in Cape Town. The rent must be extortionately high.

"This is really way too much," Celeste says, pulling her mouth into a frown. "We never had anything like this, not even after we got married. We had to be content with the house in Bloubergstrand."

"Celeste," he says in a stern tone.

"No, she's right." I walk to the edge of the pool. "I'll be more than happy with a room in the student dorm."

"It's not up for discussion." Ryan drops his hand from Celeste's back to intertwine their fingers. "If you'd like to redecorate or get different furniture—"

"That won't be necessary," I say quickly. "The place is perfect as it is. I just think—"

His mouth pulls up in one corner. "Good. Then that's settled. I'll arrange for your clothes to be moved tomorrow."

I don't have the energy to argue. I simply accept that from now on I'm living here alone.

Alone.

It's a lie. Since the day Angelo Russo walked into my life, I've never been alone. It's not going to change now. The thought sends a shiver through me.

"The breeze is cold," Ryan says. "Let's go back inside."

His phone rings as he slides the doors closed. Taking it from his pocket, he presses it against his ear. Whatever the person on the other end of the line says darkens his expression. He clenches the phone in a white-knuckled grip.

"I see," he says after a moment. "Keep me posted."

"What happened?" Celeste asks when he ends the call.

Ryan looks at me. "Santino Russo is dead."

The words sink in slowly. Someone's death shouldn't

make me happy, but after what he did to my dad, I can't help but feel a measure of satisfaction. Relief.

There are many things I could ask, but the question that takes priority is, "How?" Because I hope he suffered.

Ryan sneers. "Heart attack."

The first thought that runs through my mind is if Angelo had time to say goodbye. "When?"

"Yesterday."

I search my brother's eyes. "Who told you?"

"I have informants in high places who keep me updated with the current state of affairs."

That sounds sinister. It sounds too much like having spies in dangerous organizations.

"The universe served justice," Celeste says. "I always tell you not to fuck with karma, Ryan."

Too late.

Ryan is already knee-deep in crime, running Dad's legitimate as well as illegitimate business. Our silence implicates us in those crimes.

We're accomplices.

If karma decides to come for the rest of us, we can only hope we'll already be dead.

CHAPTER
EIGHTEEN

The double funeral took place not even two weeks ago, and here I am again, laying my father to rest. We didn't have an open-coffin burial for my mother and sister because of how the accident mutilated Adeline. For my father, it's different. I adhered to tradition, having him laid out in his bespoke black suit. I had his coffin placed among flowers, candles, and incense in the lounge where people can pay their last respects.

My uncles and cousins arrive first, then colleagues and business associates, and lastly the staff. Roch is among the guards. Seeing his face bugs me, but before I can act on it, Uncle Nico pushes a tumbler with amber liquor in my hand. I sniff the alcohol out of pure habit, registering in the back of my mind that it's Scotch as I swallow. Just like the previous time, I sit at the table amidst an abundance of food and shake the hands that people thrust at me. Only, this time, I'm at the head of the table. And this time, I drink. I shoot back the Scotch and pour another. And another. Until I'm slightly drunk.

Instead of numbing me, the alcohol intensifies the feelings I suppressed under the muck in my chest. The one that floats to the surface like oil drifting on water is anger. The one that ignites is fury. How I manage to keep a lid on it is a miracle. It brews quietly. Deadly. It waits for a spark so it can finally explode.

I force it down, because I'm not going to show my true nature at my father's funeral. Everyone is watching. They want me to step out of line. I can't afford to do that. Not now. Not here. I have to show these motherfuckers I have control. That I'm capable of running the business.

I don't miss that no one from the village is attending. I take note of that slap in the face. Let them despise and hate me. Fear is a much stronger bargaining chip than kindness.

When it's time for the staff to queue and Roch shakes my hand, I stand. My feet are steady, but my insides are shaking. It's the wrong time to do this. I know. Can I help myself? No.

"You're fired," I say.

He stumbles back a step, looking as if I slapped him. "I've been in your employ since I turned fifteen."

"Exactly." My smile is cold. "Now you're not. Gather your things and leave my property. If I ever see you here again, I'll kill you."

A hand falls on my arm. I look at the face of the owner, my muscles tensing for action. It's my uncle.

"Angelo," Uncle Nico says under his breath.

I don't care who hears me make death threats. No one will dare to speak up against me.

I shake off my uncle's touch and direct a single word at Roch. "Now."

Roch blinks.

"Angelo," Uncle Nico says again.

I raise a hand, silencing my uncle. He shuts his mouth. I'm in charge now. And no one lays a fucking finger on Sabella.

No one but me.

"You're not yourself," Uncle Nico whispers.

Uncle Enzo is the wiser brother. "Go, Roch. You heard Angelo."

Roch clenches his jaw, but he doesn't argue. He knows when it's dangerous to open his mouth. Bowing slightly, he says, "It was an honor to work for you, Mr. Russo." Then he turns and walks from the room.

"That was a mistake," Uncle Nico says in my ear.

I fix him with a stare. "Are you questioning my decisions?"

He doesn't falter under my look. "It was a mistake to let him go." He says the last part with meaning, making sure I get it.

I do. He's telling me I should've killed Roch instead of firing him, not because of what he did but because my father always said it's unwise to leave loose ends.

Roch shouldn't have pushed and insulted my future wife, but he paid for his actions. I promised my mother I'd look out for him, and I'm not going to break my promise by killing him.

Unable to stand the curious eyes trained on me for a minute longer, I go outside.

Heidi runs after me. "Mr. Russo. Angelo. Wait."

I turn.

Her face is scrunched up with concern. "Where are you going? You have guests. You can't just leave."

My smile is grim. "Watch me."

I get into my car and drive off without looking back. I have no idea where I'm going. All I know is that I need space. It's only when I pull up at the new house on the other side of the property thirty minutes later that I realize where I am.

The building supervisor steps outside. He gives me a speculative look when I get out of the car.

"Mr. Russo, I didn't expect you." He doesn't say, *not today*, but the words hang in the air between us.

I nod at the house. "When will it be ready?"

"By next week latest. The pipes were laid for the water. The electricity should be connected in a couple of days."

"Good."

I look at the stone and wood structure. It's a handsome house, big enough for a large family. The style is similar to that of the big house. I wanted continuity, even if this one stands more than twenty kilometers away from the main mansion. There's even a coop and a shed for animals. My maternal grandfather can bring his goats and chickens. I haven't seen the herd or the flock, but the people living nearby who I questioned said the old man keeps them a short distance down the stream. Apparently, he's inseparable from his animals. It's a pity he doesn't feel the same about his children and grandchildren. He's also said to be an abusive drunk. I'll have to keep a tight leash on him.

"Would you like a visit?" the supervisor asks.

It's a good, solid house. When the building site has been cleaned and the landscaper has done his work, the garden will be pretty. I should be proud of the project, but it's not me who should've been standing here. It should've been my mother. Only, now she'll never see it.

She'll never know.

The supervisor sounds uncertain. "Sir?"

I turn for my car. "No."

His baffled gaze burns on the back of my head as I get in and start the engine. It's time to throw myself into work, not only to turn my father's business into his dream, but also to forget.

Before taking the road, I type out an order on my phone that I send to the head of my security team, informing him to gather the old man and his troop of children and to move them here.

CHAPTER
NINETEEN

Sabella

When I come home from class, I leave my coat and bag on the stand, kick off my sneakers, and go to the kitchen to switch on the kettle. It's a typical wet winter's day with a constant drizzle, and I forgot my umbrella this morning. The long run from my lecture building to the parking lot left me soaked. The cold has penetrated my bones.

Grateful for the underfloor heating, I pull off my wet socks and take a clean sweater and yoga pants straight from the dryer. The comfortable clothes warm my cold skin instantly. I can do with a shower, but I first want a cup of tea to melt the icy coldness inside me. Having a snack isn't a bad idea either. I'm so hungry I'm shaking. My afternoon lecture ran late, and I didn't have time for lunch. All I ate since breakfast was a cereal bar.

After dumping my soggy garments in the washing

machine, I grab a clean towel from the laundry cupboard to dry the worst of the wetness from my hair.

I'm in the midst of shaking drops all over the floor when the doorbell rings. I freeze. I'm not expecting anyone. Colin is the only person who visits me at home, and he's at a student meeting this afternoon.

Even though I haven't seen Angelo since that day on the beach, my stomach tightens as I pad barefoot to the wall panel. The face staring at the camera doesn't belong to the man of my nightmares. It belongs to my half-sister.

I hesitate. Mattie and Mom still want nothing to do with Daisy and Laura, not that either of them tried to make contact with us after the funeral. Why is she here? Loyalty to my family and guilt about the fact that she's family too war in my chest. Finally, my curiosity wins.

The tenseness doesn't ease from my muscles as I deactivate the alarm and push the button to open the security gate. Schooling my features, I go to the entrance and unlock the door. Daisy's wide smile greets me when I open it. She's wearing a red silk blouse and black leather pants under a raincoat. Drops of water drips from the umbrella in her hand.

"Hi," she says, shaking out her blond hair. "Can I come in?" She squints at the gray sky. "It's rather wet out here."

I step aside for her to enter. She leaves the umbrella in the stand next to the door and walks to the lounge while I lock up. I take a deep breath before following.

"How did you find me?" I ask. "My address isn't listed."

"Student records."

"Those are confidential."

"I know someone who owed me a favor. Anyway, for the right price, you can buy any information these days."

Wandering through the room, she looks around. "Nice place." She stops in front of the sliding doors. "Prime beachfront position. It must cost a pretty penny."

I cross my arms. "You didn't come here to discuss my cost of living."

She turns and cocks a shoulder. "I was just wondering who's paying for it." Studying me with piercing attention, she says, "Your brother, I suppose. He took over the business after all."

Keeping my annoyance in check, I ask, "Is there a purpose to this visit?"

"I'm just saying it must be nice to have a brother who looks out for you."

"You can afford a place three times this size."

"With my inheritance money, you mean." Her lips tilt. "I suppose I could, but I don't need a place of my own. The mansion in Hout Bay is more than big enough for Mommy and me."

"I'm sure it is."

She saunters to the center of the room. "Of all his children, he talked the most about you, you know."

My heart squeezes.

Picking up a silver statue of an elephant from the coffee table, she studies it. "He loved you very much."

Miraculously, I manage to keep my voice even. "I know."

She looks at me, her wise little smile saying she's not falling for my faked confidence. "Of course, he loved Ryan and Matilde too." She adds with a wistful air, "He did always tell me I was his favorite. I thought that was sweet."

Something twists inside me. I can't help the jealousy that blackens my heart or the betrayal that drives the blade deeper.

"Our time together was always special," she continues. "We were very close."

My tone is flat. "I'm happy for you. If there's nothing else you wanted to tell me, I have to study."

"He was a great man." She puts the elephant back in its place. "Daddy will always be my idol. He was an example in every way."

She doesn't know about his clandestine business or how he truly died. He kept that part of his life from them too. In a way, I envy her. Ignorance can be bliss. Still, I'll always choose truth over illusion, and for this, I pity her.

"He said you loved the sea and swimming." She traces a finger over the back of the sofa as she strolls to the fire pit. "Is that still so?"

I clench my jaw, hating that he discussed me with her when I know nothing about her.

When I don't reply, she stops to look at me. "You must have questions for me. I sure have a lot for you."

I do have questions, plenty of them, but the only person who can answer them is dead. I doubt she understands how that feels, how living with not knowing eats a hole into your soul. I want to know why Mom wasn't enough. I want to know if he felt guilty every time he lied to me or if it simply didn't bother him. I want to know how many people he killed and if he ever thought about the families they left behind. I want to know when he decided to smuggle arms and why. What swayed him? Was it the money? The power? Was the wealth he already accumulated not enough? The petty part of me wants to know if he really loved Laura and Daisy more. And I want to know if he'd do it again if given another chance. But I'll never know, will I? That's the hardest part—accepting to live with all those unanswered questions.

"Well?" she says, raising her hands. "Here am I. So, ask me."

"What do you really want, Daisy? Why did you truly come here? To rub my face in the affection my dad had for you? Or in the money he left you? In the fact that he was more honest with you than with me? If you came here to find out which one of us was better off, I can assure you it was you."

"I didn't mean to hurt you." She pouts. "I just want to get to know you better. There were so many things I always wondered about, and now I can finally get some answers."

I don't believe her. She's not here for a bonding session. "You got your answers. Now please go."

Not waiting to see if she's following, I walk to the door and open it.

A moment later, she appears in the entrance. Her stylish rain boots squeak on the floor as she goes to the stand and takes her umbrella. She steps over the threshold and opens the umbrella.

Turning in the doorframe, she says, "I learned a lot about business from Daddy. I should've been given a place in the company. You know what it's like to be a woman. When it comes to business, we're always shunned as if we don't matter. If you could be a go-between for me and your brother, I—"

Ah. So this is the reason for the surprise visit. "Ryan will never give you a position in the company."

The muscles around her eyes tighten. "I could fight for it."

"Trust me, you don't want to. You got your share. If you learned so much about business, why don't you start your own company?"

"Mommy said that's how you all would be, that you'd never let me take my rightful place."

I don't know what game she's playing, but I don't like it. "Let's be honest for a moment. We owe you nothing. The only person who did was my dad, and he made sure to leave you financially comfortable. We don't have anything more to say to each other."

"It's a pity that's the way you're looking at it. We could've been friends."

If there's one thing I do know, it's that she's not my friend.

"Goodbye, Daisy," I say, shutting the door in her face.

Exhaling a long, shaky breath, I turn the lock and lean on the wood.

I may choose not to have contact with Daisy or her mother, but I'll never be free from my past.

The message that pings on my phone proves that point with impeccable timing. The sound I selected for the alert tells me that the message came through on the phone Angelo gave me. Taking the phone from my bag, I consider not reading the text, but I can't help seeing the words that show on the lock screen.

No sorry for my loss this time?

The phone shakes in my hand. What is wrong with him? Does he get off on terrorizing me?

Another text comes through. *Thought so.*

What does he want me to say?

And another. *I suppose you're celebrating. Champagne? Your favorite, right? I remember from your party at the casino.*

Blood rushes to my cheeks while my stomach bottoms out. Reminding me of my weakness makes my face burn with shame. It's that very weakness that compelled me to go on birth control last week. Even as I popped the first pill into my mouth, I told myself sex with Angelo would never happen again. How easily my body ruled my mind in a moment of passion scared me. That's why I'm taking that little pill every day at the same time without fail.

My phone pings with another message.

You must be happy.

I can't do this.

After switching off the phone, I chuck it on the kitchen counter. My other phone rings immediately, making me jump, but it's the ringtone I use for Colin. I all but run for it, snatching it out of my bag.

"Hey," Colin says. "Our meeting was cancelled. Too much rain. Some streets are flooded. Do you want to grab a bite to eat?"

"Yes," I say too quickly. "That will be nice."

"Are you all right?"

"It's just…" I blow out a sigh. "Angelo's father died. The funeral was today. He sent me a text message."

"Why?" he asks, anger creeping into his voice.

"I don't know. I think he likes to make me suffer."

"That motherfucker. When will you listen to me, Bella? You need to cut that asshole out of your life."

"Can we not talk about it?" I sink down on a chair. "Please?"

"You sound tired."

"It's been a tough day."

"How about I get pizza, and we eat at your place? We can study a little if you're up for it after dinner."

"Actually, that sounds kind of amazing." I wipe a hand over my brow. "I really appreciate it, Colin."

I can hear the smile in his voice when he says, "That's what friends are for. I'll be over at six. Do you have wine?"

"Ryan left some bottles from the bulk he bought at a wine farm."

"Open one so long," he says before hanging up.

I glance at the darkening sky through the windows.

Roch is no longer around. I remember what Angelo told him when he pushed me out of the boat. I deserved that push. I overreacted, not having been myself on that awful day. Angelo didn't have to pull Roch off the job. It was a severe act, but I'm not complaining about the fact that he's gone. However, I'm under no illusion that Angelo replaced him. There's someone else watching now, someone I don't know.

Jumping into action, I rush to the wall panel and push on the button to lower the shutters.

CHAPTER
TWENTY

Angelo

Sitting behind the desk in the chair that belonged to my father, I stare at the dark screen of the phone in my hand. The house is never empty. There's always Heidi and the rest of the staff. Double the number of guards patrol the perimeter of the property. Yet the silence creeps up on me at times like this, mocking me with the voices that nowadays only sound in my head. Adeline's laughter. The rattle of my father's cough. My mother humming to the radio in the kitchen.

My uncles and cousins are often here, a lot more than before. They probably think it's wiser to check in on me. I haven't been myself in a long time. I've never been drunk as often as I am of late.

I turn the phone over. I was drunk when I sent that message to Sabella seven months ago. I came home from a house I'd built to honor my mother's family, polished half a bottle of Scotch, and typed the inappropriate text. I still don't know why. I only know I was raging. Angry. Blaming myself for everything. Blaming Sabella. Blaming her for not being well enough or strong enough to be here with me.

In two weeks, she'll turn nineteen. I've been patient. More than patient. I want what's mine. I want what I paid for, and I paid dearly. We both have. It's time to turn the page and start a new chapter. It's time to lay down the ghosts and fill this house with voices again. Real voices.

The ringtone of the phone pulls me from my dark thoughts. I check the screen. It's Toma. Uncle Nico must've put him on babysitting duty again. I consider ignoring my cousin, but I'm not focusing on the investment analysis on the laptop screen in front of me. Even as I take the call, I pour four fingers of Scotch.

"Toma."

"Angelo, you need to come over to the house."

I swallow a mouthful of alcohol. "I am in the house."

"The new house."

I clench my fingers around the glass. Since I moved the old man and his family into that house, he's given me nothing but trouble. I haven't set foot in it in a month. Work kept me busy. It takes time to run a multibillion-euro business, and it takes more time turning that business into a global empire.

"What's wrong?" I ask with a grunt, setting the glass aside. I don't need these complications.

"You've got to come and see this."

I want to tell him to deal with whatever it is, but I created this problem. My father warned me, and I didn't listen. Solving yet another tricky situation is fair punishment.

"I'll be there in thirty," I say.

On my way out, I tell Heidi I'll be late for lunch. In the car, I can think. I always reflect better when I'm driving. My senses are alert despite the fact that I just downed a drink. I shouldn't be driving, but there are a lot of things I shouldn't do.

The old man and the kids didn't want to move here. You'd think I offered them a pigsty instead of a house with every possible luxury and comfort. I organized a cook and a cleaner, but the women resigned after a few weeks. They couldn't put up with my grandfather's verbal and physical abuse. The cook said he threw a pot of boiling water at her. She said if she hadn't been so fast, her face would've needed skin grafts.

I punished him by withholding his allowance. Food and commodities are always delivered to the house. He doesn't need the money, but that's what he cares about most. Nothing hits him harder than losing the cash.

Things went better after that. Until he started again. It's always the same. He causes trouble and promises to be good when I don't pay the euros into his account. As soon as he gets the next installment, he acts out again.

Those devious kids don't help. They stole the cleaning lady's phone and bank cards from her purse. They emptied a bucket of piss over her head while laughing their asses off. I thought sending them to school in Bastia would help, but they created so many problems that I ended up hiring a tutor to do home schooling. That lasted for little more than a week before the woman stormed through my door and demanded her money before getting off my property as fast as she could.

What's it going to take? Sending them to a military boarding school? I was no model child, but I knew how to behave civilized when necessary. If I'm being honest with myself, moving them into the house had less to do with feeling charitable and more with wanting to wipe away the stigma that clings to my family name. I wanted my mother to walk down the street in the village and be met with respect instead of scorn. Sure, after I made an example of the grocery store owner, people served her when she went into a shop, but they still despised her. They just hid it better.

Toma waits outside when I pull up at the house. What in the name of the gods happened here? I cut the engine and get out of the car.

Not a single plank remains where the coop and shed were situated in the distance. The garden—or what's left of it—is one big slush pile of mud and junk. The flowers are chomped down to stalks, probably by the goats. The grass is trampled, and the terracotta pots in which herbs and succulents were planted are broken. A mattress that's more brown than white with a hole burned in the center lies in a corner. Pieces of crockery stick out from the wet soil. A fork shines among the dirt in the winter sun.

Toma stands on the seat of a chair that's missing all four feet to keep his pants from dragging in the muck.

"What the fuck?" I say, raking my fingers through my hair.

"Wait until you see the inside."

I climb the steps to the porch. Goat manure covers the veranda. The front door stands open. A few pigeons moved in. They fly to the ceiling, flapping their wings in a flurry when we enter.

The place inside is no better than outside. It stinks of rot and mold. Everywhere I look, there's chaos. A curtain that's been torn off the rail is spanned between the two living room pillars to form a hammock. The drawers are turned over on the floor. The silver and cutlery are gone. Only the plastic picnic eating utensils are left.

"They emptied out the place," Toma says behind me.

"When?"

"Must've been recently. They were still here last week when the delivery guy dropped off the food." He waves an arm through the space. "I brought the water fountain refill to find this."

"What about upstairs?"

"The same. They left the heavy mattress in the main bedroom. Most of everything else is missing."

I turn in a circle, taking in the destruction. "Where have they gone?"

"Back to the valley. Kids, goats, chickens, and all."

"Motherfucker," I say under my breath.

He makes a face. "You tried."

Stomping back outside, I say from over my shoulder, "Get this fucking mess cleaned up."

"Do you want us to bring them back?" he calls after me.

"No." I climb down the steps. "Let them rot in that damn valley."

He runs to keep up with me, sidestepping a pile of goat shit. "What about the house?"

"Lock it up."

I get into the car and slam the door.

So much for trying to turn dirt into gold. Some families are born to be scum. I'm the perfect living proof.

CHAPTER
TWENTY-ONE

Sabella

Christmas comes and goes. My family and Colin's spend a quiet New Year's evening in Great Brak River. I go to the beach and swim every day, but the cave brings back memories, so I return to my comfortable villa in Cape Town before the year is one week old.

Mom wanted me to stay until after my birthday. She suggested organizing a cocktail party. Disappointment was etched on her features when I declined. I made up an excuse of going out with my university friends in the city. The truth is that I'm scared. I'm scared Angelo will return. If he does, it's best I don't lure him to my family.

The closer the day of my nineteenth birthday gets, the more anxious I grow. Healing takes time, but I haven't healed much since my dad's murder. I started getting nightmares. As my birthday draws nearer, those horrific dreams become more frequent.

Guilt eats me alive. The lies and secrets are killing me. Keeping up a front is becoming more difficult with each passing day. The acting is exhausting.

For the world, I'm happy and carefree. For anyone looking in from the outside, I'm just another spoiled rich girl who lives in a fancy villa in Camps Bay and who drives a brand-new electric car every year. They're not sports cars. However, the brands are reliable and on the upper end of the scale. Ryan insists it's for my safety. He won't let me buy a smaller, second-hand car, and I'm too worn-out to fight him on this.

I don't want for anything. Ryan makes sure of that. He covers all my expenses, including my grocery and clothing bills. The allowance he gives me for entertainment goes straight into a savings account. Next year, my lecture hours will decrease. Having more time available will allow me to get a part-time job. There are many restaurants in Camps Bay, and the staff turnover is high. They're always looking for waitresses. I'll save every penny until I can afford plastic surgery to remove the brand on my skin.

Colin calls and offers to take me out for my birthday, knowing how much I dread the day, but I don't have the energy to sit through a dinner in a fancy restaurant and pretend to be okay. I don't want to cry on his shoulder either. I'd rather be alone. It takes a lot of convincing before he backs down, but he buys my lie of needing some pampering me-time and going out for a girls' night on the town.

When the day finally dawns, I get up early and go for a long jog on the beach followed by a strenuous swim far out to sea. The exercise leaves me exhausted, which is exactly what I aimed for. If I'm too tired to think, the thoughts surrounding my birthday can't harass me.

I climb up the path to the villa, pressing a hand over

the stitch in my side while catching my breath. It's a glorious day with not a cloud in the sky. The sun hangs big and yellow overhead, warming my wet skin.

After a rinse-down in the outdoor shower, I relax in the Jacuzzi while sipping coconut water to replenish my energy. I'm a healthy eater, but today I need comfort food. I have peanut butter and banana toast with pancakes and cream, enjoying my meal on the veranda. I even indulge in a brunch cocktail of champagne and orange juice. The air is clean, smelling like salt and sea. The lap of the waves on the shore is the best music. If not for my nerves, this would've been the perfect birthday.

When the temperature gets too hot, I go inside and switch on the AC. To help me relax, I opt for a bath instead of a shower and add my favorite lavender bath salt. While the tub is filling, I double-check the wall panel to ensure the security gate and the doors are locked and that the alarm is on. I'm always vigilant and on the lookout for people following me or hanging around the villa. Although I never notice anyone, I always get a creepy feeling that someone is watching me. To be on the safe side, I lower the window shutters before I strip and get into the bath.

The warm water soothes my muscles, and the lavender helps to relieve the ache after the physical exertion. The tub is built into a corner of the bathroom on the lower level of the house where the shrubs on the side of the rocky garden provide privacy. Without any neighbors in front of me, I can enjoy the view of the waves crashing on the beach from the large window that walls in one side of the tub, but I feel safer with the shutter down. It's dark inside with the sun blocked out. I feel as if I'm tucked into a cocoon where no one and nothing can reach me.

I wash my hair and rinse the shampoo and conditioner with clean water, using the hand-held nozzle. Before the water has cooled completely, I pull the plug and take a towel from the hook on the wall. I step onto the bath rug and wrap the towel around me, and then I take a smaller towel to twist around my hair. Stripes of light fall through the grooves in the metal shutter onto the floor and fan over the mirror. I flip on the light switch and brush my teeth.

Despite the sinister significance of the date, I'm floating in a comfortable space after the endorphins of the exercise and the relaxing effect of the bath. As long as I stay inside, I feel safe. I make a mental note to thank Ryan for that. He went out of his way to find a place with every possible security precaution, and I've never been more grateful than today.

Since I have nothing planned and I'm not in a mindset to study, I'll make popcorn and binge-watch television. I haven't had time to do that in ages. It will be my birthday treat.

The idea perks me up as I saunter into the bedroom, heading for the closet. As soon as I enter the somber darkness, the hair stands up in my nape. A shiver crawls through me, contracting my skin.

I'm not alone.

I know it in an instant.

My heart starts pounding, every thud reverberating in my ears. My palms turn clammy where I grip the edges of the towel between my breasts. I look for a weapon even as I scan the dark corners of the room. And then I jerk to a standstill.

A man sits in the armchair in front of the sliding doors. With the shutters in front of the doors down, I can't make out more than the black outline of his shape, but I already know who broke into my house. I know from the tension emanating from his relaxed pose and the bulkiness of his frame. I know from the smell of citrus and cedar that hangs faintly in the air.

I stop breathing. I stop looking for a weapon and focus on escaping, because I can't beat the man who sits in my chair in strength.

His deep, disturbing voice washes over my senses. "Hallo, Sabella."

His accent is fainter than I remember. Or maybe he got more practice in speaking English.

I back up a step, choosing anger as my armor. "How the hell did you get in here?"

"Don't I get a hello? A, *how was your flight?*" His voice drops an octave. "A kiss?" When I don't reply, he chuckles. "I guess not."

I hate that I can't press the panic button or call the police. I don't want to endanger my family by phoning Ryan. I hate how helpless I am. The only weapon I have is pretending not to be scared. Men like Angelo feed on people's fear. All I can do is act as if I have the situation under control.

"Get out of my house," I say, keeping my voice as calm as I can. "You're trespassing."

"It's been a long time," he drawls. "Let me have a look at you."

A click sounds. The lamp on the table goes on. The light spills around him, bringing the features etched into my mind to life. He's broader. Stronger. I can see it even with him sitting. More dangerous than ever. Ominous energy rolls off him in waves. The light doesn't dispel the darkness coming from within him. His hair is longer and messier. The scruff on his jaw must be two days old. He's wearing a white shirt, smart black slacks, and dress shoes, but he looks less polished. Rougher.

The last few months haven't been good to him.

"As pretty as always," he says. "Even more beautiful as a woman than as an innocent girl."

The innocent part isn't lost on me. He took that from me, but only emotionally. He introduced me to betrayal, pain, and grief and taught me that no one can be trusted. Least of all him. That part of my innocence he stole violently.

The physical part, the part that has only known one man? That part, I gave to him. I'm still not sure why. I want to believe it was the alcohol or that I just wanted to give him a last first to stop his warped game. Yet I know that's not true. I wanted it to be him. The girl who fell in love with him was still living somewhere in my chest, but he killed her when he murdered my father.

He straightens, taking his time. I can't read the expression in his eyes, but his laser stare burns into my soul. I swallow when he slowly crosses the floor and stops in front of me.

I was right. He's large in physical form and in presence. The room is too small for him. His muscles bunch under his clothes. Where his sleeves are folded back, his skin is tanned and embossed with veins. Angelo Russo has always been a tough, hardened man, even at twenty. I think he was already a man when he was only a boy. Now, he's a god. A powerful one. Nothing short of a monster.

He reaches out and dips a finger under the towel where it covers my breasts. I try to pull back, but he's too fast. Too strong. With a single tug, he yanks me against him. My belly heats with fear and something else, something like a distant echo of a forbidden pleasure.

I look at his face. His eyes are the color of molasses. The irises are so dark they bleed into the black of his pupils. The intensity in his gaze as he measures me is startling. Frightening. He's only twenty-three, yet he looks like a man with the experience of one of forty. I know the things he's done. I know the things he's seen. No wonder he's too wise and too old for his age.

Pressing my palms on his chest, I try to create distance between us, but he traps me against the steel length of his body with a hand on my lower back, continuing to pull at the towel until it gives way. The edges fall open, revealing my breasts, but he doesn't look away from my eyes. He reads my reaction as if he's curious about what he'll find, whether I'll give him defiance or permission.

Exposed to the cool air in the room, my nipples harden. The towel slips down to my hips, his hand on my back and his body pressed against mine at the front holding it up. I suck in a breath. I have to be clever. If I run, I'm fucked. That's what he wants. I sense it. He wants to hunt and catch me. Isn't that what we've always been doing? I've been hiding, and he's been stalking.

A silent battle rages between us. He breaks our eye contact first, sweeping his gaze down to my naked curves. When he reaches out, I strain in his hold, but he tightens his grip on my back in silent warning. If he was a wolf, I swear he'd growl. Maybe he'd sink his teeth into my shoulder.

Knowing I have no chance of fighting, I keep still. My pulse hammers in my temples as I bide my time. Ever so gently, he brushes his knuckles over a nipple. The hard tip extends, the areola tightening. His cock grows hard against my stomach. It's a size and a fit I remember well, no matter how hard I try to forget.

I can't prevent the tremor that runs through me when he pulls an inch away and lifts his hand from my back. The towel drops to the floor. Goosebumps race over my body. He rakes a path over me with his gaze, all the while rubbing his knuckles over my nipple. When he fixes his attention on the triangle between my legs, his eyes darken with possession and lust.

I don't shave there. I won't ever again. Not as long as I'm branded with his mark. The knowledge of his seal being there seems to be enough for him. His lips tilt with satisfaction as he smooths the palm of his free hand over my stomach and spears his fingers into the curls that cover my sex. When he closes his fingers in a fist, the pull makes me go on tiptoes. It doesn't hurt, not much, but when he uses the leverage to yank me closer, I can't help but yelp.

I catch his shoulders to keep my balance. The knuckle of his middle finger rests on my clit. I try to ignore how it feels. It's impossible when he pulls harder and at the same time finds the right spot. I've lost yet another round even before he loosens his fingers and circles that button with his knuckle—teasing, testing.

He fastens his other hand on my breast, keeping me in place. My body responds to him, and I don't like it. My clit swells, and my folds turn slick. I don't like what that means or what that makes me. I hate that I like how he looks at the work of his hand, studying his own actions with carnal interest.

Needing to stop this before it goes further, I push harder on his chest, but he easily yanks the towel off my hair and weaves his fingers through the long, wet tresses. My neck arches as he pulls my head back and holds me in place. His focus shifts from my sex to my face. The pressure of his knuckle increases as he leans closer and lowers his head.

The softness and warmth of his mouth on mine catches me by surprise. I didn't expect the kiss. At least not one as tender. When he slants his lips over mine and parts them with gentle but insistent pressure, a gasp catches in my throat. The stroke of his tongue lights an instant fire that spreads with languid heat through my veins.

Fisting his hand in my hair, he tears his mouth from mine and stares down at me with an expression so dark it makes me shiver. The touch of his knuckle disappears. I heave a sigh of both disappointment and relief when something cold and hard replaces flesh and bone. I look down. He's rubbing me with his ring, bringing me closer to the edge with the insignia of his family name.

This is wrong. I open my mouth to protest, but when I lift my gaze to his, he's studying me with wicked intention. He wants me to fight. He wants me to lose. He wants to show me how easily he can defeat me. So, I give him the opposite. I relax in his hold. I press my knees together and arch my hips forward, chasing the friction. My eyes drift closed as pleasure slowly spreads, overtaking objections and shame.

He shakes me hard. His command is harsh, angry almost. "Open your eyes."

His tight grip on my hair makes my eyes water when I oblige.

"That's right," he says, increasing the pressure of his ring on my clit. "Show me how you come for me."

A wave of pleasure rushes through me, contracting my muscles. My orgasm is sweet and agonizing at the same time. He's not smiling with satisfaction now. Victory is shining like a burning flame in his eyes as he drags his ring down the length of my slit, gathering my arousal.

Watching me, he presses his ring on his mouth before licking his lips clean in a slow, fluent motion. He tilts my head to the side and draws his nose along the arch of my neck to the shell of my ear, inhaling deeply.

"Happy birthday, *cara*," he whispers, planting a kiss on my temple.

As soon as I can stand on my wobbly legs, I step away from him. He allows me to escape, letting my hair slip through his fingers. Turning my back on him, I walk to the dressing room and pull underwear on. His huge form fills the doorframe as I dress in a sweater and stretch pants. He's studying me with narrowed eyes and his arms crossed over his chest as I brush out my hair.

When I'm done, I walk back to him, stop, and wait. He doesn't budge. I'm acutely aware of the bulge in his pants and the tension radiating from him.

"If you're waiting for me to return the favor, you'll wait a long time," I say.

His lips curve into a humorless smile. "You reckon? I can make you go down on your knees right this moment and swallow my cock."

I lift my chin to meet his gaze. "Why don't you?"

He clenches his jaw, regarding me with a broody expression.

I'm not sure what changed. Making me come shifted something between us. I'm still scared, but I'm no longer terrified. I don't think he'll kill me. On the other hand, I'm never sure what to expect from him.

"I want you to tell me how you got into my house," I say. "And then you can leave."

A cruel glint sparks in his eyes. "You're not going to bite the hand that feeds you, are you?"

My pulse flutters in my neck. "I don't know what you're implying. This has to stop, Angelo. You got what you wanted a long time ago. I need you to leave me alone. I want you to get the hell out of my house. Now."

His smile is calculated. "You can't kick me out of my own house."

His words are like a slap in my face. I reel from the

impact. I can only look at him, shaking my head, because he can't mean what I think he does.

He raises a brow. "Didn't your brother tell you?"

A sick feeling settles in the pit of my stomach. "Tell me what?"

"This house, your car, your bills, your studies…you didn't think Ryan was paying for everything?"

I stare at him in horror.

"That's right, *cara*." He drops his arms at his sides. "I've been taking care of you for a long time already." He advances a step, putting us toe to toe. "As is my duty." He adds with a mocking tilt of his lips, "However, showing a little gratitude won't hurt you."

Gasping for air, I fight an urge to hyperventilate. It can't be true. Why would Ryan do that to me? I can't handle more lies from someone in my family I trusted.

"That's right," he says, caressing my cheek with the back of his hand. "You're mine to feed and clothe and keep safe. I hope the house pleases you. I thought you'd like it, knowing how much you love the beach and the sea."

It's too much to process. My head spins. Placing a palm over my stomach where the betrayal burns like a flaming torch, I back up to the center of the room. All this time, I lived on Angelo Russo's money. The worst is that Ryan let me.

Why?

"I can see this comes as a shock to you," Angelo says, stalking after me. "So I'll give you a little time to get over it." He takes something from his pocket. "Twenty-four hours, *bella*." Gripping my left hand in his, he slides a ring over my finger. "Then you're mine in every way."

My hand trembles in his hold. I look down. A huge solitaire diamond sparkles on my ring finger.

"No," I say, breathless, shaking my head again.

"I promised you." His tone carries a warning. "I told you I'd put that ring on your finger. Tomorrow, Sabella. In twenty-four hours, we'll get married in front of a magistrate." He drops my hand. "That should give you enough time to get your things in order."

I sound like a robot. "Married? My things in order?"

The lines of his face turn hard. "You're coming back to Corsica with me."

The statement sounds more like a threat. The declaration takes the wind out of my sails.

"What about my studies?" I exclaim. "I can't just pack up and leave."

"I already informed the university that you're dropping out."

I'm at a loss for words. I have no ammunition or defenses. Once more, I can only stand there on shaky legs and stare at him as he turns and leaves.

CHAPTER
TWENTY-TWO

Angelo

The truth hurt Sabella. I saw it in her pretty soft brown eyes, those eyes that remind me of a tigress. Her brother never told her, and I can't figure out why. To protect her feelings? Her fragile pride? I sure as hell didn't have any regard for her pride today. Slaying her wasn't my intention, especially not on her birthday, and a rare sliver of guilt pierces my conscience.

Because her birthday will never be special for her again.

There's no point in lying about it. From the day I used her, the date that's supposed to be a celebration of her existence will always leave a bitter taste in her mouth. I did what I did for us to be together. I told her more than once. But that won't matter to her, because I did it for me.

Tough luck.

I'm still marrying her tomorrow. Her beautiful face

paled when I told her I own her material life. The betrayal and humiliation that passed through her eyes did something to me. I must have a heart left somewhere in the rotten cavity of my chest because I didn't like that look on her. I wasn't going to give her flowers, a dress, or a reception for her family, but I changed my mind. In my own way, I'm offering her a consolation. The fact that I don't do consolations says how huge this sacrifice is. Granting her family this courtesy takes more than its pound of flesh from me.

I'll do it for her. I'll do it to make up for all the birthdays I'm yet to ruin. There's no turning back from how we started out, no undoing what's been done. She can never look at the eleventh of January in a happy way, but if given another chance, I'd do it again. If that's the price to be with her, so be it. We'll find a way of getting over it. We'll live around that day. There are more than enough other days in the year. We'll make those count. In time, she'll come to appreciate her new home.

When I leave the villa, I drive to the Home Affairs office and book an appointment for a marriage license. The money I pay under the table gets us in the front of the queue. I already have all the documentation I need. Then I book a restaurant on the beach and order flowers.

Whether her family joins us for lunch is up to them. Whatever the case, for this day and this day only, I'll tolerate them. I'll make this sacrifice for Sabella even though facing her brother, the man who killed my family, without slitting his throat will take every ounce of self-control I possess.

The only knowledge that pacifies me is that they'll be facing the same. I made a deal with Ryan after what happened. We both stick to the rules. As long as no one steps out of line, no more bloodshed between our families will be necessary. I suppose we can pretend to be decent human beings for a single afternoon. For Sabella's sake.

When everything is in place, I drive to an upmarket wedding boutique and do what I promised myself I wouldn't. I buy a wedding dress. The design I choose is simple and elegant. The halter neck will emphasize the proud set of her shoulders, and the low cut at the back will expose the golden expanse of her silky skin and the fragile line of her spine. The soft drape of the fabric will sweep over the top of her ass, exposing the dimples above. She'll look like a goddess.

I have no idea if the size is right or if the dress will fit over her curves and in all the right places, but it will have to do. If the sales lady finds it strange that I buy a dress without letting my bride try it on, she doesn't show it. She's too much of a businesswoman to turn down a sale. Proving that point, she also sells me a veil, a clutch bag, and silk-covered Cinderella style slippers. At least I know Sabella's shoe size.

My rightful place is in my soon-to-be wife's bed—in my house—but I grant her another reprieve by booking into a hotel. I did promise to give her a day.

Come tomorrow, I'll be done waiting.

CHAPTER
TWENTY-THREE

Sabella

The minute Angelo is gone, I get into my car and take the highway to the northeast. I clench the wheel to stop my hands from shaking, but that doesn't prevent the tears from streaming over my cheeks as I put my foot down on the accelerator.

I can't stop thinking about the fact that Angelo paid for this car. I can't get over what he said. The closer I get to Great Brak River, the sicker I feel.

It's teatime when I arrive. I dry my eyes and smooth down my hair, trying to force calm, but my stomach is twisted into a tight ball.

Doris greets me at the door with a gasp. "Happy birthday, Bella. If I'd known you were coming, I would've baked a cake. I can quickly go out and pick one up in George."

"No, thanks," I say, squeezing past her. "But it's very kind of you to offer. Where's Ryan?"

She frowns. "In the study. Is everything okay?"

I plaster a smile on my face. "Yes."

Steeling my spine, I walk down the corridor to the room in which I haven't set foot since my dad's death. I take a deep breath and open the door. The nostalgic familiarity throws me off balance.

Nothing changed. The smell of leather and wood polish still hangs in the air. The throw on the back of the sofa is folded in the same meticulous triangle. The only difference is that Ryan sits in the big swivel chair.

"Bella." My brother gets to his feet and rounds the desk, concern etched on his face. "What's wrong?"

Fishing the ring from the pocket of my sweater, I hold it on my palm. "Angelo paid me a visit."

Ryan blanches. He leans his backside on the desk and shoves his hands in his pockets, observing me in silence.

I wrap my fingers so tightly around the ring that the sharp edges of the diamond cut into my skin. "Did you hear what I said?"

Mom rushes into the room. Celeste follows short on her heels, carrying Brad on her hip. I drop my arm to my side. Brad's face lights up when he sees me. He gives a shy smile and sucks his thumb into his mouth.

The sight of my nephew in his Spiderman costume calms me. He's a timid kid. I don't want to scare him by losing my shit.

"Bella," Mom exclaims. "I thought you were having a party in Cape Town."

Sticking her head around the doorframe, Celeste calls for Doris. Brad finally gets over his shyness and extends his arms toward me.

"Hey, Brad." I take him from Celeste and kiss the top

of his curly head, inhaling the scent of his baby shampoo. "How are you, buddy?" I tickle his tummy. "I missed you."

He giggles. I almost burst into tears when he wraps his chubby arms around my neck.

In a couple of weeks, he'll already be two years old. He's growing by leaps and bounds. It goes too fast. I hate missing out on his milestones.

Doris appears on the threshold, her features drawn. "You called for me?"

"Please take Brad upstairs to play," Celeste says, giving her a meaningful look.

"Come here, big man." Doris takes him from me. "How about we read a story?" She shoots me a worried glance from over her shoulder as she carries him from the room.

"What's going on?" Mom asks when they're gone.

Taking another calming breath, I face my brother. "That's what Ryan is going to tell me."

My brother studies me with a stony expression.

"What happened?" Celeste asks, closing the door.

"Angelo happened," I say, not looking away from Ryan. "I want to know how he got into my house." I add in a bitter tone, "Or shall I say *his* house?"

Ryan's stoic demeanor doesn't falter.

Mom sinks down on the nearest sofa. "Oh dear God."

"Why didn't I know that Angelo Russo was paying my bills?" I ask, praying that Angelo lied, that it was just another one of his mean tricks to torment me. A sick joke. "My food, my clothes? My *studies*?"

Ryan's jaw bunches.

"Tell me, Ryan." I ball my hands at my sides, the ring a painful reminder in my fist. "Tell me it's not true."

"It's true," Mom says, her shoulders slouching. For

once, she doesn't adopt a proud or angry air. She looks defeated, and it scares me more than anything.

"You knew?" I ask with parted lips.

My mom looks away, refusing to meet my eyes.

I turn to Celeste, betrayal slicing through me. "Did you know too?"

She bites her lip.

"Shit." I utter a wry laugh. "It seems I'm the only ignorant fool in this room."

"It's not like that," Ryan says.

Anger surfaces again, mixing with the ache that constricts my chest. "Then explain it to me."

"Angelo Russo took over the business a long time ago," he says in a placating tone. "Right after he stole Dad's book."

The revelation hits me so hard I feel it like a physical blow. "What?" My voice is breathless. "What does that mean?"

"He didn't only demand shares," Ryan says. "He took everything."

I grip the chair back next to me for balance. "I–I don't understand."

"We've all just been earning an allowance from him since." Ryan continues with a neutral expression. "In my case, I'm nothing but an employee working for a salary."

My mouth is so dry I have to swallow before I can get another word out. "Why?"

"He's greedy." At last, emotion flickers across Ryan's face. "Why would he settle for shares if he could have everything?"

The sentiment is so rare for my brother that it takes me a moment to place it.

Hatred.

"The house…" I look around the room. "The house in Bloubergstrand?"

"No." Ryan crosses his arms. "Dad paid off the bonds. The investments and the houses were always intact." Ryan's smile is flat. "The rest is—"

"Charity," Mom says, all but spitting the word out. She's staring at the cold fireplace, rocking herself on the edge of the sofa.

"This was happening from the day he stole that book?" I ask, dread filling my veins.

Ryan nods.

How terrible. How humiliating it must've been for Dad to live on Angelo's money. No, not Angelo's money. The money Angelo stole from my dad when he blackmailed him to sign over his business.

The thought makes me want to empty my stomach. "What about Dad's savings?"

Ryan straightens and walks to the wet bar. "Most of it was invested in long-term funds. The trust funds were structured to be untouchable in case of bankruptcy." He pours Dad's favorite brand of Scotch into tumblers. "We couldn't touch that money. It could only pay out in the event of his death."

"Our inheritance." My heart thuds between my ribs. The reality weighs down on me, making everything feel too heavy. "What about that money? Mine is tied up until I turn twenty-five, but you have access to yours."

Mom sniffs. "I used all the money your father left me to pay off our debts."

Ryan carries two glasses over and hands one to Mom and the other to Celeste. "The business he left me is nothing but a small satellite office in Cape Town. It's the only part Angelo didn't take. It hardly makes enough money to be worth the effort."

"Hold on." I'm still stuck on what Mom said. "Debts?" I sit down on the chair facing her. "I thought we didn't live on credit."

She waves a hand. "Credit cards, wedding expenses, the funeral… It all adds up quickly."

Meaning there's nothing left.

"Don't forget that woman and her daughter got most of the money," Mom adds through thin lips.

Laura and Daisy.

It's expensive to keep one family, especially with the material standards my parents upheld, but two cost double that much.

Ryan pours another glass and lifts it with a raise of his eyebrow in a silent question directed at me.

I shake my head. On second thought, I reach for the drink. When he places the tumbler in my hand, I swallow everything in one go. The alcohol heats my stomach, dispelling some of the ice in my veins.

My eyes water from the burn of the strong liquor. "Then he pays for everything?" I can't say his name out loud. Not now. Not after what I just learned.

Ryan's silence is his answer. He pours a few fingers of Scotch for himself and, following my example, downs it in one shot.

That's horrible. Angelo is paying not only my expenses but also my family's. He's paying for our food, our clothes, and every luxury we care to indulge in.

Why would he do that? Does he take perverse satisfaction from making us dependent on him? Because Mom is wrong. Angelo doesn't have a charitable bone in his body. He doesn't do anything without a reason, let alone out of the goodness of his heart. Wait. He doesn't have a heart.

Hurt and confused, I ask, "Why didn't you tell me?"

"Dad never wanted to." Ryan shrugs. "You were so young at the time. He was trying to protect you."

To stop me from blaming myself more than I already was because I was the one who let Angelo into the house. Fresh guilt needles its way into my gut.

"Why?" I glance between Mom and Ryan. "Why would he pay our bills?"

Silence falls over the room.

I open my fist, showing them the big shiny diamond set in gold. "What is the meaning of this?"

Mom gasps.

"Why would he give me a ring if he hates us for what happened to his family? What the hell is going on?"

"You have to tell her, Ryan," Celeste says. "She has a right to know."

"Tell me what?"

More silence.

"Ryan?" Panic and helpless anger heat my voice. "*Tell me what?*"

Sighing, he scrubs a hand over his face and leaves his empty glass on the desk. "When Dad employed the Russo family, he made a deal. He promised to marry you to Angelo in exchange for their alliance and services."

The ground disappears underneath me.

"The Russos weren't only interested in the money he paid them." Ryan's expression is pained. "They wanted in on the business. Angelo would've received shares and a position in the company."

Slowly, the pieces click together. "That's why they came to my sixteenth birthday party."

Ryan continues, "The deal was discussed so long before then, Dad thought they'd forgotten about it."

"But they hadn't," I say, my voice sounding strange to my own ears.

"No," Ryan says with regret. "Dad denied making the deal. Things got heated. Santino and Angelo left your party angry."

I stare at Mom for confirmation. "That's why Dad didn't want me to have contact with him." I brace myself for uttering that name. "With Angelo."

"I didn't agree with not telling you," she says, pursing her lips in the way she does when she's trying not to cry. "Then you told me how guilty you felt, and I knew your father was right. Admitting the truth would've only made you feel worse. Your father believed it was better not to saddle you with the gritty details. I think he was worried you'd be disappointed in him if you knew what he'd done."

"Promising me to a Russo?" I ask on the verge of hysteria again.

Recollections of the times I caught my parents fighting flash through my mind. The memory of my sixteenth birthday party when my mom stormed out of the study with mascara running down her eyes comes back to taunt me. Mom was upset about something Dad had done. I still remember her words that drifted through the closed door.

I'm not going to say I told you so, but I did warn you not to do business with those people. You can't let this happen.

So much makes sense now, but the truth doesn't bring relief. It only brings more torment.

"Dad regretted it the moment it had been done," Ryan says. "He went along with the conditions because no one else could deliver the service the Russos could."

"The *service?* What service?" My lip curls around the accusation. "Killing people?"

Ryan winces. "Santino brought Angelo for the two of you to meet. The engagement was supposed to happen when you turned eighteen."

The world starts spinning around me. I put the empty

glass on the side table and grip the armrests to steady myself. The ring drops from my hand and falls with a clink on the floor.

"When Dad denied the promise he'd made, Angelo came back and stole the book."

"To blackmail Dad into honoring his promise," I say as the insight hits me.

"Yes." Ryan regards me from under his lashes. "He didn't only take the shares Dad promised him. He took over control of the business, leaving us with no power and no money, making sure we couldn't start a war."

"Is that why Dad ordered someone to kill them?" I ask. "To get back his business?"

Mom inhales sharply.

"Angelo sent marriage instructions on the day of your eighteenth birthday." Ryan holds my gaze unfalteringly as he deals yet another blow. "His family was preparing a big wedding in Corsica for June. Dad wanted to stop it. He wanted to get them off our backs."

But everything went wrong.

Celeste walks to the back of my chair and puts a hand on my shoulder. "If it makes you feel better, I didn't know that he was paying for your house either. Ryan only told me recently."

I shake off her touch. It doesn't make me feel better. Nothing can. "The Russos wanted an arranged marriage for shares and money. They have all the money. They have the business. Why does he still want me to honor the deal?"

"I don't know," Ryan says. "I thought he gave up that goal when we agreed to stop the bloodshed between our families. The only reason I can think of is that the Edwards name is respected everywhere we do business. The Russo name not so much. It's not a good name."

My laugh is cold. "You don't say. Not that we deserve

any of that respect. We're no better than the Russos. We just keep up the pretense."

"Don't say that," Mom exclaims. "Do not compare me with those savages."

"Come on, Mom." My smile is flat. "You know what Dad was involved in. None of us can claim to be ignorant about who we are any longer."

"Dad tried to spare you all from that part of his life." Ryan glances at Celeste. "So did I."

Another memory slips into my mind. I remember the day Angelo gave me the Ferrari for my eighteenth birthday. When Colin questioned the inappropriately expensive gift, Ryan silenced him. I had a feeling then that Ryan was hiding something.

My brother's strange behavior now makes sense. That's why he didn't make a scene. Angelo was already paying my way as far back as then. Farther still. My brother knew Angelo was planning on marrying me. That's why the gift didn't shock Ryan. Giving your future wife a Ferrari when you're a billionaire is hardly abnormal. That's why Ryan smoothed it over and deflected Colin's questions. He was keeping the truth from me while conspiring with Dad to stop the wedding from happening.

Yes, I kept a truth from him too, but damn it, the fact that I gave my v-card to Angelo didn't impact Ryan's life. The fact that Angelo supports me financially, me and my family, definitely impacts me.

"You should've told me." I jump to my feet. "You had no right to hide this."

Celeste puts a hand on my arm. "Bella, sweetie, I'm the first one to agree. Ryan was just trying to protect you."

"Don't make excuses for him." I pull away, escaping the comfort she offers. I'm too angry to accept their support or apologies. Too devastated.

"Bella, please." Mom stands, extending her palms. "We tried our best for this not to happen. You know how much your father loved you. He would've done anything to keep you from this fate."

"Including murder," I say, placing a hand on my brow as I pace to the sliding doors.

Fuck.

"Yes." Mom's tone turns hard. "Including murder. He did what he thought was best. We all want what's best for you."

I spin around to face her. "What are you saying?"

"We're not going to let Angelo win. Let him cut off our allowance. Let him remove Ryan as CEO of the South African branch and take away everything your father built his entire life. We'll find a way to survive. Ryan can work elsewhere. I can get a job."

I stare at her as horrible facts sink in. "Ryan won't find another job that pays that well, not with the current unemployment rate. And what would you do? You said yourself, that ship has sailed. What about Celeste and Brad and their future? Not to mention that Ryan will go to jail for murder if the truth comes out."

"Angelo Russo won't dare to tell the truth," Ryan says. "He's guilty too, remember?"

How can I forget? That image is burned into my brain. The nightmares still haunt my sleep.

"What are you suggesting?" I ask. "That I go on the run?"

"We stand up to him." Ryan straightens. "We say no. I'd rather be dirt fucking poor than deliver you to that monster."

I consider that, what it will be like for all of us to start from scratch, to have nothing and work our way up. I don't care about the comfort or the money. If I can't find a permanent job, I can always do small jobs to pay the bills. I don't need much.

But what about Brad and Celeste? Celeste doesn't earn a salary. A child costs money. There are things to consider, things like medical care and an education. Mom will have to lower her standards and give up her status. We'd have to let Doris go. Poor Doris. Will she find another live-in job in George? At least she has unemployment insurance. Mom will have to sell the big houses and buy a smaller place, maybe an apartment near Mattie and Jared. Thank goodness Jared isn't involved in the business, or he'd be relying on Angelo for a salary too.

Mattie and I will have a bit of money when the investment funds we inherited pay out. I can always use that cash to buy a studio apartment. If Ryan can't find another job, I can put that money at his disposal. Or we can rent a modest house in a middle class suburb, and I can board with them again until we're all on our feet. That way, we can still afford to keep Doris on.

Right now, a modest house in a middle class suburb sounds amazing. Like a dream.

"It's doable, Bella," Ryan says. "We'll survive."

Mom scoffs. "At least then that devil won't have a sword to hold over our heads any longer." She comes closer and pulls me into one of her rare hugs. "We talked about it a lot after you ended up in hospital. We all thought this way was the only solution if the push came to shove."

I chew my lip. "Including Mattie?"

My mom holds me at arm's length. "Mattie agrees."

"What about the shame?" I ask. "Your wealthy friends are going to look down on you. They won't invite you to their parties if you're not adding value to their guest list."

Mom lets me go. "I'll make new friends."

"I appreciate that you're all willing to make such huge sacrifices," I say. "Let me think about it, okay?"

Ryan gives me a dark look. "When will Angelo be back?"

My throat constricts. "Tomorrow."

"Then we know what to do." He kisses the top of Celeste's head. "You women stay here. Tomorrow at first light, I'll go to Cape Town to talk to Angelo."

"Do you think he'll just accept it?" Celeste asks in a small voice.

Ryan rubs her arm. "We won't give him a choice. What's he going to do? Dad is dead. If he decides to leak the truth about the bribes, we'll just have to keep our heads high."

"You're an accomplice in the bribes," I point out.

"It's my word against his. I can always claim I didn't know what Dad was doing. There's no evidence proving that I was involved."

I search my brother's face. "It will be a hell of a scandal."

"We already dealt with the scandal of Dad's affair and his so-called suicide." Ryan chuckles. "What's another one?"

"That's very brave of you," I say.

"I was willing to swallow my pride and not disillusion you about where the money came from as long as he didn't bother you again." Ryan frowns. "When Celeste and I moved back here, he rented the villa with a very clear instruction that he wanted you to live there. I had no idea he'd come back with a fucking ring."

My gaze shifts to the diamond that sparkles insistently on the rug, its light refusing to be extinguished, no matter how sinister the reasons that bling is meant for. It's at least four or five carats, worth a small fortune. I'll have to return it to the villa and leave it there for Angelo to find.

Bending to pick up the ring, I say, "It's not your fault. You couldn't know."

"Ryan is right," Mom says. "You better stay the night, Bella. It's too late to drive back."

She doesn't say it's probably safer for me here, but that's what we're all thinking.

I nod, trying to gather myself as I walk through the door. "Excuse me. I need some air."

None of this would've happened if Dad had honored his promise. But Dad never had any intention of keeping that promise. Of that, I'm sure. It's ironic that there was a time I would've gladly put Angelo's ring on my finger. I did, didn't I? I wore his signet ring with pride before I knew what he'd done. All that is in the past now, and things will never be the same.

Escaping outside, I take in the familiar view of the sea. Even this favorite sight has been tainted. A single, careless, forbidden moment spoiled everything.

The breeze has picked up. Grabbing a throw from the sofa on the veranda, I wrap it around my shoulders and climb down the dune.

Despite the memories, the deserted beach provides a measure of peace. I sit down at the edge of the water and dig my toes into the sand. I try to think, to come to a decision, but Ryan is right. There's only one thing I can do, and it scares me. It terrifies me, because I know what Angelo is capable of.

The only thought that soothes me is knowing he doesn't need me for anything other than my so-called good name. There are hundreds of women with good family names in the world. He can easily find someone else to make a good match. It doesn't have to be me.

A shadow falls over me.

Alarmed, I jerk.

"Hey," Colin says. "It's only me."

"Shit." I place a hand over my heart. "You scared me."

"Sorry. I didn't mean to." He sits down next to me. "I went for a jog and saw you coming down here from the top of the road." Studying me closely, he adds, "I thought you were having a girls' night in Cape Town."

I blow out a shaky sigh. "There isn't a party."

He frowns. "Why?"

Shifting sideways, I face him. "Angelo proposed."

"What?" His expression turns thunderous. "He came to see you again? That son of a bitch. Where is he now?"

"I don't know. He left after telling me I had until tomorrow."

"For what?"

"To prepare myself." I shrug. "To get used to the idea."

"I never wanted to kill someone with my bare hands, but I swear—"

"Please, no more talk of killing. I've had enough of that."

"Bella." He grips my chin. "I know you've never been completely honest with me. I know there's plenty you're not telling me."

Pulling free, I look away. "There's plenty I didn't know myself."

He's quiet for a moment. After a beat, he says, "Marry me. Tomorrow."

I look back at him quickly. "What?"

"Marry me," he says again. "Tomorrow morning. There'll be nothing he can do about it when he comes back for you."

Staring at him with disbelief, I scoot back. "It's not like that between us."

The muscles in his temples bunch. "We care about each other. We're best friends. We understand each other. I know you better than you know yourself. I already told you, in my opinion, that's the best foundation for a marriage."

"We were talking about a relationship, not marriage, and we were no more than teenagers."

"My age never prevented me from knowing what's right for me. I'm a practical man. You know that. We'll work together. I wouldn't have offered if I wasn't sure."

"Oh, Colin." I bite my lip. "You don't know half of it. If you did, you wouldn't make such an offer."

"Then tell me." He catches my ankles and pulls me closer. "Tell me everything, and don't leave a damn thing out. Go on. I dare you."

"Even if I could tell you, I wouldn't. You'll run for the hills."

"I'm not scared off that easily," he says with a crooked smile. "Try me."

"You'll never look at me the same again."

"Tell me," he says, squeezing my ankles. "If I'm still here when you're done, you'll marry me." He makes a funny face. "Won't that make all your problems go away?"

I can't help but laugh. "You're impossible."

His expression turns serious. "I'm listening."

For a moment, I wonder how it will be to be his wife. We have a good, solid friendship and mutual interests. There may not be sparks, but I love him in a different way. We *can* be good together. I can be a decent wife to him, making up for the shortcoming of passion in other ways.

We share the same values. Our families are friends. Whether his family will still be friends with us if they know the truth is to be seen. I doubt that. But Colin is different. He's never been judgmental. For a fleeting moment, I catch a glimpse of a safe, tranquil life with him, a life in which there's no crime or fear. No bad history.

The idea of that life is so appealing that I tell him. I tell him everything, starting from the beginning when my dad made the deal and ending with the ring I still carry in my pocket. I don't leave any sordid detail out.

He doesn't interrupt me once. He listens intently until I've finished. When I finally fall quiet, I hold my breath, expecting his scorn or his disgust, but Colin being Colin, he simply wraps his arms around me and hugs me.

The relief is so overwhelming that I burst into tears. It's not just the weight that lifts off my shoulders. It's that after everything I told him, he doesn't hate me.

"How can you still like me?" I ask through my tears.

He rubs circles over my back. "Oh, Bella. How can I not?"

Pulling back, I wipe a hand over my face. "I didn't want to put you in a difficult situation."

"Hey." He brushes a hand over my hair. "Your secrets are mine, remember?"

I smile at the reminder of the pact we made as kids.

"Tomorrow," he says, his gaze earnest as he catches mine. "We should get married in Cape Town. It'll be easier to organize there. We won't be able to find a marriage official last-minute here, and the minister won't do it on such short notice. He'll insist that we attend those compulsory marital sessions first."

"I don't want you to marry me just to save me."

He smiles. "I've always been saving you, haven't I?" When I frown, he takes my hand. "Look, I know you don't love me with sparks and fireworks and all that jazz. That's not what I want. My job is going to be hectic. Someone like you will get that. You won't expect me to be home for dinner at six every night. I want someone who'll give me the freedom to be me, and I'll give you the space you need to grow. We can just take it day by day. We'll figure it out."

"What about your family?"

"They'll be ecstatic." He stands, pulling me with him. "They don't have to know the details. We'll just say we decided to get married on the spur of the moment."

I better go home and tell everyone the news. Ryan won't have to drive to Cape Town after all. "I don't deserve you, Colin."

He wraps an arm around my shoulders. "You deserve happiness, Bella." Leading me toward the path, he says, "Come. We have a lot to do."

CHAPTER
TWENTY-FOUR

Angelo

Like the first time I landed in Cape Town with my father, I stop at a lookout point on the cliffside road to stare at the sun rising over the ocean. Thick bands of orange and red overlay the deep purple on the horizon. A few stars still twinkle in the dawn. The crash of the waves on the rocks is deafening. The treacherous sea is always restless. Angry. Unpredictable. No wonder they call it the Cape of Storms. The beauty is devastating. It's both hypnotizing and destructive. Much like the journey I embarked on since my path crossed Sabella's.

What would've happened if my father hadn't insisted that I meet her when she turned sixteen? Would things have been different if I knocked on her door when she was already eighteen? I often wonder.

Our history is as violent as the nature of this country in

which she has her roots. Our fate is just as destructive, but it's also a certainty. It's always been. I knew she'd be my wife from the day she turned ten.

I was only fourteen, yet I'll never forget the peace that knowledge brought me. My future was paved, my partner for life decided. It seemed so effortless and graceful at the time. Such a noble notion.

The promise I made my father on that first visit to this country rings in my head. I assured him I'd see this deal through.

My gut clenches when I inhale the salty air. I swear I smell a whiff of cigarillo smoke on the breeze. Just like on that day when my father stood here beside me on this very spot. We visited the vineyards to buy wine. He was drinking in the view, soaking up the hours he had left. He wanted to settle me in my future. He didn't want to die before his job here was done. That's why we came.

The memories are almost too much to bear. It's difficult to believe that was already three years ago. Sometimes, it feels as if my whole life is condensed into these past three years, as if nothing before that mattered.

It took a lot to get here, not in distance, time, or cost but in sacrifice. It feels as if I've waited a lifetime for this day, and now, it's finally arrived.

Our wedding day.

I stay until I can't stand the haunting emptiness beside me any longer, and then I drive back to my hotel. My rooms at the five-star hotel in Cape Town are as luxurious as the villa in Camps Bay, but the honeymoon suite isn't where I'm planning on bedding my wife for the first time. When Sabella becomes Mrs. Edwards-Russo, I'll consummate our marriage in the house where she'll bear our children. In our home.

The arrangements are in place. I booked a private jet

to fly us to Marseille in France. Private jets aren't good for the environment, but I don't want to share our first moments as husband and wife with four hundred strangers in a commercial plane. Those hours are sacred. I'm selfish like that.

From Marseille, we'll take the yacht. The skipper will pilot it. I'll have seven hours to ravish her body, but I will only come inside her when my seed can spill on the sheets of my bed. That doesn't mean I can't enjoy her until then. There are many ways to please her without using my cock.

At the hotel, I have breakfast in the courtyard before taking a shower. I check my phone as I dry myself off. Sabella hasn't seen the gown I left in the villa yet. She didn't have a chance. Instead, she went home to Great Brak River, no doubt to confront Ryan about the truth. The men I hired to keep her safe informed me she's on her way back to Cape Town. She should arrive any minute.

I dress in the bespoke suit I had tailored for the occasion and round the outfit off with a black silk tie. I'm not supposed to see the bride before the ceremony. My mother will turn in her grave. But I can't trust Sabella to make it to the Home Affairs office on her own. She won't get into a car with a chauffeur unless she's being held at gunpoint. Between driving her myself and having her dragged in front of an official with a gun pushed against her head, the first option is my choice.

I cast a critical glance in the mirror, taming my hair by combing it through with my fingers. Then I grab my overnight bag and check out. The security guards I hired wait in the street. Ryan and I have an agreement, but I trust an Edwards just as far as I can throw him.

Four men with firearms concealed under their jackets get into a bullet-proof Mercedes. Two more wait for me at my rental. One takes my bag and loads it in the trunk when I unlock the doors. The other shifts behind the wheel. I make myself at home on the backseat and fire off a quick text message to the pilot. He replies immediately, assuring me that everything is ready. I'm about to put the phone away when it rings.

It's the man I hired to keep an eye on Sabella.

My gut tightens as I take the call.

"Mr. Russo." He sounds out of breath. "We have a problem. Ms. Edwards hasn't arrived home yet."

"What the fuck is that supposed to mean?" I grip the phone hard, adding with menace, "Tell me you have a visual on her."

"That's the thing. She was on her way back from her mother's house, but I lost her in the city. She went to great lengths to shake me off."

"Where in the city?" I bite out.

"Near Greenmarket Square."

I gnash my teeth. "Has she been home at all?"

"No, sir. Her sister-in-law went into the villa an hour ago. My colleague said she exited with a suitcase."

"Why the fuck wasn't I informed?"

"We didn't think it strange. We assumed her sister-in-law helped her pack for her trip."

"Where did the sister-in-law go?"

He hesitates before continuing. "We lost her too."

I'm bristling with anger. "You what?"

"She entered the underground parking lot of a shopping mall. The lot has five levels. By the time we located her car, she was nowhere to be found. We're looking for her on the security cameras of the mall as we speak."

I pull up the app that tracks Sabella's location via her phone. The signal is dead. She must've destroyed the phone. The localization tracker is useless.

Fuck.

"Go faster," I tell the driver. "Don't worry about the speed limit."

He puts his foot down on the accelerator. The driver behind us follows his example.

"Put out an alert with your contacts and give them Miss Edwards's number plate," I instruct the man on the other end of the line. "Involve the traffic department if you must. Pay anyone who can be bought. Money isn't an issue."

"Yes, sir."

"Do a fucking better job this time," I say before ending the call and dialing the head of the security company.

When he picks up, I say, "I need the street video surveillance for the last hour in a ten-kilometer radius of Greenmarket Square."

"My men just brought me up to speed." His tone is apologetic. "Don't worry, we'll find her."

"You better hope so." He won't like the consequences if they don't.

When I hang up, I check Margaret Edwards's and Ryan's phones. They're both dead. So are Matilde's and her husband's. The whole family is in on this. Even the housekeeper's phone is off the grid.

If they think they can disappear with my bride, they better think again.

I call the guy watching Celeste Edwards' parents' house. He says the parents are still living like shipwrecked victims on a deserted West Coast beach. They haven't been at their house in months.

The man keeping watch at the Edwards's residence in Great Brak River says there's no one home. The housekeeper, Ryan, Celeste, Margaret, and the kid are gone. So is the neighbor, Colin Taylor. His parents and sister are on holiday in the Maldives.

Sabella doesn't have any other friends. Not real friends.

She's not hiding out somewhere. If she left with everyone she cares about, it can only mean one thing.

She's on the run.

When I catch her, she's going to regret her little stunt.

The driver pulls up at the villa. The man riding shotgun jumps out and follows me to the door where the guard on duty stands at attention.

"Anything new?" I ask.

He shifts his weight. "No, sir."

Cursing, I go around him, deactivate the alarm, and unlock the security gate and door to let myself in.

"Stay here," I instruct the two guards.

The house feels empty when I enter. It's not the way in which my shoes echo in the acoustic space of the kitchen. I sense her absence as if she's always been a part of me.

The kitchen is tidy. I open the dishwasher. A few dirty dishes are stacked inside. I go to the fridge and almost yank the door off its hinges in my haste. It's stocked with perishable foods. She left in a hurry.

The dread bleeding from my gut only increases as I rush downstairs and go through her dressing room. Most of her clothes are there, but the empty spots on the shelves indicate that a few outfits were taken. Her toiletries are gone too.

Taking the stairs two by two, I go back to the lounge and take out my phone. After pulling up an app, I access the videos that the hidden cameras in the house recorded and rewind to the point where I left the house. The cameras are motion sensitive. Movement triggers the recording.

Nothing happens until an hour ago when the video

shows Celeste Edwards entering the house. She hurries to the kitchen and hovers for a second by the table. Then she runs down the stairs, takes a suitcase from the closet, and hastily packs some clothes and toiletries. On her way out, she stops in front of the wedding dress in the transparent plastic cover that hangs behind the door and stares at it for a couple of beats before grabbing the dress as well as the Cinderella slippers and leaving with the wedding attire and the suitcase.

What the fuck?

Is she going to give the gown to Sabella to burn so that she can send me the ashes? It won't surprise me.

I clench the phone so hard it's a wonder the screen doesn't crack. I'll turn this country upside down, but I will find Sabella. She won't get away.

Something on the table catches my eye.

The ring.

I pick it up.

It screams rejection.

Sabella couldn't make herself clearer if she'd told me to my face she wouldn't marry me.

Pocketing the ring, I walk from the house with long strides. Brutal anger replaces the dread. I have to give it to her, she's fucking brave. I never thought she'd make such a blatant run for it.

She's going to pay for this. When I find her, I'll punish her so hard she'll never try anything as foolish again.

My phone rings as I lock up. It's the security company chief.

"We found them," he says. "A street camera recorded her driving toward Constantia. The car is parked on a lot behind a church. We picked up the sister-in-law on the shopping mall security cameras. She exited her vehicle with the luggage, went up to the ground level, and got into a car waiting in the street. The car belongs to the brother, Ryan Edwards. Guess where they went? To the same church. The rest of the family's cars are there too."

"Send me the address," I order as fury like I've never felt boils up inside me.

CHAPTER
TWENTY-FIVE

Sabella

"Really?" I say as Colin leads me by the hand through the large wooden doors. I adjust the strap of my handbag over my shoulder. "A church?"

"It takes time to get an appointment at Home Affairs," he says, walking us down the aisle. "Plus, the vicar is my mom's uncle. He only agreed to marry us on such short notice because my mom always makes big donations to the church."

The runner carpet absorbs the sound of our footsteps as we make our way to the altar at the front. Candles burn in the alcoves. The wax leaves a chalky scent in the cool air. The interior is mostly dark except for the soft light streaming from crystal chandeliers that hang from the vaulted ceiling. From a stained-glass window behind the altar, Mary regards us with a serene expression. She raises one hand in blessing and holds the smiling baby Jesus on her hip in the other.

A thin, tall man with bushy white hair wearing an alb and a stole exits from the vestry and comes over to meet us.

"This is my uncle," Colin says. "Uncle, this is Sabella."

The man nods. "How do you do? I need a minute to set up the wine for the Holy Communion."

"Is that necessary?" I ask, nerves tightening my stomach.

He gives me a hard look. "This ceremony is already highly inappropriate as it is."

"Give us a moment," Colin says, addressing me. "Why don't you take a minute to catch your breath? It's been such a race."

He shows me a cry room on the side just as my family members burst through the open doors.

"Turn around, Colin," Celeste says, charging ahead of the group with a white gown in her arms. "You can't see the dress."

She got a dress? Wherever did she find one so quickly?

Colin obediently gives us his back as the group rush toward us, Ryan wheeling my suitcase.

"Where can we get ready?" Celeste asks the vicar in a no-nonsense manner.

Pinching his lips, he motions at the room Colin indicated.

Celeste grabs my arm and drags me inside. Ryan and my mom follow. Doris runs to keep up with Brad who clings to her like a monkey. My nephew's small yellow daypack with the green turtle on the front looks ridiculous on her back.

My heart melts with a rush of tenderness when I kiss Brad's chubby cheeks. He's wearing his Spiderman costume again. Celeste must have a dozen of those. It's the only outfit he wears these days.

Doris wipes sweat from her brow and deposits Brad on his feet.

"Thank you, Doris," Celeste says, hanging the dress on a wall hook before taking the daypack. "Did you bring his snacks?"

"Everything is in there," Doris says. "Including a coloring book and crayons."

Celeste gives her a grateful smile. "Come on, Brad." She wraps her hand around his small palm. "Let's have your teatime snack while Bella gets ready."

Ryan puts the suitcase in the middle of the floor and kisses her on the cheek. "I'll be there in a sec." He closes the door when she and Brad have left and turns to me. "Are you sure this is what you want?"

"It's too late to back out," Mom says, unzipping the plastic clothes bag.

"Where on earth did Celeste find a wedding dress?" I ask, dropping my handbag on a chair.

"I have no idea." Ryan grins. "Maybe at one of the boutiques in the mall. That woman never ceases to amaze me. She can be very resourceful when she wants to be."

"Quickly," Mom says as she takes out the gown. "We don't have much time. Do you have the rings, Ryan?"

"Quickest shopping I ever did. I'll give them to Colin. I can't guarantee they'll fit though."

"While you're at it, make sure he doesn't come in here." Mom shakes out the dress. "It's bad luck for the groom to see the dress before the bride walks down the aisle."

"Did everything go okay?" I ask, removing my sandals. "No one followed you?"

"The plan worked like a charm," Ryan says. "Celeste

parked underground and left via the mall." He motions at the suitcase. "She packed a few things like you asked. It's best that you change cars as soon as possible, preferably before you leave Cape Town. I left enough money in your bag to buy a new one in cash."

My mom pulls down the zipper at the back of my dress.

"Have you decided where you're going?" Ryan asks.

"Colin's family has a chalet in the Drakensberg. We'll stay there for a couple of weeks until the worst of Angelo's wrath has blown over."

"And then?" he asks, concern pleating his brow.

I shrug as if the confrontation will be a breeze and not the storm I fear. "Then I'll send Angelo a message with the news."

"Take the rings to Colin, Ryan." Mom shoos him away. "Let your sister get ready."

Ryan offers me one of his rare smiles before he gives us privacy.

"The dress is gorgeous," Mom says, taking it from the hanger. "I don't know where Celeste found it, but it looks like your size."

I take in the classical cut and the sensual lines. "It seems a bit much. Colin doesn't even have a wedding suit."

Mom waves the comment away. "He's fine. Making a little effort to look like a bride for him is the least you can do. You'll have to take off your bra. The back is open, and it's a halter neck." She sighs. "What a pity you don't have proper wedding underwear. Something new and white and lacy. And something old and blue. I should've taken my pearls for the something old. Or my earrings."

"The dress is already more than we bargained on." I slip out of my sundress, remove my bra, and step into the dress she holds for me. "A wedding gown wasn't part of the plan."

Tightlipped, my mom says, "I have to admit, Celeste did something right for once. Remember to thank her."

I turn around with a nervous smile, letting Mom zip up the dress. The silk hugs my hips but not too tightly. The fabric is soft and comfortable, caressing my thighs where the skirt is narrow before flaring out toward the hem.

I lift my hair for Mom to fasten the button of the halter neck at the back. The top is a little loose over my breasts, but I don't mind. At least I won't battle to breathe. I'm already short of breath from stress as it is.

Mom grips my shoulders and twirls me around to face her. "Let me have a look at you." Emotions flood her features. "You look perfect, Bella. It's not the wedding I would've liked to give you, but it's something. At least you're marrying the right man. I only wish your father was here. Giving you away to Colin would've made him very happy."

My chest tightens, and tears spring to my eyes.

My mom pulls her back straight. "Now isn't the time to be emotional." She clips the suitcase open and buries her head inside, hiding non too discreetly while composing herself before rising with silk slippers. "Oh, look. Celeste even brought shoes."

Grateful for the foresight, I take the shoes and put them on. They're a little wide, but I'll be able to walk in them.

Mom steps back and studies me with a critical look. "Let's get some color on your cheeks."

When I unzip my toilet bag, I'm relieved to find that Celeste remembered to pack my birth control pills. At the same time, it's weird to think about Colin in an intimate way. There was a time when I considered losing our virginity together, but so much happened since. After Angelo, I can't imagine sleeping with Colin or any other man for that matter. I'm sure sex with Colin will be tame and safe. I have no doubt that Colin will be patient. Knowing him, he'll give me all the time I need.

While I brush out my hair, Mom rummages through my make-up bag. As she takes out my lipstick, the door opens, and my sister enters.

"Mattie," I exclaim with a mixture of joy and concern. "What are you doing here? You're nine months pregnant, for crying out loud."

She gasps, cupping her hands over her mouth. "Oh, Bella. You look gorgeous."

"No tears," Mom warns in a stern tone. "Bella is right, Mattie. You're too close to having the baby to be here."

"I'm fine." Mattie rubs her belly. "You didn't think I'd miss my sister's wedding, did you?"

"Impromptu wedding," I say.

Mom hands her the make-up bag and the lipstick. "Help me get some color on her face. Colin is waiting."

"They can wait another minute," Mattie says. "It's a big day after all. Jared bought flowers."

"Bless his soul." Mom scurries to the door. "I'll go see if I can concoct a bridal bouquet."

Mattie stares at me for a beat when Mom is gone. "Oh, Bella," she says again. "You look so beautiful."

The uncertainty plaguing me carries on my voice. "Thank you."

"Hey." She searches my face. "This is what you want, right?"

"To escape? Yes. But to do this to Colin? I'm not sure that's fair."

"Colin is happy. He's not an idiot. He knows what he's signing up for."

I bite my lip, chewing it for a couple of beats before admitting, "I don't love him like that."

"Love isn't always instantaneous. In fact, most true loves aren't. Love at first sight is often nothing but hormones. It's just infatuation. Real love takes time to develop and to grow. I don't know how things are between you and Colin, but I've known Colin since the day he was born. I know him well enough to be sure he'll put the time and effort into your relationship that it deserves. Besides, this is what Dad would've wanted."

Those are the words that sway me. No matter how my dad hurt me with his lies, his sinister business deals, and his secret life, I never stopped loving him. I never stopped missing him. I'd give anything to have him here today. To walk me down the aisle. Mattie is right. This is what he wanted. He told me so himself. It would've made him happy.

I square my shoulders. "You're right. Let's do this."

"That's my baby sister." She uncaps my lipstick. "Let's make you even prettier than you are."

She applies the red lipstick and a little make-up and gives me the hand mirror when she's finished. Except for the make-up, I look like every other day. Normal. My smile says I'm happy. Only, I'm not. I'm terrified, not only because I can't relax until I say, *I do*, but also because I'm worried that we're making a mistake.

Too late.

The door opens.

Ryan sticks his head around the doorframe. "We have to get a move on. We don't want to risk being found." His gaze rests appreciatively on me. "You look gorgeous, Bella."

"Thanks," I say, resisting the urge to wipe my clammy palms on the gown.

"Wait." Mattie goes through her handbag. "Just give me a second to take her hair up."

She finds a few pins that she uses to secure my hair in a messy bun. "There. What do you think?"

"Thank you," I say, pulling her in for a quick hug.

We both laugh as her belly gets in the way.

She takes back the mirror. "You look perfect. Now go."

"Come on." Ryan offers me his arm. He's wearing a smile, but tension emanates from him. "I'm afraid there's no music."

I return his smile. "That's okay."

Mattie kisses my cheek before slipping through the door, whispering on her way out, "Good luck, Bella."

Ryan looks down at me. "Ready?"

I swallow and nod.

He pats my hand where it rests on the crook of his arm. "Let's get you married."

His attempt at humor doesn't help to settle my nerves. It has nothing to with wedding day stress and everything with the man I'm running away from, but my escape is finally within grasp. Freedom waits at the end of the aisle, only a few steps away. I won't be able to relax until the vicar declares us legally married.

Colin stands tall as Ryan walks me down the aisle. Guilt that his family isn't here assaults me. Maybe we should have a small celebration when they return from their vacation.

We pass my mom, Mattie, and Jared, who are seated in the pew second from the front on the left. Doris, Brad, and Celeste sit in front of them. They're all dressed up. Everyone made as much of an effort as they could on such short notice.

Doris jumps to her feet and leans over Celeste to hand me a makeshift bouquet of white roses. The stems are tied together with sellotape. Brad's Spiderman pencil case lies open on the bench, his sellotape spilling out among his crayons. The sight makes me smile.

I mouth, *thank you*, aiming the gratitude at both Doris and Jared, and wink at Brad, who grins.

Colin looks me over when Ryan and I stop in front of him. Appreciation warms his eyes. Ryan kisses my cheek and takes his place next to Celeste. I smile at my family from over my shoulder as I place a hand on the arm Colin offers before facing the vicar.

Colin leans down to whisper in my ear, "Fuck. You look amazing."

I mock-frown, whispering back, "Language. We're in a church."

The vicar picks up a Bible. "Shall we begin?"

"Yes, please," Colin says, tearing his gaze away from me.

"As per the groom's request, there won't be a sermon today," the vicar says. "We'll dive straight into the formalities. Before we do, I'd like to read a passage from Psalms and say a prayer."

Standing in a wedding gown in front of the nonjudgmental eyes of Mary feels unreal. I never dreamt about a wedding. I'm only nineteen years old. I always thought I'd travel the world and build a career first. It's both scary and reassuring. My life with Colin will be stable and predictable. There won't be nasty surprises like Mom had to endure, or did Mom think the same when she married Dad? Was she as sure of him as I am of Colin?

A part of it feels wrong too, so much so that I can't breathe.

"Bella," Colin whispers, nudging me gently.

I look at him.

He tilts his head toward the vicar, who says, "Repeat after me. I, Sabella Daphne Edwards, take—"

The rest of the vow is cut short as the doors fly open, banging against the walls. Sunlight spills into the space, the rays lighting Mary's face. The vicar's eyes go wide. The muscles of Colin's forearm tense underneath my palm. The gasps of the people I love fill my ears as we spin around.

The bouquet of white roses drops from my hand.

A man stands on the threshold, the sunbeams bouncing off his dark shape. He takes a wide stance with his arms hanging loosely at his sides. He balls his left hand, drawing my gaze to the action. My heart pounds in the cage of my ribs as I focus my attention on the gun he holds in his other hand. The sight reminds me of a scene I don't want to remember.

Angelo Russo steps into the church, into the light. The chandeliers illuminate the harsh features of his handsome face. The look in his black eyes is more devious than I've ever seen. Dressed in a bespoke suit with a silk tie, he stands there like a god, flaunting the truth for the whole world to see. There's no mistaking who the real groom is.

I swallow as an army of men enter behind him, all carrying guns. A choked sound comes from the vicar behind us.

Angelo advances slowly, trailing a path with his gaze over me. What I see in those dark eyes sends shivers through my body. Possession. Fury. A promise of vengeance.

The women make themselves small. Only Doris gets up, but the men have surrounded them, cutting off all paths to the exits. Celeste covers Brad's eyes, whispering something about a game.

Someone closes the doors. They shut with a heavy bang.

I swallow again, trying to get my vocal cords to work, but Angelo beats me to it.

His smile is wicked, and his voice drips with evil sarcasm. "Did I arrive before the part where I get to object?" He lifts his arm, aiming the gun at Colin. "Or am I going to have to make you a widow before I can marry you, *cara*?"

CHAPTER
TWENTY-SIX

Angelo

My bride is a deceitful traitor. She steps in front of the man she has or is about to marry, protecting him from the bullet meant for his heart. She fucking shields him, placing the body and life that belong to me in the path of danger. By doing that, she puts herself head-on in the way of my wrath, because the fury that ravaged me a minute ago is nothing compared to the inferno of violent rage erupting inside me now.

I'll fucking kill him. Them. Every single man. Right here. I don't care if I do it in a church. The grace of a holy place won't save them. You have to possess some reverence to respect a house of religion, and I don't have a dignified bone in my body.

My voice doesn't betray the level of my anger. My tone reflects a well-practiced calm. "Aren't you going to answer me, *bella*?" I turn the gun on the vicar. "Should I ask *him*? Does he need a bullet in the stomach as motivation?"

"No," she cries out, raising her hands in a placating manner. "We haven't made the vow."

I take her in, how beautiful she looks in the dress I chose, the dress in which she was meant to marry *me*. So help me, I'll strip that dress off her perfect body and make her regret every second of her despicable, insulting betrayal.

First, I have to focus. I have to fight through the cobwebs of crazed jealousy that obscure my reason. I have to make sure my little traitor isn't also a liar.

I direct my question at the vicar. "Did they say the vow?"

He shakes his head with fervor.

Not turning the gun away from his head, I say, "Swear it on the Bible."

"I swear." He lifts trembling hands in the air. "Check for yourself. They haven't exchanged the rings."

I shift my gaze to Sabella's hand. All her fingers are naked. But under the dress, she already carries my mark. She had no right to give it to another man. How was she going to explain that to her *husband* on her wedding night?

Fuck.

The thought makes me put pressure on the trigger. I dispel the image that takes shape in my mind lest I kill the motherfucker behind her without making him suffer.

My command is cool and controlled, not giving away how close I am to snapping. "Step out of the way, Sabella."

"No, please," she says in a tremulous voice. "Don't hurt him."

She's pleading for him? She's begging me on his behalf? That does it.

"Take the women and the kid outside," I instruct the guards.

"No." Sabella jumps forward, pushing her chest against the barrel of the gun. "It was my idea. If you have to punish someone, kill me."

My eyes tighten, narrowing involuntarily to slits at the sight of the hard, black metal of the pistol caressing the silk of the wedding gown right between her breasts.

"Have you forgotten?" I ask with an icy inflection. "Your life belongs to me."

Her soft brown eyes glimmer with tears. "Please, Angelo."

The sound of my name on her lips gives me pause. It jars me, just for a second, but she senses it, because she continues quickly.

"Let them go, Angelo. They had nothing to do with it. They're innocent. I'm the guilty one." She leans into the gun, putting her weight behind it. "I'm the one who asked them to do this."

"I'm not leaving my husband," a woman says in a shaky voice. "If he stays, I stay too."

Celeste. The sister-in-law.

Stupid woman. Stupid but loyal.

Her husband, Ryan, grips her bicep and gives her a slight shake of his head.

Sabella's voice pulls my attention back to her. "We can get married. Right here." Her gaze is pleading. "The vicar can do it." She even manages a quivering smile. "Please, Angelo. Let's do it here. Now. Everything is ready. Let the others go."

She's offering me an exchange—her vow for her family's lives. Only, her vow was always supposed to be mine. She can't bargain with something that already belongs to me.

What I'm really interested in is, "Did you kiss him?"

She stares at me, her expression baffled. "What?"

My nostrils flare when she makes me repeat those blasphemous words. "*Did you fucking kiss him?*"

Catching on, she blinks. "No." She speaks fast. "No. It's not like that."

I apply pressure, feeling the resistance of her breastbone against the gun, feeling the cruel smile that manipulates the stiff muscles of my mouth, curving my lips as if they belong to a puppet and not to me. My words are measured, spoken softly like a dirty caress. "Did you fuck him?"

"No," she exclaims, fear bleeding into those expressive eyes. "Colin and I never…" She licks her lips. "I swear it."

Colin.

I grind my molars together at the sound of his name.

The man himself—fucking *Colin*—steps to the side, putting himself in my view. His manner is calm, devoid of bullshit. "She didn't."

She throws a panicked glance at him, no doubt willing him to go back to hiding behind her. "We're friends. Best friends."

I keep my gaze fixed on her before I'm tempted to shoot his head off and splatter her white dress with his blood. "Is that why you wanted to marry him? Because he's your *best friend?*" My mouth twists with a sneer around the term of endearment. On second thought, maybe I should blow his brains out all over her. It'll be a good lesson.

"Please," she says again, bravely standing her ground.

"But us, we're not friends, *cara*, are we?"

She pales, knowing exactly what I mean.

"Tell him," I command. "Tell him why we're not friends."

Her slender throat bobs as she swallows. "Angelo, please."

"Tell them why we're so much more than *friends*," I say, caressing that spot between her breasts with the barrel.

Her red, plump lips part, but no sound escapes.

"You want me to tell him?" The question is rhetorical. She's shaking her head, begging me quietly even as I continue, "I already consummated our engagement when I fucked her on her eighteenth birthday."

A gasp rises from the pew. Her mother.

"That's right." My words are as callous as my smile, but there's no stopping them, no denying the claim I have on her or the need to prove it to all the witnesses present. "I already fucked her more than once. Isn't that so, *bella*?"

A mixture of horror and shame transforms her features, but she doesn't look at her family or her *best friend*. She doesn't look away from me.

A deathly quiet stretches in the space. Our dirty secret is laid out in the open. It takes time to process, I suppose.

"I'll marry you." She's no longer throwing bait, tempting me like earlier. Her voice is raw. She sounds defeated. Humiliated. "Right now. Just let them go."

Bargaining with a vow that's rightfully mine is like trying to pay me with my own money. She needs to give me more. "Beg."

She gapes. "What?"

"Get down on your knees and beg me."

A pained look flashes across her face. "Angelo."

"You heard me. If you want to marry me so badly, show me how much you want it."

"Sabella," Ryan says from the side.

My command is harsh. "Quiet."

The kid starts crying.

"Get him and his mother out of here," I tell one of the guards.

There's a shuffle and a protest.

"Go," Ryan says, his order both authoritative and gentle.

I can relate to that. I'm not a father, but I know my father would've done the same. He would've laid his life down for me.

More shuffling and sniffling follow. The doors open and close. Silence again.

"I'm waiting," I say, addressing my bride. I raise a mocking brow. "Unless you changed your mind?"

Holding my gaze, she kneels in front of me. "Please, Angelo."

I follow her down with the gun, the barrel now aimed at her head. "Please what?"

Her voice comes out hoarse. "Please, marry me."

I click my tongue. "You can put a little more effort into it. Convince me."

A flame of defiance licks in the depth of her eyes, but she purses her lips and goes on all fours before bending down low and pressing her lips first on my right shoe and then on my left.

A single tear runs down her cheek when she sits back on her heels. "I beg you, Angelo. Marry me."

Her groveling doesn't leave me unaffected. Gripping her arm, I help her to her feet. She stares up at me with loathing and fear yet also with a glimmer of hope.

I nod at the guard flanking me. He grabs Colin and flings him into the front pew on the right.

"You heard her," I say to the vicar. "She wants to say yes. Speak the magic words so that she can give me her answer."

He glances at the pistol in my hand and says with a

nervous twitch of his left eye, "Can you put the weapon away?"

I tuck the gun into the back of my waistband under my jacket and lock my hand around Sabella's a little too tightly, making sure she's not going anywhere even though I know she won't run while I'm keeping her family hostage. She cares too much about them.

The vicar stumbles over the vow as if he can't recite the holy sacrament fast enough.

When she says, "I do," she doesn't look at me. She doesn't meet my eyes. She stares at the space in front of her as if she doesn't see anything at all.

I don't let her escape my gaze when it's my turn. Splaying my fingers over her cheeks, I turn her face to me. The pressure of my fingertips leaves white marks on her skin when I say, "I do."

A heartbeat later, I push both her engagement ring and the wedding band onto her finger before placing my own ring on her palm. She battles to slide it over my finger, but I don't help her. I let her wiggle the ring until it fits against my knuckle.

It's done.

After three long years of fighting bitter battles and paying in blood for what's always been mine, we're married. Husband and wife.

The silence is complete as I lower my head to kiss my bride. She doesn't kiss me back, but she doesn't pull away either.

Someone cries softly. Her mother, I think.

A gasp of distress cuts through the air.

Sabella stiffens.

We turn.

Her sister stands, one hand resting on her belly and the

other on her lower back. "I think my water broke," she says in a small, surprised voice.

"Mattie," Sabella exclaims, trying to dash toward her sister, but I catch my wife's wrist.

"Make sure she gets to the clinic," I instruct one of my men.

Matilde purses her lips. "I'm not going without my husband."

I tilt my head toward the exit, indicating the husband can go.

There's a commotion as Matilde, supported by Jared, is escorted outside. Everyone is on their feet except for Colin. Not that he's not trying, but the guard standing next to him holds him down.

"Finish this," I tell the vicar.

He goes to a table next to the altar, produces a register, and turns the big book toward me. "I'll need documentation to make this legal."

Dragging Sabella with me, I go to the table. She stumbles a step before righting herself. I take the papers from my inside jacket pocket and slide them over the tabletop.

The vicar unfolds the documents with trembling fingers, eyeing me suspiciously as he does so. When he's gone through the stack, he hands me a pen. "Sign your name here."

I write down the details and sign before giving the pen to Sabella. She does the same.

"We need witnesses," the vicar says in a high voice. He clears his throat and manages to utter in a somewhat more normal tone, "Two."

I turn to our audience, enjoying how they shuffle their feet even as they glare at me with hatred. "Ryan. Margaret."

They shift to the end of the pew, walk to the table, and sign the register.

Our marriage is legal, acknowledged by the church and the state. It's very convenient for me that religious marriages in this country are also legal. In my country, only a legal marriage is recognized, but any marriage certificate is accepted, which means Sabella is my wife here as well as on home soil. Everywhere. Anywhere I want her to fulfill her marital duties.

The vicar scribbles something on a perforated sheet that he tears from another register. He hesitates a moment before handing it to me.

I snatch the marriage certificate from his fingers with a taunting grin that makes him cringe.

Leaning so close to him that I can smell the garlic he ate for dinner in the sweat oozing from his pores, I ask with enough menace to turn him pale, "Do I need to come back here?"

He shakes his head, trying to cling to his dignity, but under his robe, his knees are trembling.

"Do you need an incentive?" And I don't mean money.

Understanding contracts his pupils. He knows very well I'm referring to a bullet.

"No," he says, still shaking his head.

"Good." I straighten. "Because you heard her." Looking at Sabella, I add, "She begged for this."

She flinches.

The guard next to Colin asks, "What about them?"

Sabella turns her big, pleading eyes on me. "Angelo."

A deal is a deal. She did beg very prettily on her knees.

Cupping her face, I brush a thumb over the soft skin of her cheek, giving the promise to her instead of to them. "They can go."

The housekeeper moves to the exit in a haste. Margaret

reaches for Sabella. Ryan clenches his fingers. Colin looks as if he wants to punch the man who finally releases him.

Wrapping an arm around Sabella's waist, I pin her to my side. "But…"

They all freeze.

Sabella tenses in my hold.

"If anyone causes trouble," I continue, "I *will* be back. For Sabella's sake, I hope that won't be necessary."

Ryan steps toward us. "If you hurt her, I swear to God, all bets are off."

"Don't worry." I pull her tighter against me. "I'll treat her fairly."

He gnashes his teeth, no doubt biting back an insult.

"Play nice and nothing will change." I pat his shoulder just because I know it'll irk him. "The money will arrive as promptly as before."

His nostrils flare. He hates that he's dependent on me for a living.

"Say your goodbyes, *cara*," I say without letting her go. "We have a plane to catch."

Her family, those who are left, come up one by one to kiss her cheek. They all wear ghastly expressions.

Margaret pauses in front of her daughter. "Is it true?" Her features twist. "Did you sleep with him?"

"Mom." Sabella wrings her hands together. "I didn't mean to hurt you."

"Enough," I say with a grunt.

Margaret winces and moves on.

Colin is next. He appears apologetic. "Sabella, I—"

"I'm fine," she says, trying to smile, but she doesn't quite pull it off.

She's anxious, as she should be. I still feel like offing the motherfucker with the soft hands who dared to try and steal her from me.

"Where's your phone?" I ask my wife.

"I destroyed it," she says, wrapping her free arm around her waist.

"Both of them?"

She nods.

My tone is curt. "Where's your bag?"

"In the cry room."

"Get it," I say to a guard.

A moment later, he comes jogging with her suitcase and handbag.

I grip both in my free hand and tug her into motion.

Her family is still bundled together in the back of the church, huddling like sheep when I pull Sabella behind me down the aisle. A guard opens the doors. My driver is waiting. He loads our luggage in the trunk while I shove Sabella into the back of the car and slide in beside her, caging her between her side of the car and my body.

When we pull off and she flattens herself against the door, escaping me even in the confines of the small space, my fury ignites again.

At last, she's mine, but it's not the beginning I imagined. Our story doesn't get a happy ending. In our case, we're doomed to live unhappily ever after.

TWENTY-SEVEN

Sabella

A ngelo is quiet in the car.
Too quiet.

I steal a glance at him. His features are set in hard lines. He's never looked more like the angel his name implies, but it's not a kind or gracious angel. He's darkness and danger personified, both beautiful and cruel.

The suit fits him well. The tailored cut shows off the strong muscles underneath, leaving no doubt about his strength. Next to mine, his body is enormous, his masculinity sucking up all the energy in the space.

Now isn't the moment to insist on favors, but I must know.

"My sister." I lick my dry lips. "I want to know if she's all right."

He takes his phone from his pocket and unlocks the screen.

A ringtone sounds before a man says over the speaker, "Yes, sir?"

"Are you still at the clinic?" Angelo asks.

"I was just about to leave."

"What's the update?"

"They've been transferred from the delivery wing to a private room."

I suck in a breath. Does that mean the baby is born?

"Send me the number," Angelo says before ending the call.

A second later, his phone pings with a notification. He checks it before pushing on the green button. As if he can't stomach the sight of my face, he barely looks at me when he hands me the phone.

I push it against my ear with a trembling hand.

Jared answers.

"It's me. Sabella." I dare another glance in Angelo's direction. "How is she?"

"She's fine." He sounds happy, tired, and strained all at once. "It happened very fast. We almost didn't make it to the clinic. It's a boy."

My chest deflates with a quiet sigh of relief. "Is he okay?"

"He's perfect. We decided to call him Benjamin."

A lump lodges in my throat. "I'm glad. My dad would've liked that. I'm sorry it happened like this. Will you tell Mattie I called? Please tell her I'm thinking of her. Of all three of you."

"Are you okay, Bella?" he asks.

Angelo holds out his hand, still not looking at me.

"Yes," I say quickly. "I have to go. Just tell her I love her."

Angelo takes the phone and darkens the screen before pocketing it.

We drive the rest of the way to the airport in silence. The driver takes my suitcase and handbag as well as an overnight bag from the trunk. Angelo throws the sling of the bag over his shoulder and carries my suitcase and handbag in one hand while wrapping his free hand around mine.

The guards don't follow us inside. They don't have to. I'm not going to run. I made a deal, and as long as I uphold my end of the bargain, my family will be safe.

After showing his license, Angelo hands his gun in at the firearm desk. I'm surprised when he takes two passports from his bag, one for him and one for me. How did he manage to get mine? People turn their heads as we go through customs in our wedding attire. A few travelers come up to congratulate us, their smiles radiant. Our smiles are stilted in return. We keep up the pretense until we're shown into a private lounge, and then we drop our masks.

A flight attendant collects our luggage. A waitress serves appetizers and champagne, but my stomach is twisted into too tight a knot to eat or drink. Angelo works on his phone, ignoring me.

Putting my untouched champagne aside, I dare to ask, "How did you find us?"

He looks up. "Street surveillance cameras." He leans closer, forcing me to shrink back. "Here's something you need to understand, wife." His black eyes darken, menace turning his handsome face stunningly savage. "I'll always find you, no matter where you hide."

I hold my breath, too afraid to say another word. When he leans back in his chair and spreads his legs out in front of him, I dare to blow out the air trapped in my lungs. I only breathe normally again when he turns his attention back to his phone.

A few minutes later, we walk to the boarding gate. An airport security official returns Angelo's gun. I have no idea who Angelo bribed to let him carry his gun in the airport and on the plane. Normally, he'd have to collect it at the firearm desk at our destination. Perhaps that's why two airport security guards escort us to a private plane.

Except for the pilot and copilot who greet us at the door, there's no other staff. The fact that Angelo and I are alone outside the cockpit fills me with dread and anxiety.

Angelo seats me and buckles me in. He sits down next to me without saying a word. I may as well be invisible. Ignoring me has more to do with trying to control his anger than giving me the cold shoulder, because rage rolls off him in waves. You have to be emotionally challenged not to sense it.

Trying to escape the animosity, I withdraw by looking through the window. Cape Town grows smaller as we climb in altitude. Uncertainty and fear tighten my stomach further when we finally break through the clouds and everything I know disappears.

The seatbelt light goes off.

Angelo unfastens first his safety belt and then mine. Standing, he holds his hand out in silent instruction. I swallow as I stare at that big, broad, powerful hand. I don't want to take it. I want to run. Only, there's nowhere to run to when you're fifteen thousand meters in the air.

Not having a choice, I get to my feet. I don't take his proffered hand, but even in this, he doesn't give me an option. He wraps his fingers around mine and pulls me down the short aisle to a door at the back.

My throat closes up with fear when he opens the door to reveal a cabin with a double bed. That fear is nothing compared to the anxiety that nearly cripples me as the door shuts with a soft click. Because that click? It's the quiet before the storm.

When he lets go, I back up until the bed forms a barrier between us. Daylight filters through the windows on either side of the cabin, but no one can look in. No one will hear me scream. No one can help me. Not even all the angels who ever lived in the fluffy clouds that pass with deceptive gaiety beyond the windows.

Unlike earlier, he watches me with a piercing gaze, focusing every ounce of his attention on me. He advances a step, but I stand my ground.

Danger bleeds from his pores. It surrounds me like thick smoke, invading my lungs and clouding my brain. I can't think through the fog. I can't breathe through the darkness that rolls over me, a bank of mist that swallows me whole.

When he finally speaks, it's to give me a stark, unyielding command. "Take off the dress."

The order is what I was afraid of. He wants to consummate the marriage. Before, when I gave myself to him, it was in the heat of the moment. This isn't heat. It's cold and calculated, premeditatedly staged. I can't lose myself in passion like this.

Lifting my chin, I ask, "Why?"

Wrong question to ask. His stoic anger melts, slipping into something chillier and more brutal. "Do you really want me to look at you in a dress you put on for another man?" His voice drops an octave. "A dress I fucking chose for *me*?"

His words make me stagger. "What? Celeste bought the dress."

He removes his jacket with a fluent motion. "Celeste took it from the villa where I left it when she packed your clothes." Reaching behind him, he takes the gun from his waistband and puts it on a built-in dressing table. "Didn't she tell you?"

"No," I say, the sound coming out of my mouth no more than a whisper. "I just assumed she managed to buy one."

He raises a mocking brow. "I'm afraid I lost my appetite for that dress. Now, take it off, or I'll do it for you."

That explains the mystery of the dress. I don't know what Celeste was thinking, if she believed I had a wedding gown delivered, but she shouldn't have taken it. She should've asked. Everything just happened so fast.

Angelo removes a cufflink, pulling my attention to the insignia set in platinum, the intertwined, snarling wolves that each has a diamond eye. The cufflink makes a clink as he drops it next to the gun.

"I see you've decided," he says, loosening the other cufflink.

My gaze snaps to his. "I don't want this."

"This?" His smile is taunting. "Define *this*."

"Us fucking."

"Fucking." He says it as if the idea is a joke. "Do you think I want to fuck you after what you've done?"

His hatred is so blatant it steals my breath.

He rolls back a sleeve, exposing his strong, tanned forearm. "But let me share a fact with you, *wife*. When you begged me to put that ring on your finger and to give you my name, you promised to obey me. When you begged me to spare the lives of your traitorous family and your pathetic best friend, you agreed to fulfill your marital duties." He folds back the other sleeve. "Any and every duty I deem fit. Is that clear? Or do you need a reminder?"

"No," I snap, hating him as much as he hates me. No, more. I don't think you can hate someone with more intensity.

He lifts a finger and makes a circle, indicating I should turn. Reluctantly, I give him my back. He grips the zipper above my buttocks and pulls it down slowly, his fingers brushing over my ass in the process. An involuntary shiver contracts my skin. Reversing the path, he trails his fingertips over my spine and unfastens the button at the top. The dress falls open in the front and slides down my legs before pooling around my feet.

His heat disappears at my back, making more goosebumps run over me even though the temperature in the room is comfortable.

"Turn around," he says.

I obey like a good wife, facing him with my arms held stiffly at my sides.

"Underwear too," he says, raking a path over me with his gaze.

Swallowing what's left of my pride, I push the thong down my thighs.

He studies me unabashedly, paying special attention to the spot between my legs where his mark is hidden beneath my curls.

"Shoes," he instructs.

I kick them off and wait for his next command. Despite his earlier statement, the bulge in his pants says he wants me. As much as I try not to be affected, I can't help the spark that ignites in my belly or the pulsing ache that grows between my legs. But then he douses the heat spreading from my lower body more effectively than a bucket of ice water dumped over my head when he says, "Get down on all fours and crawl to the bathroom."

I gape at him. "What?"

"You heard me." He flicks his fingers and points at the floor. "Here. Now."

My whole being protests. He observes me with the self-assurance of a man who knows I'll obey. How can I not? My family's lives depend on my actions.

Humiliation burns on my cheeks as I go down on my hands and knees. The floor is hard and the carpet thin. The thread digs into my skin as I crawl to the door at the back, which I assume leads to the bathroom. His footsteps are quiet, but I sense him following behind me. When I pause in front of the door, he walks around me to open it.

The bathroom is smaller than the cabin, and the floor is tiled. A shower and a toilet hug a small cabinet. Painfully aware of how exposed I am, I sit back on my heels, but he presses the tip of his shoe between my shoulder blades and pushes me down with a tsk of his tongue. It takes every ounce of willpower I possess to swallow an insult and stay where he wants me.

"Go to the cabinet," he says. "You'll find your toiletries inside."

I look at him from over my shoulder. "How did my things get here?"

"An attendant unpacked them before we boarded."

"That's an invasion of my privacy."

Ignoring the complaint, he gives another order. "Put on your red lipstick."

I frown. "What?"

"Stop asking questions, and do as I say."

What is he trying to do? Make me look pretty so that he can stand to look at my face?

When I don't move, he raises an eyebrow. "Do you want me to do it for you?"

Clenching my teeth, I crawl over the floor and open the cabinet. As he said, the bottom shelf is stocked with my toiletries. I have to kneel when I open my make-up bag because I need both my hands. The lipstick Mattie applied this morning has long since rubbed off. Why does he want me to reapply it? What is he playing at?

Without a mirror, I'm not sure if I'm doing a good job, but I dab the lipstick on and cap the tube when I'm done.

"Good," he says. "Put it away and crawl back to the room."

I fucking hate him so much. I repeat the words like a mantra in my head, taking strength from my loathing as I crawl back over the floor.

"Stop there," he says when I reach the foot-end of the bed. "On your knees facing me."

I do as he says, glaring up at him.

He walks over and stops in front of me. When he reaches for his buckle, my mouth goes dry. He can't be doing what I think he is, but my worst suspicion is confirmed when he pushes the button on his waistband through the hole, pulls down his zipper, and takes out his cock.

He slides a fist over his length, pumping twice. A drop of precum leaks from the slit in the broad head. Even now, even in these circumstances, I can't help but be fixated by the sight of him naked. He's the only man I've seen, the only reference I have of a male's anatomy. I have a feeling he's in a different league, that no other male can compare, and I only despise him for it more.

His voice is frosty, devoid of lust or desire. "Stay on your knees and spread your legs."

What's the use of fighting? If he wants to use my mouth as if I'm nothing but a whore, I'd rather get it over with.

When I've complied, he gives another instruction. "Put your hands on your thighs and keep them there."

I hold his gaze as I follow out the order, but his eyes remain cold and unforgiving. Fisting one hand in my hair, he grips my face in the other. The pressure he applies on the joints of my jaw has my lips part of their own accord. The minute my mouth is open, he slides his cock inside.

I've seen him, but I haven't tasted him. I never returned the favor. I'm not inclined to do so now, but he doesn't need my cooperation. He pumps through my lips with a steady rhythm of shallow strokes. The ice in his eyes melts into something different, something carnal and feverish but not less cold. There's no emotion, only the lust he refused to show earlier.

I try to swallow around him, but it's impossible. He doesn't have to push deep to stretch my lips as wide as they can go. He's big enough to make me battle to take more than the head. Saliva dribbles down my chin. The sounds I make are wet and sleazy. They belong in a porn movie or in a peep show. I consider biting, but I have to remember why I signed up for this. I have to think about my family.

Holding me in place, he pushes deeper. It's difficult to breathe. I flatten my tongue to accommodate him and to prevent myself from choking. He grunts his approval when I accidentally lick the crest. His taste comes as a surprise. I don't want to like it, but how can I not when he tastes like the ocean and salt and wind?

Tangling his fingers tighter in my hair, he tugs my head back. My eyes water from the sting on my scalp. Without warning, he shoves himself so deep down my throat he's buried balls-deep in my mouth. I gag around him, suffocating. The lack of air makes me panic. It's impossible to keep my hands on my thighs. My body goes into survival mode. Fighting for air, I dig my nails into the back of his pants, gripping handfuls of fabric.

Unlike me, he's calm and collected, staring at me with fascination. "Easy. Just take it. Take me. You can do it."

He pulls out and lets me breathe.

I gulp air in noisily, my chest heaving with the effort.

Not easing his grip on my face, he smooths a hand over my hair and wipes away the sting. "Your red lips stretching around my cock is so damn hot. When you swallow me down like that, it's hard to hold back."

Before I can find my voice, he slides his cock into my mouth again and shifts his hip, aiming for the back of my throat. I gag and renew my fight, hitting him with my fists anywhere I can reach, but he thrusts with a steady pace, his gaze fixed on my mouth.

Just as white spots pop in my vision, he comes. He empties himself with another grunt, letting go of my face to wrap his fingers around my neck instead. Satisfaction bleeds into his eyes when I swallow.

There's no mirror in the room, but I don't need one to know I'm a mess of mascara, saliva, and smeared lipstick.

When he finally sets me free and tucks his cock back into his pants, I collapse on my heels at his feet. This isn't how I imagined oral sex. I'm not keen on repeating it.

"On your knees," he says. "Turn around and face the bed."

I scowl. My throat feels raw inside. It takes effort to speak. "I was right. You really are a sick pervert."

The set of his jaw hardens. He doesn't like it when I call him out on his shit, especially not when it's true.

"I said on your knees, Sabella."

When I don't move fast enough for him, he grabs my bicep and pulls me to my knees before twisting me around and pushing my upper body down on the bed. He leans over me, takes my wrists, and arranges them above my head.

His voice is a wicked whisper in my ear. "You didn't do very well earlier when my cock was stuffed down your throat. Let's see if you can do a better job this time."

This time? If I hoped my punishment was over, I was wrong. As I look at him from over my shoulder, I realize when he pulls his belt from the loops of his waistband, it hasn't even started.

Cold sweat breaks out over my body, but I refuse to beg again.

"You betrayed me, Sabella," he says, folding the leather double with the buckle in his palm. "You deceived me. Ran from me. I can forgive you almost anything, but plotting to marry another man?"

Whack.

The leather comes down hard on my buttocks, leaving a sting that turns into a path of fire. Fuck. That hurts. I gnash my teeth and swallow my sounds. I try to prepare myself for the next blow, but my back arches when it falls. The worst isn't the sting. It's the lingering burn.

Whack.

"That was for not keeping your hands where I told you to keep them."

Whack.

The next two blows heat my thighs.

I curl my fingers into the covers, willing myself not to move, but it's almost impossible when the bite of the leather falls right over my pussy. My whole body jerks. It's only a miracle that I'm able to hold back my scream.

"That was for trying to give away what belongs to me."

Whack.

I nearly pass out when he directs the next lash at the same spot.

"It'll never happen again, Sabella."

He aims higher again, leaving a searing streak over my left ass cheek.

"Or I will discipline you."

Right cheek.

I've stopped counting. My whole backside is covered in flames. My only consolation is that I've given him neither sounds nor tears. I'd rather bite off my own tongue.

It takes me a moment to register that the lashes have stopped. My chest heaves as if I ran a marathon even though I don't understand why. It takes me an even longer moment to find my breath.

He lets me, doing nothing but standing quietly behind me and giving me time and space to process this.

I know what he did. He came in my mouth, making it clear he was only using one of my holes to humiliate me for how I humiliated him by running off with Colin. The spanking was for thinking I could escape.

His palm on my back jolts me. He has no right to touch me like this, to brush a hand over my skin as if he cares.

My hair came loose from the bun. The strands are tangled. Wisps cling to my sweaty forehead when I turn my face to the side. The heat he inflicted with his belt seeped into every part of my skin.

Pressing my cheek against the mattress, I look back at him. "You're a fucking hypocrite, Angelo Russo." My laugh is cold and mocking. "I learned about deceit and betrayal from the master. You're the one who taught me."

He clenches his jaw and retracts his hand. The reprieve doesn't last. Grabbing my arm, he pulls me up and across the floor. My feet refuse to cooperate. I stumble.

He rightens me, giving me a shake. "You wanted me to shoot you?" Taking the gun from the dressing table, he caresses the arch of my neck with the barrel. "That's the punishment I usually reserve for traitors."

I unleashed the monster, but we're both too angry to stop. We're both way past the point of no return.

"Then do it," I say, my nostrils flaring. "Pull the fucking trigger."

He smiles. I don't know why, but the gesture stills me.

"That's what you want?" he asks, his dark eyes pulled into slits. "That I pull the trigger?"

As always, I'm out of my league with him. I'm no match for this man who has life experience I can never dream of obtaining, experience I never want and don't wish on my enemies.

His fingers tighten painfully on my arm. "Have you ever taken a bullet, *cara*?"

Fear snakes up my spine as he traces my cleavage with the barrel and draws a circle around my breast.

"Do you want to know what it feels like when the metal tears through your flesh?" he asks, making that circle smaller and smaller until he's outlining my nipple.

The tip of my breast hardens under the touch of the cold metal. He flicks the barrel up and down until my nipple is rock-hard and extended. "Do you want to feel the pain when your blood drips down your skin?"

He yanks me closer, pushing the barrel over the hard point of my breast, letting the metal swallow my nipple whole. "Because if that's a game you want to play, I'm going to give you your fucking way."

My heart thunders in my chest even as I stare at him with defiance.

He slides the barrel to the valley of my breasts and farther until he finds the erratic beat of my heart. "A bullet to the heart will be lethal, but where's the fun in that? Much too fast, over too quickly, don't you think?"

I'm exhaling through my nose, trying to control my breathing. I have no doubt he'd love to shoot me.

When he pulls the gun away from my heart, I almost exhale in relief, but the air is trapped in my lungs as he draws a line down my torso and over my stomach. Before he reaches my pelvis, I'm straining in his hold, but he doesn't let me put space between us. He studies my eyes as he goes lower and lower, finally tracing my slit.

A gasp catches in my throat. I go on tiptoes to escape. Too late. I took this game too far. He parts my folds with the barrel, pulling them open to expose my clit. His smile is pure evil as he circles that button with the barrel.

My mind is thrown back to a different day not so long ago—only yesterday, in fact—when he pressed his ring on that spot. It already feels like years ago, as if what happened between yesterday and today left me old.

A smirk curves his lips when he rubs the barrel over my clit. The look on his face is smug because the stimulation makes me wet. I grab his forearm in both hands, but the pressure only increases, the pleasure igniting. Arousal turns me slicker. He massages me with that gun, harder but slower, keeping me on the edge.

I don't want to come, not like this. Not when I hate him and when he's lost control. I never want to come for him again, but my muscles are already tightening inside.

His pupils dilate as he watches me. He can see I'm fighting, willing this not to happen, and he's going to make sure I lose again.

I hiss when he palms my sore ass and curls his fingers around my globe, using the leverage to drag me closer.

"Is this where you want it?" he asks, his tone seductive as he pushes the barrel over my clit.

I'm not sure if he means the touch or a bullet. In any event, I want neither. Unable to conjure words, I shake my head.

He abandons my clit and pulls the gun lower. "Watch."

I shake my head again.

He lets go of my ass and fists a handful of my hair, using the strands like a rope around his hand to force my head down. He parts me slowly with the muzzle, gathering my arousal. My heartbeat spikes. I struggle in his hold, fighting a losing battle as that fog that defines his darkness travels over me again. The metal sight on the muzzle scrapes against my flesh as he pushes the barrel deeper, using my own slickness to fuck me with his gun.

He twists his wrist from side to side, lodging it deeper. His words are soft, cajoling. "Is this where you want it, *cara*? Do you still want to play that game?" Crueler now. "I can take out a bullet and play Russian roulette."

I whimper as he moves the barrel, imitating the act we did twice. Twice too many.

He walks me backward until my thighs hit the bed and my legs fold. It only takes a push, and I fall on the mattress. Towering over me, he teases me with the barrel inside. He's careful, not hurting me with me the sight tip on the front of the muzzle. It's more of a mild irritation like the scratch his cock left in my throat.

"Watch," he orders again, pressing the pad of his thumb on my clit.

My pulse skyrockets. It feels as if my heart is going to burst out of my chest. It's not only the warped, perverse, and foolishly dangerous situation. It's the look in his eyes, a look that reminds me I don't really know him at all. That I don't know what he's capable of.

"Do you want to finish this game?" he asks, rubbing harder and stroking deeper.

That, I feel. That isn't just uncomfortable. It's not just a scratch. It's fucking terrifying.

The way he rubs me is wrong. It's right too. He knows it. He knows this is the only way I can come. And as it starts, I see the shift in his eyes. I see the evil streak that makes him look like a demon. This isn't the man I met, the one I fell in love with.

This is the man I married.

Our gazes lock. He sees it on my face, I'm sure, the confirmation that he's won. That I've taken this too far. That's it's over, and that I come.

I don't close my eyes. I see it as well. I see it as I unravel naked in front of the fully clothed man who calls himself my husband.

Grabbing his hand, the one that's between my legs, I feel it. I feel his finger tightening on the trigger. I try to stop him, but it's only my heart that stops. My pleasure explodes, the fear somehow heightening everything. I see it even through the haze of my orgasm. The end. I don't have to look. I feel the movement of his finger when he prepares to pull the trigger.

CHAPTER
TWENTY-EIGHT

The naked woman on the bed has black rivulets of mascara running over her cheeks. The red lipstick bleeds over the lines of her lips and smears her face. Her dark hair is tangled, sticking to the damp skin of her forehead. A layer of sheen covers her golden skin. Her breasts heave with the effort of dragging air into her lungs, and her flat stomach quivers from the aftershocks of her orgasm. Her legs are spread, and my fist is buried between her thighs, the barrel of my gun lodged in her pussy.

It's a messy, crude, somewhat shocking picture. And fuck me if it's not the hottest sight I've seen, if she's not the most beautiful woman I ever laid eyes on.

Violent emotions twist her features. The ecstasy of climaxing. The uncertainty of an outcome. The fear of dying. Shame, perhaps. The most vivid is her anger. It's more an aftereffect of the shock than a result of my actions. I saw it in her pretty, wide eyes. She wasn't sure if I'd pull the trigger. She still isn't. That's why she's watching me, frozen in this spectacular display of a well-ruined woman.

Waiting.

She learned her lesson.

The game is over.

Careful not to hurt her with the sight on the muzzle, I pull the gun from between her legs. The barrel is coated with her arousal. It's not a game I intended on taking that far. She just doesn't know when to fucking stop pushing me.

I'm not unaffected. Far from it. I want her too much. I hate her too much.

Putting distance between us, I leave the gun on the dresser and head for the shower. I don't make it to the door before I sense her movement. I never quite know what to expect from Sabella, but what I see when I turn around freezes me on the spot.

She's jumped from the bed and snatched up the gun, pointing it at me with her arms locked in front of her and the shaft clutched in both hands. The gun shakes violently in her hold. It's not just her hands. Her whole body trembles. Her face is contorted in a mask of hatred and fury.

Her voice is as tremulous as the rest of her as she aims for my heart. "You sick fuck."

I raise my hands. "Calm down, Sabella."

"Calm down?" She laughs. "You could've fucking pulled the trigger."

I keep my tone even. "I didn't."

"Your finger could've slipped."

Unbuttoning my shirt, I turn back for the bathroom. "I

know how to handle a gun. I'm not shooting since yesterday."

She sounds close to hysteria. "Do not fucking take another step."

I face her again, letting my shirt hang open. "What are you going to do? Shoot me?"

"I should," she says, her teeth chattering. "You made me believe you were going to pull the trigger. You fucked with my head." Her voice rises in volume. "Did you enjoy that sick game, huh?"

I walk back to her slowly. "Are you angry that I didn't shoot you?"

Her nostrils flare. The gun shakes even more in her hands. She pushed me. Now, I'm pushing her. What are her limits? How far is she prepared to go?

"You should've just done it, you coward," she grits out.

I step right up to her, letting her press the barrel on my chest. Lowering my lips to her ear, I caress her with soft words. "Remember, *cara*, your life is mine, and I decide when I pull the trigger."

Retreating with a smile, I watch her. Faint blue bruises shaped like my fingertips mar her cheeks. I always regret the marks, but I can't deny who I am. Yet something stirs in my chest when I take her in as she stands up to me, looking too damn fragile and brave with that weapon in her hands. I doubt she's ever held a gun.

I hold out my palm. "It's over." The game. The lesson. "Give me the gun."

Mistrust flickers in her eyes. She doesn't believe me. But there's also a spark of vulnerability. She wants to believe me. In the end, a vicious mixture of shock and anger wins out, distorting her pretty features.

Not breaking our eye contact, she braces herself. She tightens her finger on the trigger, gets a feel for it. Time stops. So does my pulse. There's nothing but her, me, and that gun. As if in hindsight, she jumps back a step, making sure I can't grab her, all the while pointing the gun at my heart.

The human body is wired to function on instinct. The spiking of my heartbeat is an involuntary impulse. The organ reacts to being threatened. We're tuned in to each other, breathing each other's air and will of survival. Like a hunter and its prey, we're connected in the most intimate of ways in the second that separates life and death. In that second, we're living inside one another. I feel her intention even before I see it in the way her eyes flare at the same time as her pupils contract.

Surprising both of us, she takes the leap. She jumps over a cliff from which there's no return. Instead of going for quick and painless, she aims for my stomach.

Click.

The hammer triggers the striker, firing the empty chamber.

Her face turns ghostly white. She's shocked that she did it, that she would've killed me. Or maybe that she didn't. That she chose a long and torturous suffering instead of a quick and painless death. Perhaps she's most surprised by the latter. Hell, so am I. I didn't think she had it in her, not even for a minute, and I can only respect her for it.

The gun drops from her hand, hitting the floor with a clank. She backs up, looking from the gun to me.

"Sabella."

The commanding tone of my voice stops her. Her gaze flits to the useless weapon on the floor.

"Look at me," I say, the instruction gentle.

Her gaze snaps back to mine.

"It wasn't loaded." I advance cautiously, reaching for her. "The chamber was empty."

She shakes her head, making her hair fly around her face. She doesn't want to believe what's right in front of her eyes, let alone trust me.

I take another step. "They'd never let me carry a loaded gun in the airport."

Her eyes clear a little as the logic gets through to her.

"It's over." I close the last distance between us and trap her in my arms. "Nothing would've happened."

All that wildness caught inside her erupts. She fights me like a lioness, kicking and clawing and screaming. It doesn't take much to hold her in the vise of my arms and lift her off her feet. Pressing our naked chests together, I let her carry on until she's tired herself enough to sag like a rag doll in my hold. Dry sobs rack her shoulders.

"Shh." I brush my lips over her forehead. "I'll never let anything happen to you."

"I hate you," she says, her voice raw and broken. "However much you hate me, I'll always hate you more."

"I'm sure you will."

I hook an arm beneath her knees, lift her into my arms, and carry her to the bathroom.

She continues to fight, but her effort is feeble, her strength spent. "Put me down."

"In a minute."

When I deposit her on her feet, she wraps her arms around herself and stands there shivering. I turn on the tap in the shower, letting the water run warm while I make quick work of undressing. After testing the temperature, I pick her up and put her under the spray. She hisses as the water runs over her ass.

I don't linger. I only take as much time as necessary to wash her clean and rinse her hair. That wild look on her does things to me, things I don't like. I prefer her better like this, looking whole and normal. Not broken and unraveled.

Not ugly inside. That's me. That's reserved for the monsters.

She's gone from shivering and crazed to numb and vacant when I'm finished. I dry her off before taking a towel for myself. Making her sit on the closed lid of the toilet, I use the hairdryer to dry her hair. She lets me, not saying a word or looking at me or herself in the mirror.

She remains quiet while I dry my own hair, accepting whatever fate I choose for her. That's all right. Now isn't the time for talking.

I carry her to the bed, pull back the covers, and lay her down. She curls into a ball like Pirate used to do. Maybe I should get her another cat when we get home. Ryan informed me about what happened. Knowing how much she loved that cat, I can only imagine how hard it must've been for her.

When I've tucked her in, I pull down the shutters in front of the windows to shut out the daylight. Casting a glance at her, I pick up the gun. She's not looking at me. She's staring with non-seeing eyes at the wall.

I lock the gun in the safe—I'll clean it later—and get into bed beside her. She doesn't protest as I spoon her from behind and wrap my arms around her. Her body is soft and warm, the curve of her back and ass fitting perfectly against my chest and groin. I've never held a woman like this, and I take a moment to revel in the warmth that seeps from her skin.

I wait until her breathing changes to a slow, even rhythm before untangling myself from her. Taking care not to wake her, I make sure she's covered before I get dressed. Then I go to the lounge to make arrangements for when we'll land in Marseille.

Half an hour before the pilot announces our descent, I go back to the cabin. I stop at the side of the bed and study the sleeping form of my wife. Even under a heap of fluffy goose feathers, her shape is slender and fragile. With her palms pressed together and forming a cushion for her cheek, she looks innocent.

Blameless.

She *is* innocent, but she's also guilty. She's always been guilty, even before she pulled the trigger. The mere fact that she breathes earned her the liability that comes with the blood of her family name. That very name, the name of my enemy, is the means to recognition and honor, to opening the doors that have been closed to me until now. Her father may have turned us into the rivals we became, but she's mine. She's always been mine. For as long as I live, she'll belong to me.

Wiping the hair from her face, I say in a quiet voice, "Wake up, *cara*."

She stirs but fights consciousness, no doubt preferring to hide in the dark.

I give her shoulder a gentle shake. "Open your eyes, *bella*."

She lifts her eyelids and blinks. Her gaze is soft and hazy, and then it becomes shuttered as reality sets in.

"We're landing soon," I say. "You better get dressed. Your suitcase is next to the closet. Do you want me to help you?"

"No." She sits up and swings her legs over the side of the bed. "I'm fine."

"Come out when you're ready." Something tightens in my chest when I watch her naked curves. My cock stirs as I look at the juncture of her legs, remembering the sight of my gun there. "You have to buckle up for the landing."

Going to pains not to touch me, she shifts all the way to the headboard before standing. I remain on the spot as she walks a wide circle around me, goes into the bathroom, and shuts the door. The lock clicks in place.

I don't give sound to the sigh trapped in my lungs. It's going to take time. This thing between us, this hatred that binds us, knows no other way. It's not going away. We'll have to learn how to live with it and how to get around it. It doesn't help that I have no experience in this minefield called a relationship. Adeline was much better at people skills.

The thought of my sister twists my gut. Her absence is still like a visceral hole in my life. Hardening my feelings, I return to my seat and lose myself in work until Sabella returns. She's wearing the clothes Celeste packed for her—a pair of ripped skinny jeans, a tight T-shirt, ankle boots, and a leather jacket. Her hair is brushed out, and her face is free of make-up.

My gaze is drawn to the beauty spot at the corner of her mouth. I've always found that pretty. Cute. I haven't had many opportunities to study her, but I know every inch of her body as if it's my own. She's ingrained in my memory, a living entity beating alongside my heart under my breastbone.

I don't miss her flinch when she puts her ass on the seat. Leaning over, I secure her safety belt. She lets me but flattens herself against the backrest to prevent my arm from brushing against her breast.

It's past dinner time. I had meals prepared. They're in the kitchen, ready to be nuked, but with what happened, food wasn't on my mind. I doubt she had an appetite. Even so, we also skipped lunch. The growl of her stomach confirms that she's hungry.

"We'll eat on the yacht," I say. "We're about to go in for the landing."

She turns her face toward the window without answering.

It's the middle of the night when we land. A hostess boards to pack our bags. She eyes me with interest in the passing but quickly averts her eyes at my hostile look. I take the coat I bought for the occasion from the closet and hold it open for Sabella. When I helped her to fit her arms, I button it up. Through it all, she refuses to meet my gaze.

A car waits at the airport to transport us to the marina. The skipper greets us at the yacht. A helper takes our luggage and carries it to the cabin. We'll spend the night on the yacht and leave at first daylight.

Sabella follows me wordlessly to the lounge where a table is set. The chef prepared a meal of grilled chicken and roasted vegetables. A waiter pours wine while I remove Sabella's coat.

Once I've seated her, my wife allows the waiter to spread the napkin over her lap, but she doesn't pick up her knife and fork when he leaves.

"Eat," I say. "You need your strength."

Pursing her lips, she pins me with an antagonistic glare.

I take a bite of the chicken and swallow it down with some wine. "See? It's not poisoned."

My attempt at humor isn't appreciated. She narrows her pretty eyes, staring at me as if she'd rather stab me with the butter knife.

"It's delicious," I say. "I promise."

She scoffs and looks away.

My tone is stern. "Eat, Sabella."

She blinks fast but not fast enough to clear the glimmer of tears that shines in her eyes. Picking up her fork, she toys with it for a while. Finally, she stabs a cube of butternut and brings it to her mouth.

The food really is delicious. I hired the best chef in

Corsica. Once she's tasted the creamy squash with hints of nutmeg and passionfruit, she digs in.

I watch her between forkfuls of food, noting with satisfaction that she cleans her plate. She polishes the chocolate and vanilla mousse cake topped with raspberries too but declines the waiter's offer of herbal tea or coffee.

"Still hungry?" I ask when our plates are cleared.

She replies in a barely audible voice. "No, thank you."

I stand, go around the table, and pull out her chair. "Tired?"

She gets to her feet. "No."

"I can give you something to help you sleep."

Her spine stiffens. "I said I'm not tired. I slept the whole afternoon."

The waiter hands me her coat, which I hang around her shoulders. "You needed the rest."

She doesn't reply.

She tenses more when I take her elbow to steer her across the deck and downstairs to our cabin. The rocking of the yacht is gentle, but it's easy to lose your balance if you're not stable on your feet on the sea. Even though she doesn't seem to need my help, I insist anyway.

The yacht is a work of art. The Sea Hawk is fitted with the best quality stainless steel railings and Burmese teak decks. Blue floor lights illuminate our way.

"Here," I say, indicating the door at the end of the passageway.

I open it and step aside for her to enter. When she spots the woman in the white tunic waiting inside, she stops abruptly.

The esthetician smiles warmly. "Good evening, Mrs. Russo." She nods at me. "Sir. Everything is ready."

Sabella flings around, facing me with borderline panic. "Ready for what?"

"For preparing you for our wedding night," I say as I take her coat and throw it over the back of a chair.

"Preparing me how?"

I close the door and lock it. "You can start by undressing and lying down on the bed."

CHAPTER
TWENTY-NINE

Sabella

The woman has a professional air, but I sense kindness too. I address her rather than Angelo. I have a better chance of finding sympathy with her than with my husband. "I don't want to."

If I thought she'd show me compassion, I was mistaken. She irons out the white towel on the bed as if she hasn't heard me.

It becomes clear what she—or rather, Angelo—has planned when I take in the preparations on the nightstand. Wax is heating in a bowl over a tea light candle. A pair of scissors and tubes of cream are set out next to it.

"Gloria is very good," Angelo says to my back. "You can trust her."

I don't move an inch. My muscles tense, everything inside me begging for violence. I want to hurt him, and the sentiment scares me. The person I don't like, the one who rears her head whenever Angelo is around, is becoming a little stronger with every minute I'm in his presence. I'm yet to deal with what I almost did, what I would've done if the gun was loaded. I hate who that makes me. I can't even face myself right now. I don't want to be that woman, but I already am. Losing myself frightens me more than life as my husband's prisoner.

Brushing my hair over my shoulder, Angelo presses a kiss on my neck before saying softly in my ear, "I can always strip you and tie you up."

It's futile to resist. My arguments don't matter to him. What I want is of no consequence. I learned that the hard way. I have no doubt he'll humiliate me in front of the woman by executing his threat.

Escaping his touch, I walk to the bed and start removing my clothes. Gloria takes every item as it comes off and lays it on a bench in front of a dresser. When it comes to my underwear, I refuse to hand it to her. I place them on top of the pile of clothes, my cheeks burning as I stand naked in front of her while Angelo bears witness.

"Here," she says, taking my hand and helping me onto the bed. "You can lie down."

I stare at the ceiling as I obey, hating them both even though she's very gentle. I'm grateful for the folded towel she drapes over my upper body, leaving me naked from the waist down.

Angelo pulls a chair up to the end of the bed and makes himself comfortable while the woman busies herself with stirring the wax. He leans his arms on the padded armrests and stretches out his legs in front of him.

I clench my teeth. "Getting ready for the show?"

He smiles. "I wasn't seeing it like that, but if that's what you want, I'm happy to oblige."

Asshole. "If you're not watching like the pervert you are, then why are you here?"

His tone remains reasonable. "To make sure you're treated as I instructed."

"Being tortured?"

He seems amused. "Pampered."

I snort. "Right."

"You don't believe me."

"Have you ever been waxed?" I ask, letting my gaze drop to his groin. "Down there?"

He raises an eyebrow while suppressing a smile I wish I could slap off his face. The minute I thought about inflicting that violence, disappointment bleeds through my chest. I hate him for getting a rise out of me. I hate that his reactions affect me.

"No," he deadpans. "Have you?"

I haven't, but I don't bother to reply.

"Gloria assured me it doesn't hurt," he says. "You should only feel mild discomfort."

Right.

"Are you cold?" the woman asks. "Would you like me to turn up the temperature?"

My manner is curt. "No."

Coming from summer, the night here is freezing, but the cabin is warm.

"What would you like?" she asks, directing her smile at me. "Just a bit of tidying up or the full monty?"

I quickly look at Angelo. He's giving me an option?

As if reading my mind, he says, "The choice is yours."

"Then why are we doing this?"

His voice is low and soft. "Why do you think, *cara*?"

"To see your mark," I say with the anger I didn't want to show bubbling to the surface again.

"You already understand me so well."

I'm not sure if he's teasing or mocking me, but I'm not taking the bait this time.

Addressing Gloria, I say, "As little as necessary."

"Okay." She pats my thigh. "Just relax. Like your husband said, it's not as bad as it seems."

I swallow the retort on the tip of my tongue.

After fitting surgical gloves, she spreads my legs a little and gets to work. First, she trims my curls and lathers my skin with a soapy liquid, and then she pats it dry and applies talc.

"I hope you're enjoying this," I tell my husband in a biting tone as Gloria tests the temperature of the wax before applying it.

I think up a hundred insults to hurl at Angelo, but my thoughts are interrupted abruptly when, a short while later, Gloria rips off a strip of wax. It doesn't hurt as much as I expected it to, but it's not comfortable either. Closing my eyes, I shut out the man in the chair and the unwanted ministrations, wishing it was over already.

After what feels like hours, she says, "All done. What do you think?"

I lift my head and look down. My curls are trimmed into a neat triangle that will allow me to wear a bikini. The mark Angelo branded on my skin is visible at the top.

He gets up and walks to the edge of the bed, inspecting the junction of my legs. "Very pretty. This'll do nicely." He slides his gaze to mine. "I like your pussy naked, but this look is hot on you too. No? What do you think, *bella*?"

Blood rushes to my cheeks. I glance at Gloria, but she's packing away the wax, not showing any reaction to Angelo's crass remark. "What I think doesn't matter, so why do you ask?"

"It *was* your choice," he says, brushing his fingers over

his mark. "If your opinion didn't matter, I would've just told her what I wanted done."

"May I use the bathroom to wash my hands?" Gloria asks, removing the gloves and discarding them in the trashcan.

Angelo indicates a door on the side. "Go ahead."

Silence stretches between us as she disappears into the adjoining room. I immediately regret her absence. I haven't realized what a buffer she's been. Closing my legs, I try to sit up, but Angelo prevents me with a hand on my shoulder.

"We're not done," he says.

Alarm quickens my breathing. "What do you mean we're not done? What else do you want to do? Wax my—" I bite off my words, not wanting to give him ideas.

Gloria steps out, cutting our unpleasant exchange short, and comes back to the bed. When she starts fitting a new pair of surgical gloves, I shoot upright.

Angelo stops her with a hand on her arm. "I've got it from here. You can go."

Offering me a warm greeting, she packs up the rest of her equipment, minus the tubes of cream, and leaves.

"What are you doing?" I ask, leaning on my elbows as Angelo uncaps a tube.

"Stop fussing." He squirts a blob on his finger. "It's an antiseptic lotion to prevent infection."

"I can do that."

"Be still."

I jerk when he rubs the lotion over the top of my pelvis, outlining his mark before tracing a line to the seam of my inner thigh.

"I'm already doing it," he continues.

I relax only marginally. I don't want him to touch me, especially not like this. It's too intimate. Too caring. And he doesn't care about me. The only thing that matters to him is the business deal our marriage sealed.

The light brush of his fingertips over the sensitive areas between my legs makes my stomach contract with a flutter. It's an involuntary reaction, but it's no less potent. His touch is like poison, a very sweet poison that's both deadly and alluring. I can't help but feel it where it matters, all the way to my core and deeper, right in the bruise that grows in my heart.

The most disturbing fact is that the reaction isn't only physical. A part of me needs the meticulous gentleness he administers. I need it to compensate for the brutality of his intentions, yet I can't allow myself to derive comfort from him. That would be a mistake. He's a hardened murderer, a selfish criminal only interested in furthering his own agenda.

A voice in the back of my head says my silence made me an accomplice to murder, that we're cut from the same cloth, but I don't allow that thought to linger.

Steeling myself, I push his hand away. "That's enough. You covered everything."

He grins. "Not by a long shot. Turn over."

My fake show of confidence slips. "What?"

He caps the tube and opens the second. Arnica. "Turn on your stomach."

"I don't need arnica."

"Don't tell me my belt hasn't left welts."

"Whose fault is that?"

"Come on, wisecrack. Don't test me." He lifts the towel from my breasts. "I'm not in the mood to repeat the lesson of earlier."

Gritting my teeth, I do as he says while watching him from over my shoulder.

He warms the lotion in his palms before massaging it into my globes. He's careful to keep his touch light.

When he's done, he instructs me to stay while he washes his hands. Bending my elbows and resting my cheek on my forearm, I watch him through the open door of the bathroom as he dries his hands and folds back his sleeves. He flicks off the light before returning, only leaving the dim ceiling lights in the cabin on.

"Gloria was supposed to give you a massage," he says, stopping at the side of the bed. "I decided it would be more fun to do it myself."

I tense all over again. "I don't need a massage."

"It'll help you relax."

"I don't need to relax."

He chuckles. "Stop being so obstinate. You'll make things easier for yourself if you learn to cooperate."

"If I obey, you mean."

He takes a bottle from the nightstand and pours oil into his palm. "That's what you promised. Must I remind you? I can have your vow framed and hung above our bed."

"Fuck you," I say, making to get up, but he pushes me down with a hand on my lower back.

"Keep still. You'll get oil on the sheets."

"Not my problem."

"That mouth of yours." He shakes his head. "It *is* very pretty. Can't say the same for the words coming out of it. I can always find a better use for those luscious lips."

I bite my tongue to prevent myself from replying.

"However," he says, "I'm glad you recovered your spirit."

The reference to my earlier meltdown makes my spine goes rigid. I don't relax when he brushes my hair aside and rubs the oil over my shoulders. The oriental fragrance of ylang ylang fills my nostrils. It's strange that he chose an oil known for its aphrodisiac properties when his goal is to relax me.

I remain on edge even as he kneads my muscles with firm but gentle pressure. He's thorough, covering every inch of my skin as he works his way down to my lower back. I groan when he presses on sensitive points at the base of my spine. Skipping my globes, he pays attention to my thighs and calves and finally to my feet. When he gets to my toes, it feels so good I close my eyes.

He slaps my ass playfully. "On your hands and knees."

"Why?" I ask, quickly opening my eyes again.

Instead of waiting for me to comply, he grips my hips and pulls me into a kneeling position. Then he flattens his palms on my inner thighs and pushes my legs apart. "Stay like that."

"Why?" I ask again, watching him as he takes his phone from his pocket and puts it on the nightstand before unbuttoning his shirt and pulling the tail ends from his pants.

The black ink that covers half of his chest captures my attention. No matter how many times I see it, every time feels like the first time. The artwork fascinates me. It's a replica of the mark branded on my skin, just much bigger, the detail more intricate. I both admire the work of art and loathe it.

My gaze snaps to the word inked above the line of his waistband when he unbuckles his belt.

Resilience.

He pulls down his zipper. "You pointed a gun at me today."

"So did you," I exclaim, trying to sit back on my heels, but the slap he delivers with a flat hand on my ass cheek stings so much that I freeze in place.

"If you move, you'll get another lashing tonight."

"You're such a damn hypocrite."

"I didn't point a gun at you to shoot you." He pushes down his briefs and pants. "That was to teach you a lesson. You, however, pulled the trigger."

The reminder tightens my chest. I don't want to think about it. I can't. I can't admit what that means.

"I'm going to punish you, *bella*, like you deserve, but if you relax, you may love it more than hate it."

My mind races ahead, trying to figure out what he has in mind. Not another lashing. Something different. Yet if he went to the lengths of massaging me to coax my muscles into softening, what he has in store for me can only be bad. I'm tense again in an instant, all his effort to relax me for nothing.

I swallow. "You don't have to do this."

"I'm afraid I must." His voice doesn't hold an ounce of regret. "What kind of husband will I be if I let you believe you can get away with killing me?"

Before I have time to formulate a reply, he cups my sex and rubs his fingers over my clit. My body responds in an instant, my muscles tightening.

"I wasn't going to do this," he says, rubbing oil over his cock. "Not tonight."

The warning registers too late. I feel his intention when he presses the head of his cock on the wrong hole and breaches it with a punch of his hips. My scream bounces off the walls. My first reaction is to crawl away from him, but he digs his fingers into my hips and holds me in place.

"Relax," he says, breathing hard. "It'll make it easier to take me."

Reaching behind me, I grab his wrist, not sure if I'm pushing him away or holding on. "I can't."

"You can, and you will. You will take all of me in your tight little ass."

As if to prove his point, he shoves deeper. It hurts too much.

"You'll tear me," I shout, not caring who hears.

"I won't." He rubs his hands up my sides and closes his fingers around my breasts. "Just work with me."

My breath catches when he moves. He's too thick, too long. "I don't have to do anything for you."

"It's not for my sake. I'm already enjoying this. It's entirely for yours."

He punches his hips, making me yelp.

"Play with yourself," he orders, his cock sinking deeper. "It'll help."

He can't know that it will. He doesn't feel what I'm feeling. A part of me doesn't want to make this easier on myself. I want to remember that he's cruel and unfeeling, and he's proving it so effectively.

When I don't oblige, he lets go of one breast and slips his hands around my waist and between my legs. In this, he's a fast learner, knowing exactly how to touch me to wrench pleasure from my body. The signals are mixed. It feels as if he'll tear me apart even as the slow build of an orgasm contracts my core. The overbearing sensations increase when he parts my folds and sinks a finger inside. I'm too full. Too close.

He finds purchase on my hip again while pumping his finger. My inner muscles clench around the intrusion. My pleasure spikes. It's not that I don't feel the discomfort. It's just muddled in the haze of my need. It's absorbed in the explosion of unbearable pleasure that destroys me like a bomb would flatten a landscape. It happens as fast as it's intense, leaving me legless in seconds. It's only Angelo's grip on my hip that keeps me on my knees.

The moment my muscles give and my body softens, he buries his whole length inside me. I don't have to look to know. I feel. The pummeling of his groin against my ass is almost too much to bear, but I don't have the energy or the will to stop it. I can only take it, half sagging and half choking as he beats out a rhythm that leaves me raw. I'm down and I can't get up, not when a pleasure much darker and deeper ravages the wreckage he's made of my body, making me clench around his cock.

He groans and curses and then doubles his onslaught.

I lose all sense of time and place. The pleasure pebbles out again but differently this time. With too much force. I jerk when something makes contact with my oversensitive clit. His hand, I think. I couldn't care. I can't focus. Can't move. Can't distinguish one sensation from another. Everything is pleasure. Everything is pain.

"Fuck," he utters, his voice strangled as he slams his groin against my ass and stills.

Warmth bathes me inside. The sting follows a second later.

"Fuck, Sabella."

Another curse aimed at himself or me, I can't be sure.

He bends over me, chasing me down as he finally allows my body to collapse on the mattress.

"You're so fucking tight like this." He pushes onto his elbows and kisses my neck. "The sight of your asshole swallowing my cock with those red welts painted over your ass made me lose my fucking mind." He presses his chest against my back, covering my body with his, and nips my shoulder. "Stay."

Even if I wanted to, I couldn't move.

He gets off me, pulls out. The burn flares.

The mattress dips, and then his heat is gone.

From the corner of my eye, I see him adjusting his clothes before walking to the bathroom.

I sink deeper into the mattress, letting it absorb my

weight. When I was little, I fell off my bike while driving at full speed down the hill. I'll never forget that feeling while I was lying on the ground. I couldn't move. I registered the hurt, but I felt more paralyzed than I felt pain. This is the same. And I know from experience when my limbs regain their ability to move, I'll be worse for it. The adrenaline numbs the intensity. It's the scrapes and burns that linger.

Angelo returns with a wet facecloth and carefully cleans me. In my semi-lucid state, I'm aware that the only consequence he suffers in the aftermath of our sex is pleasure. I suppose it's one of the advantages of being a man.

I watch him through my lashes as he discards the cloth on the nightstand and undresses, letting his clothes fall in a heap on the floor. When he's naked, he lies down beside me. Brushing the hair from my face, he presses a tender kiss on my lips. "Do you need a painkiller? Water?"

I close my eyes. I want nothing from him.

"Come here," he says, dragging me against him before removing the towel from under my body and pulling the comforter over us.

We're laying face to face, his breath fanning over my lips. I don't open my eyes for fear that I'll cry. I didn't think it was possible for him to ruin me more than he already has. With every passing moment, I hate him more passionately.

He kisses my temple. "Try to rest. We have a long journey ahead tomorrow."

When I strain in his grip, trying to roll onto my side, he tightens his arms around me.

"And if you ever point a gun at me again," he continues in a soft, deep voice, "I'll do a lot more than come in your ass."

The threat makes my eyes fly open, but I immediately

regret it. His dark gaze burns on my face with so much heat and possession that my heart falters in its beat.

I bite down hard on my tongue, willing myself not to speak, but I'm a damn masochist, because the question tumbles from my lips anyway. "What will you do, Angelo? Define *a lot more*. Kill me?"

"Kill you?" His smile is brutal even as he traces the seam of my lips with a fingertip. "No, *cara*. That's too easy. I'll shackle you in irons and whip you so hard you'll beg me to rather take my cock in your ass."

My chest deflates, the air in my lungs escaping with a gasp, because I believe him. If there's one thing Angelo Russo taught me, it's that he never makes idle threats.

"Now, sleep." He kisses me again. "You'll feel better in the morning."

Rebellious emotions rise inside me. I always knew Angelo could be devious, but he's even more inhumane and savage now than when we lost our virginity together.

I'm swallowing down my bitterness when a hard knock falls on the door.

Angelo stiffens. "I said I don't want to be disturbed."

"Sorry, sir." It sounds like the captain. "We have a problem."

Cursing, Angelo gets from the bed and pulls on his pants. He makes sure I'm covered up to my chin before he almost yanks the door off its hinges. "Can't you handle it?"

The captain, a middle-aged man with a salt-and-pepper beard, shifts his weight. "I'm truly sorry for the interruption." He makes a point of not looking at me even though Angelo blocks the view with his body. "The gendarmerie is here. They want to come aboard and search the yacht."

Angelo mutters a string of curses as he picks his shirt up from the floor. His voice is strained. "I'll be right there."

The captain doesn't budge.

"Was there anything else?" Angelo asks, fitting the shirt with jerky movements.

"They asked to see Mrs. Russo." He dares a glance in my direction, but at the growl that reverberates in Angelo's chest, he lowers his gaze. "Apparently, they need to ask her some questions."

CHAPTER
THIRTY

Angelo

The set of my jaw is hard as I walk down the bridge to the marina. A man in a gendarmerie uniform and parka jacket waits at the bottom, standing with his feet wide apart. A team of five men hover behind him, flaunting their weapons.

I recognize his bulky frame and tufts of blond hair. Lieutenant Lavigne is in charge of drug trafficking investigations. Not my domain.

My smile is dismissive. "Can I help you?"

"Mr. Russo." He smirks. "Welcome back to Marseille." He glances over my shoulder at the yacht. "Arriving or going?"

It doesn't surprise me that he knows my name or that I'm only passing through. He knows my destination is Corsica. I've been on their radar for as long as I've been running my father's business. *My* business now.

"Both." I cross my arms, barely feeling the icy Mistral that blows in from the northwest despite not wearing a jacket. "What can I do for you?"

He measures me with a narrowed gaze. "We're doing a routine check of the marina." His question is posed like a challenge. "You won't mind if we take a look on your yacht?"

"Do you have a search warrant?"

"Do I need one?"

His reputation exceeds him. He's tougher than the others. Bribes aren't going to sway him.

"No," I drawl, "but I'm on honeymoon. Unfortunately, the timing doesn't suit me."

Nodding, he pulls his face into an expression of surprise. Bullshit. He knew the minute I set foot on French soil with my bride. Customs would've alerted him. It's flattering really, how closely they track my movements.

"Congratulations." All traces of agreeability vanish from his face as he folds his arms behind his back and steps right up to me. "We'd like a word with Mrs. Russo."

Every muscle in my body tenses. "She's resting."

His smile is fake. "It'll only take a minute."

I make a show of checking my watch. "It's late. If you don't have a search warrant, either go get one or leave."

A glint of malice sparks in his eyes. No, more than malice. I see it often enough to know the sentiment well by now. Disgust.

"We have to investigate." He sizes me up with a smug look. "Your neighbors lodged a complaint."

"What complaint?"

"They heard a woman screaming." He nods at my yacht without breaking eye contact. "Said it came from the Sea Hawk."

I turn my head a fraction. Lights burn on the deck of

the Casablanca that bobs next to Sea Hawk. A Moroccan flag flies on the mast. A woman stands at the rail, pulling a coat tightly around her as she watches us. A man with gray hair is at her side. Just my luck that my nosy neighbors are sleeping on their yacht tonight.

I clench my teeth. "My wife is perfectly happy and well."

His smile thins, not reaching his eyes. "Then you won't mind if she tells us herself." He steps closer still, bumping our chests like a rooster heading for a cock fight. "For that, I don't need a warrant."

The curve of my lips is mocking in return, but my voice drips with acid. "By all means, be my guest."

He doesn't let me invite him twice. Holding my gaze with that annoying smile plastered on his ugly features, he bulldozes past me and flicks his fingers at his men. They cross the bridge and stop at the top where the captain blocks their path.

I take my time to follow. The captain waits for my command. When I incline my head, he stands aside.

"This way," I say, leading them to the lounge while I pin the man and woman next door with a stare.

The curious couple scurry over their deck and disappear inside a cabin.

I open the lounge door for the men and make a point of not inviting them to sit. "Wait here. I'll fetch my wife."

I catch the captain's gaze. He nods, understanding the silent instruction to watch them. I keep them in my visual through the window as I walk with long, measured strides down the passageway. When I reach the stairs, I quicken my steps, heading toward the master cabin at the back of the yacht.

Sabella sits up, clutching the comforter against her chest when I enter.

"What's going on?" she asks.

Her dark hair hangs in tangled tresses over her naked shoulders. Her pretty face looks tired and pale.

A deckhand unpacked our bags while we had dinner. Going to the closet, I take out a pair of leggings and a warm sweater that I throw on the bed. "Get dressed."

"Why?" she asks, sounding scared.

I open the drawer and grab a set of underwear, which I dump on the bed as well. "The neighbors called in a domestic disturbance. They probably heard your screams."

She stares at me with wide eyes, following my movements with her gaze.

"Come on, *bella*."

I tug the comforter from her tight grip and pull it off her body. Goosebumps run over her arms.

Regret slips into my voice. "You have to get ready."

She swings her legs over the side of the bed. Fucking perfect timing. It's not the moment to drag her out into the cold, but we don't have a choice. I can't not let her show her face.

Taking her elbow, I help her up, but she pushes me away. The rejection stings, and that comes as a surprise. It's not as if I don't deserve it. I took her hard, and I didn't prepare her. But punishment is punishment, and I'll do well not to go soft on her. I shouldn't forget how quick she was to betray me, how ready to marry another man.

I take the panties and hold them open. "Here."

She snatches them from my hands and gathers the rest of the clothes before making for the bathroom.

"Sabella," I say in protest, reaching for her again, but she stops me short with a raised palm and pursed lips, her chest rising with a deep breath.

It takes every ounce of control I possess and then some to give her the space she wants, especially now. Especially when the men in the lounge are waiting. I don't miss the small steps she takes or how the proud set of her shoulders is designed to hide her discomfort. She doesn't want me to know. But I do.

The shutting of the door and the lock that turns with a firm click is a very clear message. It takes even more restraint not to go after her and break down that fucking door. Pacing is all I can do until she steps out a minute later, dressed but still looking disheveled with her hair hanging wild around her face.

"Sit," I say, pushing her down onto the bench in front of the dresser. It's padded, but she winces when her ass hits the surface.

I find socks and a pair of sneakers and go down on my haunches in front of her. This time, she doesn't object as I pull the socks over her feet before tying the sneakers.

"Listen to me, Sabella." I straighten, gripping her chin. "They're just going to ask you a few questions, and then, they're going to leave."

She stares up at me without blinking, her dark eyes hazy. Is she even processing what I'm saying?

"Do you understand?" The next words pain me. "Do not even think about betraying me again. Remember what's at stake."

She swallows. Nods.

"Good girl." I bend down and plant a kiss on her lips. "It'll only take a few minutes. Soon, you can go back to bed."

She doesn't reply.

Taking the brush from the dresser, I try to be gentle as I pull it through her hair, but the bristles catch on the knots. My ministrations move her head this way and that. She doesn't resist or complain when the brush gets stuck.

When she's more or less presentable, I put the brush

aside and grasp her elbows to help her to her feet. "How are you doing?"

She pulls away. "I'm fine."

Clenching my hands to stop myself from reaching for her again, I take her coat from the back of the chair and hang it over her shoulders.

The wind is like a blast of ice in our faces when I open the door. Her just-brushed hair blows in every direction as she grabs the rail and walks down the passageway.

A gust of wind creates a swell that rocks the yacht. I wrap my hands around her waist from behind when she almost loses her balance and, despite her protest, hold her steady as I steer her ahead of me up the stairs. Her ribcage expands under my palms with the long breath she takes as we pass in front of the window through which the men in their blue uniforms are visible. When we turn the corner, she blows it out slowly.

By the time I open the door and usher her inside, her manner is composed.

Lavigne stands at attention. He takes Sabella in with a practiced glance. "Mrs. Russo, my apologies for interrupting your rest."

"That's all right," she says.

I take a position beside her, placing my hand on her lower back.

Lavigne's gaze slips to the action. "Do you know why we're here?"

She doesn't skip a beat. "My husband told me there's been a complaint about the noise." Her cheeks flush as she continues, "We're on honeymoon. I'm sorry about disturbing our neighbors." She even manages to flash me a smile. "We'll keep it down until we're on the open sea."

Lavigne squints. "We all remember how it is to be newlyweds. Do you mind if we have a word alone?"

"I prefer that my husband stays."

"Are you sure, Mrs. Russo?"

Damn son of a bitch.

She wraps her arms around herself under the coat. "Yes."

"We can go down to the station," he says. "We can talk in private there. Do you prefer that?"

"She prefers nothing of the kind," I bite out. "She's not going anywhere with you."

"Is this yours?" Lavigne asks, motioning at the cashmere coat draped around her shoulders.

She frowns. "Yes."

"Do you mind if we have a look at it?"

"No," she says while I simultaneously say, "Yes."

"Yes," I repeat, my jaw clenched. "We do mind."

Lavigne ignores me. "You said no, Mrs. Russo, didn't you? I heard you correctly. My hearing is good."

What the fuck is he playing at?

"I–If my husband—"

"I'm asking you, not your husband," he says. "The coat does belong to you." He raises a brow. "You said so yourself."

She shoots me a nervous look.

"What are you implying, Lavigne?" I ask, nailing him with a stare. "We'd like to get back to bed."

He shrugs. "Just a routine check while we're here. I do apologize for keeping you from your sleep." Turning to Sabella, he adds, "You don't have anything to hide, do you?"

"Of course not." She shrugs the coat off her shoulders. "See for yourself."

Lavigne catches the garment too eagerly. He passes it on to one of his colleagues who pats the coat down.

"Sir," the man says, taking something out of the pocket.

A small plastic bag with white powder.

Sabella stands glued to the spot, her mouth dropping open.

In two long strides, I'm in front of Lavigne, reaching for his neck. "You son of a bitch."

"Angelo," Sabella cries out, grabbing my arm before my fingers can lock around their target.

Lavigne stands his ground, silently daring me to follow through with the action. It's what he wants. He's pushing me, waiting for me to lash out.

"Don't," Sabella says, her voice soft behind me.

"Well, well," Lavigne says. "What have we here, Mrs. Russo?"

Her tone is innocent and her expression shocked. "That's not mine."

She doesn't realize it's a setup. My muscles tense, gearing for action again. I'll fucking kill him. All of them.

"Mr. Russo." The captain's voice reaches me through the haze of fury obscuring my reason. "I advise you to call your lawyer. Now."

"You do that," Lavigne says, motioning at his men.

Two of them grab Sabella. The other three draw guns.

"You're under arrest for the possession of drugs, Mrs. Russo." Lavigne gives me a shit-eating grin. "We're taking you down to the station."

I bounce forward with a growl, ready to rip the motherfucker to pieces, but the captain steps in front of me and shoves me hard on the chest.

"Calm down, Mr. Russo." Emphasizing every word, he repeats, "Call your lawyer."

"Get your fucking hands off her," I say, raging like a beast.

The captain's tone turns hard. Stern. "Do you want them to arrest you too?"

I still at that. They easily can. For obstruction of justice or whatever flimsy reason they'll concoct. Whatever it'll be, they won't dare to be as bold as to plant fucking drugs on me.

"Take her away," Lavigne instructs his men. To me, he says, "You know where to find her. If charges are filed, you'll need bail money."

Sabella glances at me from over her shoulder, her eyes round and panicked as they push her toward the exit. The wind barrels inside when one of the men opens the door. She's dressed in a sweater and leggings, for Christ's sake. She'll freeze out there.

I reach for her, but the captain grabs my bicep and holds me back.

"Wait," I say, shaking off the captain's hand and suppressing the urge to bash the men's heads in. "She needs a jacket."

The bastards ignore me, dragging her into the cold night farther away from me. Violence pushes up inside me as I go after them. At the bridge, the captain fists a hand in my shirt, all but tearing it in his effort to stop me.

"You can't get her back like this," he says in a calm voice. "Not with violence. Think with your head."

His reasonable tone gets through to me. He's right. There's only one way of getting her out, and that's not by pulling their limbs from their bodies. Sadly.

The rail is cold under my palms where I grip it as I watch them handcuff her, *fucking handcuff her*, before pushing her into the back of a branded police car. I'm like a grenade about to explode as the driver starts the engine and the vehicle pulls off.

"Get my phone," I tell the captain, unwilling to look away from the car. "I left it in the cabin."

He runs to execute the order.

I stare at the red taillights of the car as it speeds down the road with a blaring siren before turning the corner. Then, there's only darkness. Me. Sabella gone. And I find that I can't stand it. I can't stand the sudden emptiness of the winter night or the anguish that eats a hole in my gut.

"Here," the captain says, returning with my phone.

I take it without moving my gaze from the road where the second vehicle pulls off with screeching tires. I keep looking at the spot on the marina where my wife stood only a few seconds ago while dialing my lawyer with a voice command. He'll pick up, no matter the hour. He's in Marseille. It shouldn't take him long to get to the station.

When the line connects, I'm already stalking to the cabin for my keys and coat, my hand shaking with rage.

Those motherfuckers. They know Sabella is out of her depth. They're not taking her in for questioning about a complaint or for concern about her welfare. They're taking her in to press her for information on me. And I don't know how long she'll last before they break her.

CHAPTER
THIRTY-ONE

Sabella

The police station is a cold and miserable place with lime-green doorframes and yellowed tiles. The interrogation room is freezing cold. I'm sure it's on purpose. So is the humiliating full body search that a female officer executes with surgical gloves and probing fingers.

She asks me to open my mouth before pushing down my tongue. Then she instructs me to bend over and touch my toes. I die a thousand deaths as she does a thorough feel-around in all my private places.

I'm shivering from cold and embarrassment when she's done. She tells me in a neutral tone to get dressed, watching me as I do so. Her gaze slides over me until I've tied my laces, her expression giving nothing away. No words are exchanged and no explanations offered. She simply grabs my arm and escorts me to another room with a metal table and two chairs. A camera that sits in the corner of the ceiling is pointed toward the table. One-sided glass forms a window in the back wall.

A guard enters and handcuffs me to the table. After securing my ankles with chains, they leave and shut the door.

For a long time, nothing happens. I'm alone, shivering with cold. I'm hurting both inside and outside. The hard seat of the wooden chair doesn't help. I breathe in and out, trying to still my violent trembling and to simply exist without thinking, but as I'm filling my lungs with the stale air that smells of urine and bleach, the time ticks by slowly, and nobody comes.

I know what they're doing. I know why they stripped me and searched me so thoroughly. I know why they're letting me sit here in the cold, chained to a table and the floor. They want to break me. They're hoping I'll cooperate when they finally come back for me, and I understand why.

The answer is Angelo Russo.

That's why they planted the drugs on me. I've been an idiot to give them my coat. It's a hard lesson, but one I learned well. I won't make the same stupid mistake again.

After what feels like hours, the door finally opens and the man who brought me here enters with a file in his hands. I watch him closely as he crosses the floor and takes a seat. His sympathetic look doesn't fool me. Underneath the surface, I sense his excitement.

He opens the file and studies the piece of paper that lies on top. "Mrs. Russo." He looks up from the paper and catches my gaze. "My name is Lieutenant Lavigne. I just got the report from the officer who searched you." He watches me with a penetrating stare. "The report states signs of abuse."

Not making it easy for him, I raise an eyebrow and wait.

"Marks on your body that indicate a beating," he says after a couple of seconds.

I tilt my head. "We've just been married."

"Exactly." He drops the paper and folds his hands on the table. "That doesn't seem very romantic."

"Yes, well, each to his own. We have different sexual preferences, if you know what I mean. Have you never tried spanking in the bedroom?" I shrug. "I suppose that's not your taste."

He stares at me for a long moment before speaking again. "I'm not a fool, Mrs. Russo. I know who Angelo Russo is and where he comes from." He leans back with a self-satisfied grin. "I also did a little search on you and where you are from. You come from a prestigious family with ties in high places. It seems very unlikely for someone of your standing to marry a person like Mr. Russo out of your own free will."

My laugh is nervous despite the confidence I'm striving for. "I don't think it's your job to make assumptions. Isn't your job gathering facts?"

He continues as if he hasn't heard me. "I'm going to offer you a way out. Give me information on Angelo Russo, any evidence that will help me to put him away, and all your problems will be solved. When he's behind bars, you can divorce him and go home."

Wow. I didn't expect him to be so direct. I suppose he has limited time. He must know Angelo is most probably trying to bail me out as we speak. Not because my husband cares about me. He just wants to make sure I don't talk.

He crosses his arms. "It's something to consider—your freedom."

If only he knew. I don't dare open my mouth. Ever. It

won't bear well for Ryan or my family who are accomplices in murder. No, I'm stuck. I'm in this marriage for better or worse, for as long as I live, and judging by the way it's going, it's leaning toward the worse end of the scale.

"Mrs. Russo." He sighs. "I'm going to put Angelo Russo behind bars if it's the last thing I do. There are only two sides in this war. You better make sure you choose the right one. Silence makes you guilty too. When the time comes to lock him away for life, you don't want to share that sentence."

"Is that why you planted the drugs on me?" I ask, looking straight at the camera. "So that you could drag me down here to offer me a deal?"

He only smiles. "Take a little time to think about it." Leaning forward, he says in a tone soft enough not to be caught on the recording, "I'll be back for you."

The threat hangs between us, our breaths making white puffs as the words dissipate into the frigid air. The promise feels like a noose around my neck, and the rope is in Lieutenant Lavigne's hands. Is he bluffing? I can't get a read on him. There's no way of telling.

Taking a business card from the pocket of his padded jacket, he pins it with a finger on the table and slides it toward me. "That's my number. Memorize it. You can call me when you have an answer or information." He adds in a dark tone, "Or anytime you need my help."

I look from the card to his face. "Your help? After what you just did, what makes you think I'll ever trust you?"

"Your husband has a reputation. Let's just say he has an appetite for violence. You may need me sooner than you think."

I swallow at that, because he may be right. Only, I can never turn to him for help. I can't turn to anyone for that matter.

The door opens with a squeak. We both turn our heads that way. A tall man in a three-piece suit carrying a briefcase in his hand enters. His dark-blond hair and pale blue eyes remind me of Colin. My chest tightens at the thought of my friend and how I left him. I hope he's all right. I wish I could check on him. I wish I could call Ryan and make sure they're fine.

The newcomer glances briefly at me before settling his gaze on the lieutenant. "I'm Gervais Laurent, Mr. Russo's lawyer. I'll be representing Mrs. Russo. What are the charges?"

Lieutenant Lavigne faces me squarely, his signature smile curving his lips. "No charges." He adds with emphasis, "This time."

Mr. Laurent's manner is business-like. "Unlock her hands and feet. If Mrs. Russo has been maltreated, you'll hear from me again."

"Oh, she has," the lieutenant says. "But not by us."

Mr. Laurent ignores the comment. He waits for Lieutenant Lavigne to uncuff me and to remove the chains from my ankles. When I'm free, Mr. Laurent takes my arm and helps me to stand. I'm grateful for the support. My body is stiff after sitting for so long, and my legs are uncooperative. I feel cold and brittle from the lack of blood circulation, and by the time the lawyer guides me into the lobby of the station, my teeth are chattering.

The space is crowed with people, but Angelo immediately draws my gaze. He's a head taller than everyone, his black hair shining under the flickering lights. Even if he didn't stand out because of his height, the fury rolling off him in waves would've caught my attention. Quiet violence glimmers in the depths of his dark eyes.

The people clear a path as he comes toward me with long, powerful strides. He carries my coat in one hand and a travel mug in the other. His gaze drills into mine, a thousand turbulent emotions transmitted as he hands Mr. Laurent the mug and helps me to pull on the coat, but not a word is said. Not here. I understand that.

Angelo holds my gaze as he buttons up the coat. I don't make sense of all those emotions. I do however register the questions burning in his eyes.

Did I talk?

Did I break?

Did I betray him?

These questions are the only explanation for the cold, silent anger that pulsates around him.

He drapes an arm around my shoulders and pulls me into the warmth and protection of his body. Shielding me against him, he leads me outside as fast as my feet allow.

He stops on the pavement, takes the mug from Mr. Laurent, and puts it in my hand. "Chamomile tea with honey. It's warm."

I'm grateful for his foresight as I drink the hot, sweet tea. It warms my stomach, helping to dispel some of the cold. I'm thirsty and my throat is still sore. The relief when I swallow is instantaneous. Even though my pride doesn't want me to take any comfort from him, I'm too exhausted and frozen to argue with myself or to refuse.

I take small sips, trying to make the treat last as Angelo walks me to a waiting car. He opens the backdoor and helps me inside. The interior is warm. The engine is running, and the heater is on. A driver turns in his seat and greets me in French. I don't manage more than a nod.

Angelo shuts the door. He exchanges a few words with Mr. Laurent before coming around the car and getting in beside me. Once he's buckled first my safety belt and then his, the driver takes off.

I lean my head on the backrest and turn my face

toward the window, noting the lights that blur into a continuous line as we speed toward the city, but I don't take in the sight. Not really.

"Sabella." Angelo grips my face, the fingers of his large hand splayed over my cheeks as he forces me to look at him. "Did you tell them anything?"

"You can relax." I sag deeper into the seat, exhaustion stealing over me. "You're safe."

The muscles in his jaw bunch, creating hollows under his high cheekbones in the shadows that play over his handsome features under the fast-shifting lights. Such a beautiful face. An angel's face. I can never forget he has the heart of a devil.

"I'm sorry you had to go through that," he says, brushing a thumb over my jaw. "I had no idea Lavigne was going to play that dirty."

"It's over."

I tremble when I think about the lie. It'll never be over. Not for me. Lieutenant Lavigne and Angelo have one thing in common. They're both determined. Neither of them is going to let me go. This is only the beginning. I try to pull free, but Angelo doesn't let me escape his touch or his piercing gaze.

Holding fast, he stares into my eyes. Too deeply. Seeing too much. "I should kill him." Then softer, more seriously, "I will."

Stiffening at the sound of that word on his lips, that single, small word that can decide a man's fate, I glance in the driver's direction. Angelo throws that threat around as if he's a god, as if it's his right to say who lives and who dies.

"Don't worry." Angelo finally sets me free. "He's on my payroll."

The driver, he means.

My face burns where his fingers branded me. "Nothing happened." I finish the last of the tea and stare through the window again. "Just let it go."

"Nothing?" Anger slips into his voice. "You call what happened to you *nothing*?"

"Please." I turn my face to him with a beseeching look. "I don't want to talk about it."

A muscle ticks in his temple, but he drops the subject. For now, at least.

We carry on driving deeper into the city. I can't even bring myself to ask him where we're going. At this point, it doesn't really matter. Anyway, I can change my destination as little as I can change my fate. What's waiting for me can't be worse than how my wedding day started and ended. My wedding night must be the worst night of my life, excluding that fatal early winter evening when Angelo killed my dad. But I can't think about that now. If I do, I'll break down, and I need to hold on to my strength, even if only for appearances. I don't want to show Angelo how shaken I am. He'll only exploit my weakness.

The driver pulls up in front of a luxury hotel. Angelo gets out and opens my door. He extends his hand, but I ignore the offer of assistance. Does he take no for an answer? Never. Not Angelo. That word doesn't exist in his vocabulary. Locking his fingers around my wrist, he helps me from the car whether I want him to or not.

A memory of the day we met flashes through my mind, how his eyes had flared when I'd said no to him. I should've known then, but I was young and inexperienced. Falling in love. Falling for the wrong man. That man took my heart, and he never returned it. There's no hope of ever getting it back, because the man I gave my love to is an illusion. The man who holds my affections in a beautiful prison constructed of never-ending pain is nothing but a pretty pretense. He's like a character from a book, and I'm the fool who bought into the story. I can never get back what I gave him, not my virtue and not my innocence. None of my firsts. Least of all my love. I gave that to a man who doesn't exist, and that's a bitter pill to swallow.

As I don't have a say, I simply let it happen, let things unfold. My control is limited, and the war stretches a lifetime ahead of me. I have to choose my battles wisely.

The coat he provided is warm, but I can't stop shivering. The frost inside me refuses to melt. While the driver takes two travel bags from the trunk, Angelo removes his own coat and hangs it over my shoulders too. His smell wraps around me like a favorite memory, cedar and citrus bringing me comfort despite myself. I cling to the false sense of safety, clutching the edges of the coat together as if I'm hanging on to it for dear life.

Angelo guides me inside, holding me under the hollow of his arm while the driver carries the bags. We bypass the reception and walk straight to the elevators. Angelo must've already checked in.

As we wait for the elevator, he smiles down at me and tilts his head toward the mug in my hand. His tone is uncharacteristically soft. "Finished?"

I nod.

He takes the mug and pulls me inside when the doors open. The driver follows with the bags. Angelo obviously doesn't trust the hotel staff with his luggage. After what just happened, I can't blame him.

We get out on the top floor. He unlocks the first door with a keycard and holds onto me as he brings me inside a spacious lounge. The room is richly decorated in beige and gold. The style is baroque. The driver drops the bags in the adjoining room and leaves. Only when we're alone does Angelo drop his arm and give me space.

Stepping sideways, I hug myself. He watches me, never moving his gaze from my face as he takes off his jacket and throws it over a chair.

I tense when he walks to me. He reaches out carefully but with determination. Going about it slowly, he brushes his coat from my shoulders. He catches it over his arm, searching my eyes as he lays it over his jacket before removing the coat he gave me, which fits me surprisingly well.

I stand quietly, allowing him to strip off the coat, but when he cups my face between his palms, I duck and put distance between us.

My voice is shaky. "I need a shower." I need to wash what's happened away.

"Of course," he says, standing with his empty palms raised for a second before lowering his arms to his sides.

I'm glad he doesn't ask why. I'm relieved that he gives me quiet understanding as he takes my hand and leads me through a large bedroom into a bathroom where he turns on the water in the shower.

"Can you give me a moment?" I ask, biting my lip. For some reason, I don't want him to see me naked. Not now. I have to do this alone.

"What have they done, Sabella?"

"Nothing," I say quickly. I didn't want to talk about it in the car, and I still don't.

Steam billows in a white cloud over the door of the shower cubicle, turning the air warm and humid, but he doesn't budge. "No, *bella*. It wasn't nothing. I know how the system works."

Exasperated, I say, "Then you know what happened."

"Tell me anyway."

"Why?" I exclaim. "Why do you want me to say it if you already know?"

"Because I'm asking you."

I huff a laugh. "I think you have no idea. You just want to make sure I didn't sing like a canary."

"That's not true," he says, his long legs eating up the distance between us.

I take in the wide set of his shoulders and how the fitted shirt hugs his frame. How the muscles weave and string together underneath. How strong he is. Has he ever been forced to do something he didn't want to do? I doubt that. Very much. Not a man like him. No officer has ever laid a finger on him.

Testing my theory, I ask, "Have you ever been inside?"

He purses his lips.

A victorious smile curves my lips. "Thought so."

"I don't have to be arrested to imagine what it's like."

It's hard to hold that smile when my mouth is so stiff from the effort. "You can't imagine feelings you'll never know."

"You're right." His manner is demure. "I've never set foot in an interrogation room."

"Then you can't have any idea what it's like to strip naked, to bend over, and to be examined by a stranger in parts too private for strangers to see. You can't know what it's like to be chained to a table and the floor in a room for hours. You don't know how it feels to be so cold that the pain in your hands and feet becomes needles under your skin."

The violence that flows so shallowly under the surface of the man who's now my husband surfaces in the rage that contorts his features. In contrast, his voice is calm as he reaches for me again. "Then tell me."

"Don't touch me," I cry out, trying to flee, but the bathroom is too small.

He easily catches me in the tender vise of his arms, breathing soft, insistent words in my neck. "Tell me."

I fight his hold, not wanting his comfort. Not wanting him to be nice to me. Because this part of Angelo? I don't trust it. I don't understand it. I don't understand how he can be so cruel the one moment and so kind the next.

He gives me gentle words again. A cruel command. "Tell me, *cara*."

The emotions that have been building since he walked into the church and married me at gunpoint reach a breaking point. My earlier meltdown after I pulled the trigger was about something different, about who I am deep inside, about not wanting to look at that woman too closely for fear of what I'll find. Now? It all comes pouring out in a pathetic display of anger as I fight him for all I'm worth, flailing my arms and twisting in his hold to free myself. Because I'm too ashamed to admit what I feel.

"Tell me," he says, pinning my arms to my sides and lifting me off my feet.

The helplessness only makes the anger worse. It spills over my lips in a truthful confession I never intended to give him. "It feels dirty," I yell. "Like my body has been invaded."

He stills. Another breath tickles my temple, disturbing wisps of hair. The only sound in the room is the water running in the shower. My shame is flayed open and laid at my enemy's feet.

Carefully, he lowers me to the floor, but he doesn't let me go when my toes touch the ground. He holds me against him, hugging me while the storm inside me does its damage, until my shivering stops and my body goes still.

"Sabella," he says with something close to a growl. "I'll fucking kill them."

"Just stop saying that." My shoulders sag. "Please."

The storm wreaked its havoc. The aftermath is a quiet landscape of brutal devastation. I don't know how much more of this I can take. Not in one day. Not even a lifetime is enough.

Angelo is a man of contrasts. True to his nature, he gives me one wish while denying me the other. He doesn't speak of killing any longer. Instead, he undresses me, not granting me the luxury of privacy.

He takes off his own clothes and carries me into the shower. Like the night I first gave myself to him, he cleans me, washing away the touch of unfamiliar hands. The humiliation. He wipes away my thoughts and replaces them with physical feelings, forcing me to focus on nothing but pleasure as he slides inside me slowly under a cascade of cleansing water. The rock of his hips is gentle. His grip in my hair is hard. The look in his eyes is fierce as he holds me in place, his gaze fixed on my face as he makes love to me.

The steel grip of his fingers is painful around my wrist as he pushes my hand between my legs. He holds it there, setting the pace while making me use my own fingers to rub my clit. I place the palm of my free hand over the black ink on his chest. His heart is the same color inside, yet it beats strongly under warm flesh. Sometimes, when I touch that picture, I expect it to feel differently—cold and dead.

When I come, he releases my arm and wraps a hand around my neck to hold me against the wall while he kisses me. His lips are warm and soft on mine, wet with drops of water. The kiss is tender and urgent at the same time, demanding all my attention. He grunts into the kiss and punches his groin against mine like he does when he finds his release. He's still pumping inside me while tangling our tongues with his eyes wide open long after the spasms have rippled out.

Both the sex and the aftermath are different than before. Surprisingly, this gentleness takes everything from me. It's not a punishment that requires resistance and pulling up walls around my heart. It allows me to let go. In its wake follows an overpowering knowledge that I'm ruined for other men.

The admission isn't new. It's just never stared me with so much finality in the face.

I lean on the wall, letting it hold my weight when he pulls out. Letting him wash between my legs. The earlier feelings are gone, someone else's clinical touch eradicated by his heated gaze and meticulous passion.

He turns off the water and wraps a towel around me before securing one around his waist. I know the routine. He dries me first before taking care of himself. We're silent, absorbed in our own thoughts as he towels his hair dry and I brush mine.

Back in the bedroom, I'm grateful for the warm, comfortable pajama set he takes out of one of the bags. It still has the price tag on.

"Where did you get all of this?" I ask, motioning at the rest of the women's clothes in the bag.

He drops the towel and takes a pair of pajama bottoms from the other bag. "Personal shopper."

My gaze is drawn to the heavy, thick cock between his legs that's already semi-hard again.

"It'll take some time for your own things to arrive." He steps into the pants and pulls them over his hips. "Even with air freight. The clothes Celeste packed for you is hardly enough for a week." He walks over and stares down at me with dark, brooding eyes. "What were you planning on doing?"

This is dangerous ground. We're not going there again. I turn, but he stops me with a hand on my bicep.

"I think I deserve an answer, *bella*." His smile is flat. "Don't you?"

"I don't know." I blink, trying to hold his gaze without faltering. "I didn't really think about it. Hide out for a couple of weeks in the Drakensberg. It was just an idea."

The muscles around his mouth draw tight. "Just an idea?"

"You punished me. Can we please move on?"

He considers that before unlocking his fingers and releasing my arm.

"Aren't we going back to the yacht?" I ask to change the subject.

"It's more comfortable for you here." He lifts the covers, a quiet instruction for me to get into bed. "We'll leave after breakfast."

Just like that, my animosity flares. I cross my arms. "Are you concerned about my comfort now?"

"Of course."

"That wasn't the case earlier."

"I took care of your pleasure, didn't I? I could've simply gotten myself off."

I grit my teeth. "I didn't enjoy that."

"That wasn't the point."

"I don't want it to happen again."

"You have a short memory." He brushes his knuckles over my cheek. "You promised to fulfill any marital duties I see fit, and this is very much part of the duties I expect my wife to fulfill."

"Liar. You're only saying this so you can punish me again. Admit it, Angelo, hurting me turned you on."

"Yes," he says with brutal honesty that takes me aback,

tilting his hips and letting me feel his hard-on. "But as I said, it's up to you how much you enjoy it."

I utter a yelp when he catches me in his arms and pulls me down on top of him on the bed.

"Now close your pretty eyes and shut that cheeky mouth so that we can get some sleep." He presses a soft kiss on my neck. "Tomorrow, you're meeting your new home."

My ribcage squeezes, the air in my lungs compressing, and it has nothing to do with the tightness of his arms around my body and everything with the way in which he made that declaration, as if the worst is yet to come.

CHAPTER
THIRTY-TWO

Angelo

The water is choppy. Sabella isn't bothered by the rough boat ride. She quickly found her sea legs. From how motionless she stands at the rail, not losing a step as the swell tips the yacht, she was probably born with those long, slender, toned sea legs. The notion makes someone like me with pirates for ancestors proud.

Now that I had her, breaking my own intention in doing so, I consider fucking her for the whole seven hours of the trip. My body agrees, my cock hardening at the thought of what I can do with her. I can push her down on her knees again or have her on all fours. I could spend the entire journey with my head buried between her legs and my tongue in the delicious heat of her pussy. The temptation is huge, but my concern is bigger.

What happened at the police station shook her. Her meltdown proved as much. Despite honoring her wish to not talk about it, I still want to off those motherfuckers for laying their hands on her. For what they did to her.

And I will.

In good time.

Once I've gathered the information I need.

For now, I let it be, let *her* be, however difficult it is for me to give her space. That doesn't stop me from staring, greedily drinking in every small detail with my eyes.

She leans her elbows on the upper deck rail, the icy wind whipping her ponytail around her beautiful face.

The image is breathtaking. Except for that attractive beauty spot, her honey-gold skin is flawless. She's so perfectly created she seems unreal—like a wax doll with long legs, curvy hips, and a small waist. Firm, pert breasts.

She looks as if she has herself together, as if nothing can derail her. Only, on the inside she's not a vision of perfect calm. I know what she's been through because I've put her through part of it. Fine. Most of it. She's strong though. She neither bends nor breaks easily. And that makes my chest swell with more pride. She's a brave woman, a perfect fit for me. I never doubted that.

Yet it's the very courage I admire in her that won't let me shed my gnawing concern. Being clever and brave are characteristics of a fearless traitor.

Staying close enough to grab her in case she slips, I take my phone from my pocket. I keep one eye on her while I fire off a message to my informant in the bureau, instructing him to pull the tape from the interrogation room.

I know how officers like Lavigne operate. He would've cut her a deal. Most likely, he offered her freedom in exchange for getting him the evidence he needs to slap a life sentence on me.

And if there's anything my beautiful bride wants, it's her freedom.

The only sword hanging over her head is her family. Exposing me will implicate them. She won't risk their reputation, let alone their safety. No. She'd negotiate. It would have to go all the way to the top, to governments and higher, because the French law can't ensure her family's indemnity. It would have to be an agreement made with her country's leaders, one favor exchanged for another. That's how these things work.

"Come on," I say, going over when I can't resist the pull any longer. "The temperature is sub-zero with the wind factor." Linking my arm through hers is just an excuse to touch her. "Let's get you inside."

The wool coat and scarf she wears over a cashmere sweater and a pair of skinny jeans aren't enough protection for the spray blowing over the deck. I don't want her to catch pneumonia.

In the lounge where it's warm, I make sure she's comfortably seated before sitting down opposite her and catching up with emails on my phone.

My attention isn't on work however. It's focused on the woman in front of me. She's staring through the window, a fast-growing habit. It's nothing but a tactic to avoid looking at my face.

One of the deckhands brings her a cup of tea. She thanks him politely and cups the warm drink between her palms. Making an effort to ignore her, I open the encrypted reply from my informer. The news isn't good. The recording was wiped clean. There's no record of what was said between Lavigne and Sabella. That can only mean one thing. Lavigne is covering something up.

Drumming my fingers on the armrest, I consider the

turn of events. I'll have to be extra careful around Sabella. I can't let her hear or see anything she can use against me.

It's going to make living together complicated, seeing that my office is at home and most of my business deals are discussed and concluded there. I host many men from crime organizations who are high up in the hierarchy. The comings and goings in Corsica are both vital and sensitive.

Unless she proves herself one hundred and ten percent trustworthy, which is, considering our circumstances, highly unlikely, I won't have a choice but to lock her up. The thought twists my gut. It's not what I want or what I planned. Far from it. I can only hope it won't come to that.

The early darkness of winter has set in when the captain steers the yacht into the bay and moors it next to the jetty. The path lights are lit for our arrival, forming a twinkling golden line that runs up the rocky hill.

I try to see it through her eyes. I've always been proud of my home. The architectural beauty of the fortress is undeniably handsome. The garden with its Olympic size pool is featured in many landscape magazines across the globe. The isolated location on the rugged coastline is a natural gem. I suppose it's easy to admire if you're invited for a visit. For a stranger coming to live here, it must seem remote. Imposing even.

I take Sabella's hand and help her down the bridge onto the jetty. Her dark eyes flare when she looks toward the house. She's used to living in luxury dwellings on beaches, both in Great Brak River and in Camps Bay, but her parents' house and the villa I rented for her don't compare to the small castle stretching over the expanse of the cliff. Thick streams of soft, golden light from garden spotlights illuminate the towers and ramparts. Beyond, a ripe moon rises over the vineyard.

We make the steep climb in silence. My father

contemplated the logistical difficulties of the house as his retirement approached. The roads are manageable, but climbing up and down to the beach becomes difficult if not impossible at a certain age. For that reason, he was going to install an elevator like one of those that Valparaiso is famous for. Fortunately, it's not a project I have to tackle for the foreseeable future. Not until we're both old. I like the sound of that—growing old together. Raising a few children.

I steal a glance at my wife, noting the rise and fall of her chest from the exertion as we reach the top. I imagine her belly round with my baby. I imagine how she'd look, and a protective rage already washes over me.

I'm getting too soft around her. I have to be careful.

Heidi opens the door. The captain would've alerted her to our arrival.

"Mr. Russo," she says, barely nodding at me before turning her attention to my bride. "Mrs. Russo." She beams. "Welcome home. Come inside. You must be freezing after having been on the water all day."

Sabella appears lost as Heidi takes both her hands and pulls her into the warmth of the house. Flavors of oregano, garlic, and portobello mushrooms hang in the air.

"I prepared a welcoming dinner," Heidi says, taking Sabella's coat. "After all, it's a special day. It merits a celebration."

I observe the exchange quietly, shrugging out of my coat as Heidi makes small talk about the weather, which gives Sabella time to remove her scarf and find her bearings. What kind of a mistress will my wife make for my house? Will she be mousy and too afraid to breathe like my mother or buoyant and over-present in every corner like Adeline?

As always, the memories tighten my chest. A dark

cloud drifts over my mood. It's difficult to witness Sabella in the house where only the ghosts of the people I loved remain and not to hold grudges. A voice deep down says that my mother and Adeline paid the price for Sabella's presence. They paid with their lives so I could finally bring my bride home, and I can't help but think the same thing as always—that it's my fault they're dead. That we are where we are because of Sabella. That my mother and sister should've been here, that they *would've* been here if I hadn't been so adamant about marrying Sabella. But I've always been selfish. No one can accuse me of possessing a bleeding heart.

"This way." Heidi gives Sabella a warm smile before leading the way to the dining room.

Sabella glances at me from over her shoulder, her expression uncertain.

"Come," Heidi says, entering the dining room and waving Sabella in. "You must be starving."

Sabella stops dead in front of me. I cup her waist to prevent her from tripping. Her body is warm under the layers of clothes, her muscles tense beneath my palms.

The reason for her apprehension becomes apparent as I lift my gaze over her head. My uncles and cousins sit around the big table. They're not in a hurry to get to their feet. Animosity hangs like a thick cloud of poison in the air. My uncles size my wife up with unfriendly stares while my cousins take her in with curiosity as they slowly stand.

"Uncle Nico, Uncle Enzo, it's good to see you." I nod at each in turn. "Toma. Gianni. This is my wife, Sabella." I walk her deeper into the room. "Sabella, meet my uncles and cousins."

Uncle Enzo steps up first. He doesn't kiss her cheek or shake her hand. He scrutinizes her with shrewd eyes. "Welcome to Angelo's home."

Not *your* home.

The jab doesn't escape anyone. Toma and Gianni exchange a glance. Sabella tenses more under my hold.

The hostile smile that curves Uncle Nico's lips says he already despises her. "Yes. Welcome."

"Thank you," she says, lifting her chin.

Heidi is either oblivious to the strained atmosphere or pretending not to notice. "I'll let you take care of the seating arrangement while I get the starters, Mr. Russo."

I acknowledge her with a curt, "Thank you, Heidi."

In the uncomfortable silence that follows when she walks from the room, I seat Sabella on my left before taking my place at the head of the table.

"As you were," I say, indicating they're free to sit where they please.

A bottle of rare red from my father's cellar—not from our own vineyard—was opened to breathe and left on the table. I pour a generous amount of wine for Sabella and then serve everyone else.

"A toast," I say, raising my glass. "To the new Mrs. Russo."

Sabella flushes, hiding her face behind her glass as the men dissect her with their glares. Uncle Nico tips back his glass but barely wets his lips. Uncle Enzo mumbles something unintelligible.

The grandfather clock ticks in the background, counting down every awkward second.

"Oh, um." Toma clears his throat. "I'm also marrying soon." At the cutting look his effort to strike up a conversation earns him from his father, his enthusiasm slips. His voice wavers. "Um, in one year's time."

Uncle Nico scowls at him. Toma swallows a gulp of wine and hangs his head.

Heidi enters with bowls of asparagus soup on a tray.

She convinced a few guards to play waiters. They follow behind her, carrying more bowls, baskets of freshly baked bread rolls, and dishes of salted butter.

I utter a silent sigh, wishing this night was over already so that I can take Sabella to bed.

Heidi went to a lot of effort with the menu. The main dish is her specialty—marinated wild boar in a red wine reduction sauce with young carrots and mushrooms on the side. It's one of my favorites.

My uncles clean their plates. Sabella only picks at the food while the conversation turns to business—only the legal parts, that is—that doesn't concern her.

By the time the chocolate fondant and crème anglaise are served, she's yawning. We got to the hotel in the early hours of the morning. We only slept for a short while. It's been an exhausting two days on more than a physical level.

The minute the dessert plates are cleared, I get to my feet, signaling that the dinner is over. I open my mouth to bid them good night, but Uncle Nico beats me to it.

"Cognac, Angelo?" he asks. "There's a matter we need to discuss with you."

I push back my chair. "It can wait."

He smiles even as he clenches his jaw. "I'm afraid it can't."

Uncle Enzo adds with ill-staged regret, "We wouldn't keep you from your wedding bed if it wasn't important."

Sabella stares at the place setting in front of her, two red circles growing on her cheeks.

"Fine." I motion at the corridor. "You know the way."

They file through the door, Toma and Gianni in tow. When Gianni twists his neck to stare at Sabella, I slap him upside the head.

On my way out, I stop next to her chair. Her chest stills with the breath she's taken.

Kissing the top of her head, I whisper in her ear, "You may as well make yourself useful."

She pulls away and tilts her face up to frown at me.

In case she's unclear about my meaning, I clarify, "I'm sure Heidi can do with a hand in the kitchen."

From how she glowers, I suspect she took the suggestion as an insult. My intention is good. Being useful made my mother happy. The sooner I involve Sabella in my household, the sooner she'll integrate.

Her eyes burn holes in the back of my head as I walk from the room.

My uncles and cousins sit on the sofas facing the fireplace in the study. A fire already burns high, no doubt thanks to Heidi's foresight. Cognac and cigars are set out on the coffee table. I pour and hand the glasses around, but I don't touch the cigars. I'm not going down the same road as my father, not after what happened to him.

"Angelo," Uncle Nico says.

I sip my cognac, waiting for him to continue.

"We heard BAC took your wife in for questioning in Marseille."

I raise a brow. "That was fast."

His stilted nod is placating. "It's our business to know everything that concerns them."

"Your point?"

The leather creaks as Uncle Enzo shifts to the edge of his seat. "How long did they keep her?"

I clench my jaw as I relay that fact. "A few hours."

Uncle Enzo watches me with sly attention. "That's a long time."

"They put a lot of red tape in place." My hold on the glass tightens in a reflex reaction. "It took my lawyer time to work through it."

Uncle Enzo licks his bottom lip as he studies the rug

before flicking his gaze back to me. "A lot can happen in a few hours."

"I understand your concern—"

Uncle Nico cuts me short. "We need the tape of the interrogation." He dips his head. "You know why."

"They erased it." I work my jaw. "My informant already tried to get his hands on it."

Uncle Nico's tone is laced with caution. "Then you can't trust her."

"You know what your father would've done," Uncle Enzo says.

My rage ignites in a second. I don't take the bait. I don't ask what my father would've done because I know.

My flat voice doesn't give the violence simmering inside me away. "I'm not my father."

"You are the head of this business now," Uncle Nico says, letting the unspoken meaning hang between us and making it clear to everyone in the room.

I pin him with a stare. "If you have something to say, say it."

His docile calmness vanishes. Determination hardens his jaw. "He wanted her dead. It was his dying wish. He told you to deal with her the day he avenged your mother and sister's deaths. Yet she's alive." His look is cunning. "And most probably working with the cops against you."

The bang as I slam my glass down on the table makes my cousins jump. "She's my wife. I'll deal with her how and when I see fit."

"She's an Edwards," Uncle Enzo says. "Giving her your name can't change that. She is and will always be your enemy's daughter, the man who killed your—"

"I fucking know what he did," I say through clenched teeth. "You'd be wise not to bring that up now."

Uncle Enzo stands. "You may not want to be reminded

of the facts, but your father was our brother, and we know what he would've done in your position. What he would've wanted. He'd never take a risk. If there was the slightest chance of betrayal, he would've killed that spark long before it had a chance of kindling a flame. You and I both know that the most logical, safest decision is to get rid of her."

Fury boils the blood in my veins. I'm about to reach over the table and grab him by the throat when I notice a movement in the doorframe.

Sabella.

She's as pale as a ghost, supporting herself with a hand on the wall.

Fuck.

The men turn their heads in the direction of my gaze. Silence stretches as they look at her, branding her as guilty for nothing but standing there, for hearing something she shouldn't have.

"I—" She swallows. "Heidi sent me to ask if you want coffee."

"No," I say, my tone harsh. "They're leaving."

Uncle Nico puts his glass on the table and gets up with a sneer. "Good night, Angelo. Congratulations again." He doesn't look at Sabella as he walks from the room.

Uncle Enzo follows his twin's example. Toma and Gianni push to their feet, stealing uncertain glances at me before leaving without saying a word.

Sabella folds her arms behind her back and leans on the wall, watching me quietly. I want to pick up my glass and down what's left of my drink, but I don't. I'm volatile enough as it is. My uncles questioned my authority, and even though I'm respectful of their age, I'll have to put them back in their place lest I lose mine in the hierarchy.

Because if I do, God knows, I won't be able to keep Sabella safe.

Her voice is soft, her question loaded. "So, are you?"

"Am I what?"

"Are you going to kill me when I've served my purpose?"

On second thought, I grab that drink and swallow it down in one go. I school my features before I look at her, keeping my expression devoid of emotions. I can't show her the turmoil in my chest. "Only if I have to, so make sure you don't give me a reason."

She digests the statement, taking a second to let it sink in. Then she turns on her heel and flees from the room.

That's all right.

I let her run.

There's nowhere in this house she can hide.

Sabella

The thought of Angelo killing me has crossed my mind. Many times. I of all people know what he's capable of. He never wanted me for me. He only needed my family name. Now that he has that, he's going to make the best use of it he can. He won't waste a minute in securing business ties. He may not kill me soon, but that doesn't mean he won't do it one day. Or that he won't do it in a fit of temper. I have to tread lightly around him. I can't lower my guard. Not for a second.

Wariness weighs me down as I walk down the long hallway toward the kitchen. I can't help but glance over my shoulder as a shiver runs down my spine. The house is voluminous and basked in soft light, but the ambiance is dark. Despite the tasteful furniture and decorations, it feels empty and hollow, as if something is missing.

I quicken my steps, the echo of my soles chasing after

me until I burst into the brightly lit kitchen where Heidi is loading the dishwasher. The housekeeper can't protect me, not against the master of the house, but I do feel better for another human being's presence, especially one who's friendly and kind.

"They don't want coffee," I say, trying to keep my voice normal and not let her hear how scared I am. I can't afford to let anyone suspect that I'm anything less than confident and strong.

She straightens with a smile. "Well, then." After drying her hands on a kitchen towel, she drops it on the counter. "Why don't I show you to your room?"

"I'll help you tidy up first."

"Nonsense." She marches out ahead of me, her blond braid swinging between her shoulder blades. "You had an eventful time with the wedding, not to mention a long day of traveling." She glances over her shoulder. "Of course, it's your house, and you're free to do whatever you like. I'm sure you have lots of instructions for me. We can talk about that tomorrow when you're rested." In the stillness of the house, our steps sound loud on the polished yellow stone floor. "We can start with the menu for the week if you like, unless you prefer to do your own cooking like the late Mrs. Russo." We go up a staircase with a red carpet runner. "You don't have to worry. I'm a fast learner." She stops on the landing. "I'm good at mastering new recipes."

I admit a little sheepishly, "I haven't done much cooking, to be honest. My parents—" I quickly rectify, "My mom has a housekeeper who's also a wonderful cook, and I mostly lived on ready-made meals when I moved out."

"That's what I'm here for," she says, patting my arm. "Don't worry about a thing. We'll sort it out together."

I offer her a grateful smile.

She waves a hand toward the left. "The west wing is

where Mr. Russo's parents resided." She crosses herself. "Bless their souls. Mrs. Russo didn't like to be on the ocean side because of the breeze coming from the sea. She preferred the rooms looking out over the vineyard."

Guilt tightens my stomach at the mention of Angelo's late mother.

"You and Mr. Russo are in the east wing," Heidi continues.

She walks briskly down a broad hallway. I follow behind, taking in the paintings that depict wild cliffs and tranquil beaches or dense forests and snow-capped mountains.

I point at one of the paintings. "Are these scenes from around here?"

"They're all landscapes from the property. They're beautiful, aren't they?"

The house is stunning, but I had no idea the surroundings are so diverse and gorgeous. "How big is it?"

"The property?" She pauses in front of the second-last door on the right. "I don't know exactly over how many hectares it stretches, but it's vast. The farthest border must be about twenty kilometers away." She opens the door. "This is your bedroom."

I enter the large space that's furnished with a king size bed and a small sitting area arranged around a fireplace. Sliding doors give access to a balcony. The night beyond the doors is dark, but I can make out the long line of lights running down to the beach and the water in the distance.

While Heidi fluffs out the pillows and turns the bedcovers down, I take in the rest of my new domain. The room is decorated in neutral colors. A writing desk and an antique armoire stand against the wall opposite the sliding doors. I stop dead as my gaze lands on the dress that hangs against the armoire, its hem sweeping the floor.

A wedding dress.

The classical cut with thin shoulder straps, a plunging V-neckline, and a narrow skirt is striking in its simplicity. The glittery, pure-white fabric adds texture and richness to the design. It's without a doubt the most beautiful dress I've seen.

"It's lovely, isn't it?" Heidi asks in a wistful voice behind me.

Startled, I look over my shoulder to catch her studying the dress with a sad light in her eyes.

"I couldn't get it over my heart to put it away," she says, sounding far-off. "Mrs. Russo had it made for you."

"She did?" I ask, simultaneously surprised and moved.

"For the big day. Adeline was so excited about it. The dress, I mean. The wedding also, but I still remember how she ran downstairs to tell Mr. Russo—Angelo—how perfect the gown was." She smiles, focusing on a spot on the wall with a non-seeing gaze. "Mrs. Russo warned her not to spoil the surprise for her brother. He wasn't supposed to know what the dress looked like. It was right before…" She trails off, getting lost in her own thoughts, and then shakes her head as if trying to dislodge the memory. "Never mind."

The dress draws my gaze again. I can't look away from it. I can't stop thinking about Angelo's mother and sister, about their fates.

"It's terrible what happened," Heidi says, more sadness spilling into her tone. "Such a tragedy."

In my mind's eye, I see Angelo's mother telling her daughter it's bad luck for the groom to see the dress before the wedding. It's something my mom would say, something she *did* say when I got ready to marry Colin. It already feels so long ago.

Tearing my gaze away from the stunning creation, I

turn to look at Heidi. I can't help myself from asking, "Did Angelo see it?"

"The dress?" Heidi shakes her head again. "After what happened, he just locked everything up, left their rooms exactly like that. He couldn't go in there. Wouldn't let me. The dress was in Mrs. Russo's workroom. I just thought you deserved to see it."

Not sure what to say to that, I remain quiet.

"Anyway," she says, wiggling her shoulders. "I aired your room and put sheets on the bed." She points at a door in the corner. "Your suitcase is in the dressing room." Motioning at another door on the side of the bed, she continues, "That one gives access to Mr. Russo's room."

I only nod.

"I took the liberty of stocking your bathroom with toiletries." Heidi brushes down her skirt. "Just shout if you need anything. I can always send a driver to Bastia to pick up supplies."

I clutch my hands together in front of me, accepting the hospitality I don't deserve. "Thank you."

If she knows why Angelo's sister and mother are dead, she'll want to throw me over the balcony herself.

"I'm sure you'd like to get some rest." She walks to the door. "I sleep in the apartment next to the kitchen. If you want anything, you can use the phone on the nightstand to dial me. My extension is marked as *housekeeper* on the phone. If I don't answer, try the kitchen."

I follow her to the door. "Thanks again for the delicious dinner."

"You're welcome, dear," she says before slipping into the hallway.

I close the door and stand there for a moment, not sure what to do. When the door opens again, I assume it's Heidi who forgot to tell me something, but a gasp escapes my lips when Angelo enters.

He opens his mouth and freezes when his gaze falls on the dress. A spectrum of emotions washes over his features before settling on something disturbingly dark. The anger that tightens his eyes and hardens the line of his jaw scares me, because this anger is fueled by grief, and I'm the person responsible for that grief. My family. We're to blame.

Not taking his eyes off me, he puts his head around the doorframe and calls in a thunderous voice, "Heidi."

Hurried footsteps fall in the corridor.

The housekeeper appears on the threshold. "Yes, Mr. Russo?"

He points at the dress, all the while staring daggers at me. "What's the fucking meaning of this?"

Her cheeks pale. "I just thought—"

"Do not think," he grits out. "That's not what I pay you for. Take it away."

"Yes, sir," she says, scurrying across the floor and plucking the hanger with the dress from the armoire.

Angelo and I face each other like war opponents as she runs from the room and softly closes the door.

"She wanted to give you the wedding of the year," he says, hatred pouring into the words. "A beautiful wedding."

"I'm sorry," I whisper, backtracking to the bed, because there's nothing I can do but apologize. I can't change what happened. I can only run from my husband as he chooses the monster inside him instead of the man.

He comes after me. Furious. Hard.

"Angelo," I whisper, not knowing how to stop this. Him.

"That's right. You better get used to my name on your lips. You belong to me, and nothing will be given to you without my permission, so you can practice saying my name when you go down on your knees and beg me."

"Beg you for what?" I ask, my throat closing up.

The smile he gives me as he stalks closer is the cruel one. The statement he delivers is a vicious blow. "For everything."

Understanding blooms. He doesn't only want to make me kneel. He wants to make me crawl. This is how he wants me to pay. He wants to punish me for the dress I never wore, for the wedding that never happened, and for everything else that was outside of my control.

I stand my ground even as he unbuckles his belt and pulls it from his waistband.

"You'll beg me for the food you eat and the air you breathe." He unbuttons his shirt, revealing the black ink that decorates his chest. "For the bed you sleep in." Finishing the task of undressing, he drops his clothes on the floor. "For my cock." He closes the distance between us and stops flush against me. Stark naked. "Beg for it, *bella*, and maybe I'll let you come."

The dress and what transpired with his uncles triggered something inside him. I'm not insensitive to his pain. I know how much unexpected reminders can hurt. However, I already begged for my family. I begged him to marry me, but I won't beg him for a single thing more. Especially not to fuck me.

His smile grows sinister. "Fine. Have it your way, *wife*."

"It's been a long day."

"Exactly. So, let's not drag this out."

I square my shoulders. "I need a shower and sleep."

"You will have both when you beg me."

Clenching my hands into balls at my sides, I can only stare at him with hatred seeping from my heart.

"Beg, Sabella, on your knees, and you can have a shower and your bed. After you fuck me."

"No, thanks," I say, my nostrils flaring. "I'd rather stay dirty and sleep on the floor."

Calculation tightens his features. "If that's what you want, that's what you'll get."

I'm trembling with anger. I should've taken a knife in the kitchen, preferably a blunt one. I could've stabbed it into his cold, sadistic heart.

"Strip," he says. "Or do you prefer that I undress you? I can promise you it won't be romantic."

I spit the words at him. "Go to hell."

"We're consummating our marriage in my family home tonight. Cooperate, and it'll be over sooner."

"You're such a jerk."

"Strip, Sabella. You're not shy, are you? I've already seen every part of you."

Biting back an ugly retort, I tear out of my clothes. He follows my actions with his gaze, not giving me a reprieve from his invasive stare.

When I'm naked, he says, "Get onto the bed on your hands and knees."

I'm not getting out of this. He won't let it go. I may as well just give him what I signed up for and, like he said, *get it over with*.

My lip curls as I get on the bed and look back at him. "Are you going to spank me again? Is that what you need to get hard? What does that make you, Angelo? A fucking sadist?"

The jab I aimed at his character is useless. He laughs it off, stepping up to the edge of the bed and tracing my opening with a finger.

The touch jolts me. My body jerks.

"Play with yourself," he commands.

"Why?" I ask, infusing my tone with more snideness. "Does the show get you off?"

"I don't want to milk my cock with a dry cunt."

The crude words turn me cold inside even as heat pushes up in my neck. "Is it fun being an asshole?"

"Only to you." He grabs his cock in his fist and pumps twice. "Get yourself wet, wife. It'll be nicer for my dick, but you're the one who'll benefit most."

I want to slap him so hard I have to fist my hands in the covers to prevent myself from attacking him again. He makes it difficult to hold on to my dignity.

"There's a woman at the pleasure house," he says when I don't react. "She's called in to prepare new brides for their wedding nights. Shall I call her? I'm sure she won't mind coming out, despite the hour. I can watch while she gets your body ready. She'll ask me which method I prefer. A lubricant will be quick. She'll make sure to get it deep inside you. But watching her get you wet with a vibrator may be more fun."

Tears burn behind my eyes. I face forward lest he notices. He's trying to humiliate me, and he's succeeding. I shouldn't let him get to me. I simply shouldn't think about it.

"Make your choice, Sabella."

There is no choice. Slipping a hand between my legs, I touch myself with trembling fingers.

"Spread your legs," he says. "Let me see if you're getting the job done."

He can fuck right off. Cringing inwardly, I set my knees apart and put myself on display like he wants. I give him the show he demands by rubbing my clit with two fingers pressed together.

As always, a spark of pleasure ignites at the touch. A glance over my shoulder almost stills me. He's pumping into his fist while fondling his sac in his free hand. Lust burns hot in his black eyes as he watches my hand between my legs. Every perfectly cut muscle in his powerful body is taut, drawing a striking picture of masculinity. The wolves on his chest come alive, snarling viciously when those muscles bunch. Beneath his broad shoulders and hard pecs his washboard stomach is flat. The V of his groin runs deep. The cursive letters inked above his hipline sum him up in a single word. Resilience. Strong legs with big calves are well proportioned. The dark hair that covers his legs grows denser around his groin. His cock juts out proudly, the head already slick with pre-cum.

I don't want the image to arouse me, but the heat spreading through my belly is an involuntary reaction. Finally, it's not the ministrations of my own hand that turns me wet. It's how my body responds to the visual sight of him getting himself ready. It's simple nature, one body reacting to the arousal of another, and he's not unaffected. He likes what he sees. I test the theory by sinking a finger inside, studying him from over my shoulder. His jaw bunches as he pumps faster into his fist. When I pull my finger out and slowly push deeper, he utters a growl.

His voice is guttural, rough like an animal's. "You've gotten yourself so wet it's dripping down your thighs." He steps up and traces my crease with the head of his cock. "Such a dirty girl." He fastens a hand on my hip. "Spread your legs wider and push out your ass. Show me what a good job you can do of presenting yourself for my cock."

When I don't move, he plants his hands on my inner thighs and pushes them apart as far as they can go. His cock brushes against my glute as he puts a palm between my shoulders and applies pressure. I have to pull my hand from between my legs to catch myself when he continues to press down until my upper body is flattened on the mattress.

"There," he says. "Just like that. Fuck, Sabella. You're a sight for sore eyes."

Pinching my eyes shut, I press my cheek against the covers. I tense when he buries his fingers in the flesh of my hips. Anticipation ripples through me as he parts my folds with the broad head of his cock. Knowing what's to come doesn't prepare me for the pleasure as he slides all the way in. Holding me in place, he rubs his groin against my ass and keeps still. My body welcomes the intrusion, my inner muscles already clenching around him.

"That's right, dirty girl," he says with a groan. "Milk my cock. You're so hot when you beg without words."

I tune him out, trying not to listen to his wicked praise, because he's moving, and it's all I can focus on. I can only hold on, clawing at the bedsheets as he pulls almost all the way out before slamming back again. He pumps his hips with a leisurely pace, dragging his cock over sensitive nerve endings and punctuating each thrust with a slap on the fleshy part of my right ass cheek. The sting doesn't hurt as much as it heats my skin, and strangely, it makes me hotter. Needier.

Taking what I need, I push back when he thrusts. The fall of his palm on my ass is rhythmic, matching the pace of his pumping. Intense need throbs between my legs. I can't get enough. He swaps hands, gripping my right hip to tan my left globe while timing the rhythm. I'm burning up on the inside and the outside, but he doesn't allow me to go faster. He keeps me still, the force of his fingers bruising, while taking me at his own sweet pace.

My inner walls clench hard. He utters a curse but maintains the lazy pivoting of his hips. His palms no longer heat the skin of my ass. Instead, he massages my globes, wiping away the burn. Digging his fingers into my sensitive flesh, he spreads my ass cheeks and drives home with enough force to wrench a gasp from my lungs.

Finally, he gives me what I want. He bends over me and slips a hand around my waist and between my legs to massage my clit in circular movements. His pace doesn't falter as he quickly and effectively brings me to the edge before violently pushing me over.

An orgasm rips through me at the same time as he surges deep and stills. Warmth bathes me inside. My release is instantaneous and powerful, leaving me legless and weak. When he pulls out and pins me in place to watch his seed leak from my body, I don't have the energy to fight him.

"You're so pretty with my handprints on your ass and my cum dripping down your thighs," he says, finally letting me go.

I collapse flat on the bed, shame not only for the crass remark but also for how cold it leaves me creeping over my cheeks. His feet are quiet on the floor. I don't need to open my eyes to know he's gone. The water that comes on in the bathroom confirms it. That's how he leaves me—discarded after being used.

I take a moment to catch my breath. To deal with the aftermath. I've long since accepted the awful fact that I find pleasure in the arms of my dad's killer. It doesn't make me feel less despicable. It's just another bitter pill to swallow.

The room is warm, but I shiver. I'm about to get off the bed when Angelo returns. I feel him rather than hear him as he stops next to me. Despite my better judgement, I open my eyes. He stands tall and proud, the familiar hatred as he studies me darkening his eyes.

"Get up," he says.

Fear knots my stomach. "Why?"

"It's late. I have a long day of work ahead. I need my sleep."

"Then sleep," I say, unable to keep the bite from my tone.

The smile that curves his lips doesn't reach his eyes. "You're sleeping in my room. Come."

He doesn't wait. He goes ahead and opens the interconnecting door, knowing I'll follow.

It takes effort to peel myself off the bed. Steeling my spine, I say to his back, "I'll shower first."

He turns to face me, that evil grin intact. "You won't."

I gape at him. He can't be serious. I know what he said, but he can't expect me to crawl into bed with a sticky skin and his cum drying on my thighs.

His eyes crinkle in the corners. "You should've begged when you had the chance. It's too late now. Come before I decide to drag you in here."

Turning his back on me, he walks through the door. I stand rooted to the spot, disbelief and a hot wave of fresh anger running through me.

"Sabella," he says from the other room. "Now."

"I need to get my pajamas."

"You're sleeping naked," he calls back.

Bastard.

I bite my tongue as I cross the floor and enter a room that's almost an exact replica of mine. The sight that greets me steals my breath. Candles are burning on every surface, and rose petals are strewn over the bed. I guess Heidi is responsible for the effort. She must've assumed we'd consummate the marriage in his bedroom.

The romantic setting doesn't faze him. He grips the comforter and shakes off the petals, making them sift down over the floor.

"Blow out the candles," he instructs. "We don't want the house to burn down."

Swallowing a retort, I go around the room and blow them all out. The sharp smell of smoke and wax hangs in the air when I'm done.

Angelo lifts the covers and gets into bed. I hover for a moment, starting to feel cold. When I make my way to the other side of the bed, he says, "No."

I stop. "What?"

He points at the floor next to his side of the bed. "Here."

My mouth drops open. "You're joking."

"I'm afraid not, *cara*. That's what you chose, and that's what you'll get until you learn to beg."

Fuck him.

I'm spinning on my heel when his words stop me.

"Don't make me tie you up and dish out another punishment. You're keeping both of us from our sleep."

Angry tears burn at the back of my eyes. He doesn't only want to punish me for my family's sins. He wants to break me. Well, good luck to him. I refuse to break. Not for him.

Lifting my chin, I go over to the side of the bed and lie down.

"That's a good girl," he says, reaching over and switching off the lamp on the nightstand. Darkness folds around us. "Sleep well, *bella*."

I suppress an urge to punch him. In the dark, tears of humiliation and helpless anger finally run over my cheeks. The rug is scratchy, the wool scraping my skin. The flagstones under the rug are hard and uneven, the edges digging into my hip and shoulder. I use my arm as a pillow, but it's difficult to get comfortable.

It's colder on the floor. Soon, I'm shivering. The lesson

isn't lost on me. The price for a shower and sleeping in a warm, soft bed is humiliating myself over and over, night after night, on my knees. I don't know if I can do it. My pride won't let me, but how long will my pride last? How many skipped showers and nights on the floor will it take before my pride bends and I give in?

When I start itching from the wool, I turn on my other side to scratch the irritated skin. Angelo's slow, even breathing only rubs salt in my wound. He's sleeping cozily in his bed while making me suffer. There's no way I'll last the whole night like this.

Getting up quietly, I tiptoe back to my room. Afraid to make noise, I leave the door open. I don't want to switch on a light and risk waking him, so I feel around on the floor until I find his discarded clothes. My fingers brush over his shirt. I pull it on and button it up. A smell of cedar and citrus wraps around me, reminding me of the man I fell in love with. He's like Jekyll and Hyde. I'm never sure which one I'll get. I have a feeling that here, in the environment where he lost his family, he's not going to be the kinder Angelo often. The memories are too raw. There are too many reminders in his home.

I don't want to wear his clothes, but I haven't unpacked my suitcase, and I don't want to run into anyone while stalking naked through the house. There were guards when we arrived. For all I know, they're patrolling inside at night.

The big bed in my room is tempting, but I don't want to give Angelo a reason for punishing me if I can avoid it. The last two punishments are still too fresh in my mind. I'll have a hot drink to warm up, and then I'll find a sofa where I can make myself comfortable. If I'm lucky, I may even locate a blanket.

My bare feet are quiet on the cold floor. Moonlight sifts through the big windows, painting black shadows in the corners as I go downstairs. It's eerily quiet. No guards are moving about. The hallway to the kitchen is lit with dim floor lights. Heidi must've clocked off for the night because the kitchen is dark.

I feel for a light switch on the wall and flip it on. A single bulb flickers to life over the island counter. The kitchen is fitted with modern appliances, but with baskets of dried herbs and fresh ones growing in pots on the windowsill, it has a rustic feel.

After putting water on to boil, I go through the cupboards until I find a mug and jars of tea leaves. Choosing chamomile, I brew an infusion and stand by the window while sipping the drink. Beyond the vegetable garden, the moonlit vineyard is visible. If the property is as big as Heidi said, I'm effectively a prisoner here.

The herbal tea quickly warms me inside. My muscles are sore, and my skin is itchy from the wool carpet and Angelo's dried seed on my thighs, but I try not to think about it. Maybe I can quickly rinse down while he's sleeping. I'm yet to come up with a plan to avoid begging for basic living necessities, but I don't think about that either. I'm too tired.

I carry the mug upstairs, heading back to my room. On the landing, I stop. It wasn't my plan to go there, but my feet carry me left instead of right. I tread carefully, like a trespasser, driven forward by curiosity and a strange, invisible pull.

The hallway is dark except for a sliver of light that falls from a door that's open a crack. The decision to go there isn't conscious, but I find myself in front of it, pushing a palm on the heavy wood.

The door swings open soundlessly. The light comes from a desk lamp with a stained-glass lampshade. The room is fitted with bookshelves and a writing desk. A sewing machine stands on a large table. A cozy sitting area with a well-worn sofa and armchair faces the window. On a rail pushed against the wall hangs the wedding dress.

I step into the room. It looks like a study. The books on the shelves include an eclectic collection of fiction, romance, biographies, and recipes. A framed photograph of the Eiffel Tower hangs on the wall. The space looks well lived in, much warmer than the rest of the beautifully decorated house.

Going over to the desk, I trace a finger over the dust-covered wood. Brochures are stacked in neat piles on the surface. I tilt my head to study them. They depict flowers and formal place settings with fancy crockery. Wedding brochures. Some have photos of cakes. Others show chair covers and tablecloths. All the colors are in shades of apricot. This is what Angelo's mother had planned for us.

Something twists in my chest as I stare at the pictures of a wedding that never came to fruition, a wedding my dad kept a secret. I understand why he tried to stop it from happening. He knew Angelo. He understood the duality of my dangerous husband's personality. He did what he did to protect me from this fate, but the price was heavy. Unthinkable. The price was this—a deserted room layered in bitter-sweet memories and covered in dust.

It's unbearably sad.

I shouldn't be here. I won't be welcome.

Leaning over the desk, I switch off the lamp. Heidi must've left it on when she returned the dress. I leave quietly, shutting the door behind me. When I turn, I come face to face with a picture in a frame hanging on the door on the opposite side of the hallway. Pressed flowers in all the colors of the rainbow are glued on a painted background of pink, spelling a name.

Adeline.

I go closer and squint at the name and date written in the corner in thick black ink. Angelo's sister made this when she was ten years old. The tightness in my chest increases, squeezing the air from my lungs. Sadness wraps around me like the emptiness in the house. How hard it must be for Angelo to have lost his twin.

Did she look like him? Was her personality the same? Was she also cursed with cruelty and kindness living side by side in her heart? Were they close?

I hesitate. I should go back to my room, but I'm riveted by the past, curious about my husband and his history. It's the notion that I'll never know that part of his life that sways me, that makes me open the door and flick on the light.

The room is similar in design to mine, but it's an explosion of colors. Bright yellows, oranges, reds, and pinks fill every nook and cranny. The wallpaper is pink with a sunflower motive. A hand-knitted blanket in purple, blue, and turquoise covers a wrought-iron bed. Porcelain trinkets, bottles of perfume, and glass bowls filled with costume jewelry stand on a dresser. Rows of bead necklaces hang over the frame of the mirror. A red sweater is carelessly draped over the back of a chair, and a pair of yellow ballerina flats lie askew in front of the bed as if they'd been kicked off in a hurry.

The photo frames on the dresser catch my attention. Clearing a small space, I leave my mug on the corner and pick up a heavy silver ornate frame.

The young woman in the picture smiles at the camera. It's a happy, contagious smile that dominates the image. It's a smile you see even before you notice the long hair that billows in the wind.

She stands on a clifftop with the sea behind her like in one of those scenes from the paintings. Sunbeams pierce through the clouds in the sky as if the angels themselves projected them to shine on her. Her hair isn't as dark as Angelo's. The sunlight that falls like a spotlight on her reflects an auburn tint. Her features bear a striking resemblance to her brother's. They have the same olive-toned skin and black eyes as well as the same good bone structure except that hers is more feminine and the lines of her face are softer.

I return the photo and pick up one in a Swarovski frame. It's one of those family portraits that's done in a professional studio. Judging by her and Angelo's age, the photo was taken a couple of years ago at the most. I recognize Santino although his image in my memory is vague.

With thick, white hair and Angelo's angular features, he looks the same as when I saw him at my sixteenth birthday party. A petite woman poses between Adeline and Angelo—their mother. They got their almost pure-black eyes and dark hair from her. Unlike the twins who are tall and toned, Mrs. Russo is small and frail. She's well-dressed, but there's a vulnerability and shyness in the manner she clutches her hands together in front of her.

I bet it's not the photo from the shoot that Mr. and Mrs. Russo chose to have framed, because Adeline is making bunny ears behind Angelo's head and wearing a mischievous grin on her stunningly beautiful face. Like his father's smile, Angelo's is proud.

The image gives me somewhat of an insight into their family dynamic. My gaze is drawn to Angelo, to how handsome he looks in a designer three-piece suit, how deceptively civil and well-bred. It's just a front though, the one he shows the world when he has to function in it among mere mortals while hiding the demon lurking under his skin.

After taking my fill of the image, I put it back in its place and open a jewelry box with an intricate inlay of triangular mirror pieces in the lid. A ballerina pops to life, doing a pirouette on the tune of The Blue Danube. Two compartments are filled with earrings and rings, most of them costume jewelry. The bigger one holds a cross on a gold chain and various bracelets and baubles. A short necklace of Venetian glass beads lies on the top. I take it out and lift it to the light. I'm admiring the kaleidoscope of colors inside a bead when Angelo's cold, furious voice cuts through the tinny notes of the waltz.

"What the fuck are you doing?"

I give a start, dropping the necklace and knocking the jewelry box down in the process. The necklace falls on the floor with the unmistakable clink of glass breaking. The box hits the stones with a thud, the metallic notes screeching with a hollow vibration before dying as the box cracks in the middle and the ballerina stops dead.

Jewelry is scattered everywhere. The bottom of the box is split open, revealing the skeleton of wheels and mechanics. Splintered glass beads litter the space around my feet. Some have rolled under the bed and the dresser. The broken string lies like an accusation over my bare toes.

I stare at the destruction, unable to breathe.

"What have you fucking done?" Angelo yells, beside himself with fury.

"I'm sorry," I say in a trembling voice. "I'm so sorry, Angelo. It was an accident." I kneel and start to gather the pieces. "You gave me a fright and—"

In two long strides, he's next to me, hauling me up by my arm. "What were you doing in here?" He shakes me hard as he drags me to the door. "Snooping? What were you looking for, Sabella?"

"Nothing," I cry out as he pulls me behind him toward the stairs. "I swear."

"You're a bad liar, wife," he utters in a cold, haunted tone. "You're a fucking traitor. A betrayer."

This Angelo is the one I'm terrified of. This is the monster, not the man.

"Angelo, please."

My protest falls on deaf ears. He manhandles me down the stairs. I almost trip trying to keep up with him, barely managing to find my footing. My feet leave bloody prints on the pristine, yellow floor, but I don't feel pain. I vaguely register that I must've cut my soles on the glass shards.

He drags me across the foyer to the front door.

"Angelo," I say again, trembling in his bruising hold.

He punches a code into a wall panel. "Do not say my name. You don't deserve that privilege."

The door clicks open. A blast of cold air hits me in the face. He shoves me outside, making me lose my balance. I go down, catching myself on my hands and knees. Lights go on in the garden and on the porch. The bright glare that shines in my eyes blinds me. I have nowhere to run, but I know one thing. I have to. And I can't let him catch me, because Angelo isn't human right now.

I struggle to my feet, slipping on the tiles that are wet from dew, but before I can straighten, he catches me again, his fingers finding purchase around my bicep and in my hair. He pushes me ahead of him down the steps and along the side of the house.

Running not to fall, I knock my toes against rocks. The cliffside of the house is dark. Another few steps, and a spray light goes on. The light must be motion triggered. I'm shivering with cold and fear when he stops in front of a metal door.

I fight him, but he easily constrains me by gripping both my wrists in one of his hands behind my back.

"Angelo," I try again when he punches another code into a wall panel.

"I said not to fucking utter my name."

The door clicks open, revealing a staircase. The inside is dark. Freezing. I don't want to go down there, but I don't have a choice when he wraps his arms around me in a steel vise and lifts me off my feet.

I twist in his hold, trying to free myself, but when we get to the bottom, I still. It's so dark I can't see my hand in front of my face. Yet I don't have to see to know this place is shrouded in death. I smell it in the strong scent of bleach that hangs in the air.

When he drops me to my feet, I scurry away from him. A single, naked bulb flicks on, throwing a circle of weak light into the shadows. Angelo stands in that pool of illumination like a dark angel, hatred bleeding from his pores.

Swallowing, I retreat until my back hits the wall. Something clanks as I stumble into it. Chains. If I didn't know before, I now know without a doubt what the cellar is for. What he does here.

This is where he kills people.

The realization restricts my throat. The air is cold and brittle. It hurts to breathe.

I try again. "Angelo."

What he does next makes my knees buckle. He takes a whip from a hook on the wall.

"Angelo, please," I say, raising my palms as he advances on me.

He tests the whip by lashing it on the damp floor. A sharp slash cuts through the air. Pausing in front of me, he says, "Stop fucking saying my name."

"Then what am I supposed to call you?"

The way his knuckles turn white around the handle draws my gaze. I shiver so violently my teeth chatters. He swings the whip past my face, hitting the wall behind me. I jump. He's going to kill me. He's going to beat me to death.

"I'm sorry," I say, tears streaking over my cheeks. "I shouldn't have gone in there. I was just curious."

Swishing the whip next to me again, he says in an icy tone filled with loathing, "You have no business being curious about them. Not about my mother, and not about Adeline."

"Stop," I say, flattening my body against the wall when another thwack falls on the other side of me. "Stop before it's too late."

"I should fucking kill you," he says, clenching his jaw. "My father would've."

I try to make myself small. "Then why did you marry me? Why didn't you just kill me that night when he told you to do it?"

He stills at that, stabbing the fingers of one hand into his hair while raising the whip in the other. The effort it takes him not to bring that whip down on me shows in his eyes, how hard he's fighting with himself.

"It's because you want me to pay," I answer for him. "If it's going to take whipping me, then do it. Do it or kill me now and get it over with."

He utters a raw cry, throwing the whip aside and cupping his head while walking in a circle with his face tilted toward the ceiling.

I stand quietly, the bones in my body rattling as I wait to see who's going to win his war, the man or the demon.

Finally, he turns to me with a wail of frustrated rage and grabs my arm. I fall, knocking my knee hard, but he doesn't give me time to straighten. He hoists me up, throws me over his shoulder, and carries me outside, jostling me like a bag of potatoes.

"What are you doing?" I ask, numb with fear.

He walks to a building a short distance away, takes a key from his pocket, and clicks on a remote that opens one of six garage doors. A sports car is parked inside. After yanking open the door on the passenger side, he dumps me on the seat and slams the door. I wrap my arms around myself, trying to still my trembling.

"Where are we going?" I ask when he gets inside.

His jaw locks as he starts the engine and pulls out of the garage with screeching tires before racing down a gravel road.

The speed at which he's driving forces me to unwrap my arms from my middle and clutch the edges of my seat.

"Where are you taking me?" I ask again.

Staring straight ahead, he puts his foot down on the accelerator.

Wherever he's taking me, it's going to be bad.

"Tell me," I say. "I have a right to know."

He turns his head and fixes his black gaze on me for so long that I want to beg him to watch the road again. The look in his eyes is filled with so much loathing there's no doubt about how much he despises me.

He changes gears and finally faces forward again. When he replies, his voice is devoid of emotion. "You're not a wife or a lover to me. You're nothing. Just a body to use. You don't deserve to be a part of my life or to live in my house. You don't deserve to breathe the same air they used to breathe."

His words are designed to inflict hurt, and they do. My heart shrivels, everything inside me icing over. "What does that mean?" I add with stupid hope, "Are you letting me go?"

His hold tightens on the wheel as he maneuvers the car around a bend in the road. "Never."

The momentum throws my body against the door. I cling to my seat. At the next straight stretch, I sit upright and exhale shakily. "Then what's going to happen now?"

The moonlight draws deep shadows over his face. The harshness of his features seems to reflect what's inside him. "You're banished from my house, Sabella." His sentence is a cold judgment that dooms me to a dark fate. "Forever."

~ TO BE CONTINUED ~

ALSO BY CHARMAINE PAULS

Diamond Magnate Novels

Standalone Novels

(Dark Arranged Marriage Romance)

Beauty in Deception

Beauty in the Broken

Diamonds are Forever Trilogy

(Dark Mafia Romance)

Diamonds in the Dust

Diamonds in the Rough

Diamonds are Forever

Beauty in the Stolen Trilogy

(Dark Kidnapping Romance)

Stolen Lust

Stolen Life

Stolen Love

Beauty in Imperfection Duology

(Dark Arranged Marriage Romance)

Imperfect Intentions

Imperfect Affections

White Nights Duet

(Contemporary Russian Billionaire Romance)

White Nights

Midnight Days

The Loan Shark Duet

(Dark Mafia Romance)

Dubious

Consent

The Age Between Us Duet

(Reverse Age Gap Stalker Romance)

Old Enough

Young Enough

Standalone Novels

(Enemies-to-Lovers Dark Romance)

Darker Than Love

(Second Chance Cheating Romance)

Catch Me Twice

Krinar World Novels

(Futuristic Romance)

The Krinar Experiment

The Krinar's Informant

---

7 Forbidden Arts Series

(Fated Mates Paranormal Romance)

Pyromancist (Fire)

Aeromancist, The Beginning (Prequel)

Aeromancist (Air)

Hydromancist (Water)

Geomancist (Earth)

Necromancist (Spirit)

Scapulimancist (Animal)

Chiromancist (Time)

Man (The Boss)

ABOUT THE AUTHOR

Charmaine loves to write dark and edgy romance that will melt both your e-reader and your heart. She's a mom of two teenagers, an adorable dog, and a dominant cat. Her country of birth is South Africa where many of her stories play off. Her French husband kidnapped her to the south of France where she currently lives with her family. When she's not writing, you'll find her in the kitchen baking cakes or in the gym lifting weights (because ... all those cakes!).

Join Charmaine's mailing list
https://charmainepauls.com/subscribe/

Join Charmaine's readers' group on Facebook
http://bit.ly/CPaulsFBGroup

Read more about Charmaine's novels and short stories on
https://charmainepauls.com

Connect with Charmaine

Facebook
http://bit.ly/Charmaine-Pauls-Facebook

Amazon
http://bit.ly/Charmaine-Pauls-Amazon

Goodreads

http://bit.ly/Charmaine-Pauls-Goodreads

Twitter

https://twitter.com/CharmainePauls

Instagram

https://instagram.com/charmainepaulsbooks

BookBub

http://bit.ly/CPaulsBB

TikTok

https://www.tiktok.com/@charmainepauls